Betrayal

International bestselling author Lesley Pearse has lived a life as rich with incidents, setbacks and joys as any found in her novels.

Resourceful, determined and willing to have a go at almost anything, Lesley left home at sixteen. By the mid sixties she was living in London, sharing flats, partying hard and married to a trumpet player in a jazz-rock band. She has also worked as a nanny and a Playboy bunny, and has designed and made clothes to sell to boutiques.

It was only after having three daughters that Lesley began to write. The hardships, traumas, close friends and lovers from those early years were inspiration for her beloved novels. She published her first book at forty-nine and has not looked back since.

Lesley is still a party girl.

Find out more about Lesley and keep
up to date with what she's been doing:

Follow her on Twitter
@LesleyPearse

Sign up for her newsletter
www.lesleypearse.com

Betrayal

LESLEY PEARSE

MICHAEL JOSEPH

PENGUIN MICHAEL JOSEPH

UK | USA | Canada | Ireland | Australia
India | New Zealand | South Africa

Penguin Michael Joseph is part of the Penguin Random House group of companies
whose addresses can be found at global.penguinrandomhouse.com

First published 2023
001

Set in 15.5/18pt Garamond MT Std
Typeset by Jouve (UK), Milton Keynes
Printed and bound in Great Britain by Clays Ltd, Elcograf S.p.A.

The authorized representative in the EEA is Penguin Random House Ireland,
Morrison Chambers, 32 Nassau Street, Dublin D02 YH68

A CIP catalogue record for this book is available from the British Library

HARDBACK ISBN: 978-0-241-54495-2
TRADE PAPERBACK ISBN: 978-0-241-54496-9

www.greenpenguin.co.uk

Penguin Random House is committed to a
sustainable future for our business, our readers
and our planet. This book is made from Forest
Stewardship Council® certified paper.

To my son Martin Hartland.

Words cannot fully express how wonderful it was that you found me in 2022. I thought you were lost forever.

I feel such joy now and the sadness of the past has vanished. You are a son to be proud of, a great husband to Svetlana and father to your three lovely daughters.

I never anticipated that my family would suddenly double in size.

I hope so much that I have many more years to catch up on all our missing years.

I love you.

I

London, 1998

Don shoved the back door open, banging it hard into the wall. Eve knew by the ferocity of his entrance he was certain to pick a fight with her tonight.

She knew there was no chance of appeasing him. She'd tried every which way in the past and it always ended the same. He would hit her. Often till she was unconscious.

It was just after eleven. That meant he hadn't found a willing candidate for more drinks after the pub and a kebab. That usually mellowed his mood.

Eve braced herself for the inevitable as he stomped into the kitchen, looking at her balefully. 'Can I make you a bacon sandwich?' she asked hopefully.

'Fuck off, you silly cow,' he snarled. 'Do I look like I want a bacon sandwich?'

You look like a pig, she thought but didn't dare say. 'Is there something else you'd like to eat?'

She didn't see the punch coming. For a big man Don could pounce as swiftly as a cat. As his fist connected with her cheek her head rattled with an explosion of pain.

'Is food the only thing you can offer?' he shouted at her, and the stink of his beer and cigarette breath made her stomach heave too.

He caught hold of her shoulders, head-butted her, punched her in the stomach so she fell to the floor and then kicked her again and again. She heard a faint crack and knew that, once again, her ribs had broken, but even as she wanted to scream out in agony, she felt the heaven-sent wooziness of unconsciousness.

She came to later to find herself lying in blood; she wasn't sure which part of her was cut, as everything hurt. An attempt at getting up proved hopeless – her ribs and head hurt too much. Don had left the kitchen light on, and she wished she could manoeuvre herself to reach the cardigan she'd left on the kitchen chair because the heating had turned off and she was very cold.

There was nothing for it but to lie in agony waiting for it to abate enough to try to get up. She would blank out the thought of all the other times she'd lain for hours in this very spot.

'You should never have married him,' she muttered as she lifted one hand to examine her face. Her left eye had already swollen so badly she couldn't see out of it, and one of her teeth was bleeding but it didn't feel as if it would fall out. The rest of the blood appeared to be from her shin, where Don had kicked it.

So many people had advised her against marrying Don, including her father. They had all witnessed various bouts of bad temper, but back then Eve always found a good reason for them. Besides, back in 1986 when they'd married, his anger had never been directed towards her.

Eve's mother Sandra had died from breast cancer when Eve was ten, and her father Jack had become a dour, difficult man, so getting married and gaining a home of her own seemed a happy solution. Don was ten years older than Eve, a big dark-haired handsome man. He was a plumber and made a very good living. He even owned a house of his own. Granted it was only a two-up two-down in a scruffy road in Lewisham, and in bad repair, but Eve felt she could make it lovely.

They had only been back from their honeymoon in Spain for a week when he hit her for the first time.

'I didn't mean to hurt you,' he said almost as soon as he'd attacked her, and he got a bag of ice to put on her already swelling eye. 'I had a terrible day at work and when you began nagging me about decorating the lounge, I just saw red.'

She found herself apologizing for merely offering to paint and wallpaper it herself, something she was good at. She hadn't considered that was nagging. But as he kissed her bruised face and told her he loved her, she forgave him.

With hindsight she should've walked out of the door right then.

Don was delighted when she told him she was pregnant. When the scan showed it was a girl, he was even more thrilled; he said he'd always wanted a daughter. He didn't hit her again for quite some time, and she believed that he never would again. But when she was eight months pregnant and she said she was too tired to go to the pub with him one Friday night, he hit her again and when she tried to run away from him, he'd grabbed her, swung her round and broke her wrist.

'Don't you ever try to run away from me,' he snarled at her. 'You are my wife, and you must obey me. So if I say we are going to the pub, you go with a smile on your face.'

Her broken wrist was still in plaster when she went into labour. Her midwife pointed out she'd find a few problems with bathing and dressing a new baby. Eve remembered thinking that perhaps that would be a wake-up call for Don, seeing her struggling at such an important time. But he didn't appear to even notice.

Fear made her obedient. Not just fear of Don, but fear of what her father would do if she ran to him for help. He was not in the best of health and if he tried to stand up to Don, he might have a stroke or a heart attack. Then there was the fear of what the neighbours would say. They liked Don as he'd done plumbing work for most of them. They would believe any story he chose to tell them. Then there was the fear of having to bring her baby up alone.

A year later Oliver was born, and she told herself she had to make the best of it, as where could she go with two small children? He had always made a fuss over Tabitha, but he seemed totally disinterested in Oliver. Maybe she should have sensed what was to come instead of fooling herself into thinking one day it would all come right.

Now, as she lay on the floor, cold and in terrible pain, she glanced at a framed wedding photograph on the wall. She had looked so pretty that day, her blonde hair curling around her face, blue eyes alight with happiness at becoming Mrs Donald Hathaway at last. Eighteen, with a slim hourglass figure and an alabaster complexion. Back then Don said she was like a beauty queen, and to her he'd been a tall, dark and handsome prince.

But it had all gone sour and she knew she must finally make a plan to escape him. Her father had died five years ago; perhaps his heart attack was due to a broken heart because despite all the efforts she'd made to hide what Don was doing to her, he'd found out. He had urged her to bring the children and come and live with him. He'd planned to see a solicitor so if he should die, the proceeds of the sale of his house would go directly to Eve, not to her and Don. Tragically he had died before he could organize it. Eve couldn't help but wonder if Don had brought on his heart attack by threatening him.

So it was that Eve's old family home, a semi-detached house on one of the best roads in Eltham, passed to both Don and Eve. Don in his usual imperious way saw the money from the sale as his and made an offer on a brand-new Georgian-style detached house in Grove Park. He didn't even take her to see it until his offer had been accepted.

She had to admit it was a lovely house, with a good school nearby, a big park and direct train access to central London. But back in Lewisham she had people she knew close by, friends she'd made taking the children to playgroups and latterly at infant school. While she had never divulged to anyone what Don did to her, she was fairly certain most had guessed and sympathized. Julia, one of the mothers whose son was in the same class as Oliver back then, was a nurse and had seen Eve come into casualty one morning looking as if she'd been in a car crash.

Yet when Don had taken her to see the newly built house in Briar Road, he'd said it was to be a new beginning for them.

'I've never liked being so close to other people as

we are in Lewisham,' he said. 'It makes me nervy, like we're being spied on. It's too cramped and old-fashioned. I hate it.'

He took her face in his two hands then and kissed her tenderly. 'I know I haven't always been kind to you, Eve,' he admitted. 'But I do love you and I'm going to turn over a new leaf and spend more time with you and the kids.'

He raved about the big garden and how he'd build a shed for himself and put up a swing and climbing frame for the kids. 'We've never had enough space, but here we'll have plenty,' he said, beaming with happiness at what the new house would bring them all. 'The kids can ride their bikes on the street; it's safe and quiet here. We are going to be so happy.'

She believed him too and for almost a year after they'd moved in they were happy. They had passion-ate lovemaking like they'd had on their honeymoon, and Eve forgot to be cautious in what she said to Don. Oliver and Tabitha loved having a bedroom each and liked their new schools. It all looked so rosy, and for the first time in their marriage she was able to take control over the decor, something she had a flair for. Don even praised her for the chic and tasteful result. Eve particularly loved the spacious modern kitchen, with French windows that opened out on to the garden, and Don built his shed halfway down it, laughingly saying he might live in it.

But just as Eve thought the bad old days had gone forever, Don came in one evening from work and gave her such a terrible beating that she was in bed for days. He started to pick on Oliver around the same time; ridiculing him for not liking football, for spending too much time reading and called him a 'milksop'. Soon his spite turned to slaps and punches, and on one occasion he beat Oliver with a piece of lead piping because he claimed his son had scratched his car getting his bike out of the garage. One night when Don was attacking her, Oliver came out of his room to try to defend her, but that ended very badly when he punched the boy so hard he broke two of his ribs.

Eve could see that both Oliver and Tabitha were becoming withdrawn and fearful in their father's presence. She made them promise that if they heard any rows they would stay in their rooms. But she knew lying in bed listening to their mum being hurt must be terrible for them. She had to take them and flee to safety, somewhere he'd never find them.

The trouble was she had no money of her own. She hadn't worked since Oliver had been on the way, and although she'd been trained in curtain making at an interior design shop in Blackheath and become so good at it that Jacintha her boss had been upset to lose her, she had no job now. Maybe she could make curtains again, but how could she rent a flat without money for advance rent and a deposit? And how could she get all three of them out of this house without him suspecting anything?

Despite all Don had done to her, she also resented leaving the house when it was her father's money that had paid for it. The sale of his own little house had been spent by Don on a bigger van for work, a new BMW, his shed, and the rest frittered away at the pub.

As she lay there shivering, she wondered if there was a way she could kill him, as his death would solve everything for her. A pillow over his face while sleeping? A push down the stairs, or could she cut the brakes on his van? Poison? Or just knife him and claim it was self-defence?

2

Don was still asleep when Eve left the house with Olly and Tabby the following morning.

The children had both hugged her when they came down for their breakfast, their anxious expressions showing that although they knew how she'd got her black eye and why she was in obvious pain, they didn't know what to say about it.

Seeing her children's concern and fear Eve knew she had to speak out.

'We will leave today if possible,' she reassured them as they ate cereal. 'But I have to work it out when and how, and where we will go to. For now we just act as normal, and I pretend I'm taking you to school. But really, I'm going to try and get some advice.'

'You should go to the police and get him locked up!' Olly burst out, and he pointed to her bandaged leg. 'What did he do to that?'

'He kicked me. I think it needs a stitch; it won't stop bleeding,' Eve said. 'I'll catch the bus to Lewisham Hospital before I do anything else.'

'I wish I had big muscles, then I'd do that to him

and see how he likes it,' Olly said, his big dark eyes so like his father's, glistening with unshed tears. 'If ever I get married, I'll never hurt my wife.'

'I really hope you won't,' Eve said, smoothing back his dark hair. 'I also hope both of you will think very carefully about committing yourself to anyone until you know them inside out.'

But she knew she wouldn't have listened even if someone had told her Don was a serial killer. She had loved him on sight and to her he was perfect. She wondered how she could teach Tabby to recognize a potential brute.

They kissed her goodbye at the end of the road and Eve went to the bus stop. She had to make sure everything looked normal back home. Don's breakfast place was laid at the table; she usually made him tea and toast, plus bacon and egg if he wanted it. She hoped he wouldn't be suspicious and wonder why she'd taken the children to school. Hopefully he'd remember how hard he'd hit her last night and feel ashamed.

Before she'd left the house, she'd checked her appearance. Both her eyes were black and very puffy, she had a big bruise on her forehead, and her lip was cut and swollen. She thought she looked nearer forty now than her real age of thirty. Setting aside her present injuries, the previous ones had yellowed her skin, her neck looked scraggy, her blue eyes dull, and her blonde hair needed a wash and hung limply to her shoulders. She had only gained a few pounds since her wedding, but she no longer carried herself as well as she did back then; she'd noticed she tended to stoop. She'd put on a mid-calf skirt to cover her leg injuries, but that made her look older too. But then she'd silently reminded herself she wasn't going for a job interview or a date. Finally she'd taken her sunglasses out of the hall-table drawer and put them on. They weren't right for grey skies, but they hid her eyes. And she did her best to sound cheerful as she walked up the road with the children.

Waiting for the bus to Catford, she didn't feel so good. Her broken ribs hurt badly and washing and dressing had been agony. Plus, she was tired from the night on the kitchen floor. She just hoped her leg wouldn't start bleeding again. Bending to bandage it had been so difficult and she'd nearly passed out with the pain.

'Time to go,' she whispered to herself as the bus came. 'This time you will do the right thing.'

In Catford she went straight to the police station. Fortunately, there was no one else waiting in reception. When she took off her sunglasses as she told the duty officer she wanted to report her husband for beating her, his voice softened, and he said he would put her in an interview room and bring her a cup of tea.

A policewoman with a long nose came in and

introduced herself as WPC Sutton. To Eve she looked about thirty.

'My goodness, you look as if you've done a few rounds with Muhammad Ali,' she said. 'I'm so sorry, Mrs Hathaway, you must be in great pain.'

'The ribs and leg hurt more,' Eve said, liking her a bit more as she sounded genuinely sympathetic. 'I should have come for help years ago; each beating is worse.'

She was naturally reserved, and she'd been brought up to never tell tales on anyone, but she knew this was crunch time; she really did have to admit how often she was beaten and why.

'He always used to apologize,' she said, tears stinging her bruised, swollen eyes. 'But he doesn't any more, and I think if I don't do something now, he might eventually kill me or my son.'

'What do you want the police to do?' Sutton asked.

Surprised at such a question, Eve hardly knew what to say. 'Well, stop him, take out a restraining order, put him in prison. Anything so this nightmare ends.'

'We can certainly talk to him, and if you bring charges against him, we will arrest him. But I have to warn you that in cases like these men often wriggle out of it with just a fine. Even when an injunction is in place, when the judge says he mustn't come to your home, most violent men ignore that.'

'So are you trying to say there's no point in reporting him?' Eve asked, her voice rising to a surprised squeak.

'No, not at all. I'm just pointing out the way it is. Personally, I think men who beat women are bullies and need to be treated harshly so they take on board it's unacceptable. Sadly, Mrs Hathaway, this is still a man's world, and they get away with it. There are even some old fossils, judges, barristers and, to my shame, the police, who believe it's perfectly OK to beat your wife. What I'm going to do now, is take your statement, then get your injuries photographed. I think you should talk to a solicitor, who may be able to advise you how to proceed. Have you got relatives you could stay with?'

Eve shook her head. 'I don't even have enough money for a bed and breakfast,' she admitted. 'I told the children this morning we would get away, but where without money?'

'A solicitor will have details of a women's refuge. We have the number of one solicitor who does fight for women's rights. She's very highly thought of. Would you like me to ring her and make an appointment for later today?'

'Yes, please, but I must go to the hospital first. I think my leg needs stitching.'

'Then I'll take you straight away to our photographer. I'll ring the solicitor, then come and tell you what she said. I'll ask our nurse to meet you at the photographer's. He will re-dress your leg after the photograph.'

It was an hour later when Eve left the police station. Having the photographs taken was embarrassing, as she had to take off her top to show the terrible bruises which almost completely covered her chest and back. The close-up pictures of her facial injuries might not have been embarrassing or painful, but it still felt like an intrusion.

Gary Swinburn, the police nurse, made it easier. A rather short, stocky man, who would've made a more likely boxer than nurse, he seemed to sense how uncomfortable she was and helped her at every stage, whether putting her top on again for her and buttoning it up or getting her a drink before re-dressing her leg wound, which he agreed was a bad one. Then he insisted on driving her to Lewisham Hospital; he said she wasn't well enough to get a bus.

Gary had made her feel better; he was caring, gentle and his probing questions felt like those of a friend, not an interrogation. He made her smile when he said it was a change to take care of someone nice, as mainly he dealt with wounded criminals.

'I want to leave my husband, but it's so difficult when you have children and no money.'

'Divorce laws were put in place to protect ladies

like you,' he said as he helped her into his Mini. 'You've got to leave him, Eve. Every day you let your children stay in that toxic home, they are learning bad things. I often wonder how many of my patients are the products of learned behaviour in the home. Either becoming violent bullies themselves or allowing others to bully them.'

Eve had never looked at it like that before; the thought of Olly hitting women brought tears to her eyes. She couldn't let that happen.

It crossed her mind as Gary took her arm and helped her into the casualty department that if only she'd fallen in love with a man like him, rather than Don, how sweet her life could've been.

Gary gave her his card as he dropped her at Casualty. 'Ring me any time, Eve. If I can help, I will. Maybe just to listen or, God forbid, to dress wounds. Or to hear you are on the mend and just need a friend. I'm serious. I don't give my card to just anyone. I'm concerned about you. So call me. Good or bad, tell me where you are, how you're doing. If you need help or just someone to talk to, I'll be there.'

3

Eve could hardly believe how rapidly Hannah Gordon the solicitor acted.

In just a half-hour appointment where Eve told her the bare bones of her story, Hannah said she wanted Eve and the children out of the house at Briar Road that same day.

Eve tried to stall, making excuses about packing, talking to the children's school, and discussing it with them. But Hannah was having none of it.

She was what would be described as a handsome woman, about fifty, tall, at least five foot eight, with chestnut shoulder-length hair. She wore a grey-and-white pinstriped suit, which looked very expensive, and three-inch heels. Almost immediately Eve could imagine her in court. Her voice was well-bred Home Counties, loud enough to be commanding, yet she was compassionate and understanding about what Eve had been going through.

'If you don't leave today, you will weaken your case against your husband. He might also hurt you again. Ideally, I want to get an order so he has to leave your house, so you and the children can return; however, that outcome takes time to arrange. Yet we must make it absolutely clear to him that your marriage and his brutality is at an end.'

'But where do I go? I've got no money,' Eve began to cry.

'I shall find you a place in a women's refuge,' she said firmly. 'As for money, you can get emergency payments from social services, but for now you won't need any. I'm going to get Martha, my assistant, to drive you home now so you can pack a case for the three of you. Don't try to take stuff for every eventuality, just basic everyday things, as if you were going on a holiday. Just one case between you.'

'But their school?' Eve managed to get out through her tears.

'Don't worry about that. I'll ring them, and Martha will pick them up for you this afternoon and take you all to the refuge. Now, I need to warn you this place might be a little shabby, not what you are used to. But you'll be safe, and you'll have the chance to rest and recover. Most women we place in them make good friends there. It isn't like prison, and the children will have other children to play with, which helps them adjust.'

As Martha made it quite clear they needed to be quick with the packing, just in case Don came back unexpectedly, Eve didn't have time in Briar Road to panic about what to take or that a refuge was a bad idea. She felt she had to trust Hannah's judgement.

While Hannah had been open, firm and compassionate, Eve found Martha puzzling. She guessed her to be around forty, but her tightly permed hair, lack of make-up and greying complexion made her seem far older. Yet she was efficient, clearly having everything in hand. But she didn't make conversation and her answers to questions were straight to the point, as if she hoped that would deter Eve from asking more. She had a faint Birmingham accent, and Eve suspected she'd been a battered wife too.

'You pick out three or four outfits for the children, not forgetting pants, socks and nightclothes. Then I'll pack them as you sort out stuff for yourself. Think simple, Eve, jeans, T-shirts, jumpers, sensible shoes. You won't be going anywhere you'll need to dress up.'

'What will happen to all my other clothes?' Eve asked once she'd given the pile of selected clothes to Martha.

'They'll just stay here until you get your house back.' She looked puzzled at the question.

'I'm scared Don might destroy them all to spite me,' Eve said.

'To be honest he's unlikely to even know you've taken anything today,' Martha said with an unexpected smile. Maybe she'd noticed how many clothes were in Eve's wardrobe. 'Men are pretty gormless about clothes, I've found. By the time he realizes you aren't going to be his punchbag any more, he'll probably be cuddling one of your sweaters and crying. That tends to be how it works.'

'I can't see Don crying about me,' Eve said, but the idea made her smile.

'You'd be surprised,' Martha said, raising an eyebrow. 'We had one client whose husband built a kind of shrine to his wife in the garage. I have to admit it cracked her up; she roared with laughter when she saw it. He'd got her wedding dress, a nightdress, a swimming costume she'd worn on their first holiday together, shoes, photographs, and even copies of her favourite recipes. It was bizarre. They were snapshots of the bits about her he liked the best.'

'That's making me think Don isn't so bad,' Eve said.

'One look in the mirror should remind you just how bad Don is,' Martha said sharply. 'Take a piece of advice from me: don't ever lapse into sentimental tosh. He's a brute and you are getting away. Now let's get this suitcase shut and get out of here.'

Eve took just a moment to look around her before they left. There was the painting of water lilies she loved, the cuckoo clock that she'd taken from her parents' home after her father died. The lovely Italian table lamp like a huge golden pineapple she'd bought in Pimlico before she married Don. It had cost nearly a week's wages, but she loved it. When she thought back, Don never had any taste; he sneered at anything he thought 'arty'. She wondered now why on earth she had wanted to marry him.

Her ribs hurt like hell with just the strain of getting clothes from cupboards and her leg was even worse. When she glanced in a mirror she saw Quasimodo looking back at her; she was even a bit hunchbacked as she was leaning sideways to avoid putting any pressure on her ribs.

When they went to pick up the children from school and Martha told them they were going away to the seaside, they were thrilled.

'To Brighton?' Tabby asked. 'Is it Brighton?'

'No, not Brighton, a good deal further than that,' Martha said. 'We're going to Sidmouth in Devon. It's a long drive but there's some cushions back there so you can snuggle down and go to sleep if you like.'

As they drove out to the west of London and the M5, Eve could only think that each mile took her further from Don and the fear of being hurt.

'I'll stop for a toilet break and to get something to eat once we're right out of London,' Martha said.

The children were very quiet, and Eve thought it odd they weren't asking any questions: not if she had been to the hospital, how this had come about, or if they would see their father again. But perhaps they were just glad they hadn't got to find their mother hurt again.

They stopped for a break in the services on the M5. They all had a McDonald's meal, which pleased Olly and Tabby, and Eve bought them some chocolate too. Looking at her watch she noticed it was now six o'clock. Don would be returning home and she wondered how he would react to find they'd gone.

Soon they were in open countryside, and at last Eve could feel herself unwinding. Martha was better at talking to the children than to Eve, asking them about their hobbies and interests.

It was nearly eight when they got to Sidmouth, and Martha offered to take them on a slight detour to get an idea what it was like before she took them to the refuge. Although Eve had no preconceived ideas about the town, she was somewhat enchanted by the elegant Regency architecture and the unexpected lack of seaside-town brashness. Her first thought was that this was a place she could happily live in. Although the beach was shingle, the sea looked very blue in the early-evening sunshine; there was no litter, burger bars or noisy pubs, and beyond the end of the little town were undulating cliffs calling out to be walked on. It was true the majority of people strolling around were over fifty or couples with young children, but she felt that was another plus.

'I like it here,' Olly piped up. 'I can't wait to swim in the sea.'

'That will have to wait till tomorrow,' Martha said over her shoulder. 'Now we must go to the refuge, and I've got to go to Exeter to stay with a friend overnight.'

The street Martha drove into was a short terrace of houses with no front gardens. She drove along it to the last house in the road, a detached double-fronted one, and it was clearly built much later than the terraced ones, perhaps in the twenties. It had a front garden hidden by a tall hedge. Next to it was a car park.

'We don't tell anyone what this house is,' Martha said in a low voice to Eve. 'If you are asked, you say Marianne is an old friend of your family. If you have any problems, telephone Hannah. But don't tell anyone at the house your surname or any personal details like your former address,' she added. 'Just a precaution – you can't be too careful.'

Later that night Eve pondered on that piece of advice. Was it given because some of the women were thieves and would burgle her house while she was in Sidmouth? Or because some husbands came looking for wives, and it was best no one could tell them if she was here?

'This is it,' Martha said. 'The sea is about a fifteen-minute walk away, and you can catch a bus to pretty villages in the surrounding countryside. But for now I need to hand you over to Marianne; she owns this place. Like the house, she's a bit rough, but she's got a good heart. Then I'll say goodbye and good luck. We'll meet again when I come to take you back to London. That might be to a temporary rental place if Hannah hasn't managed to get an order for your husband to leave the family home by then.'

She kissed both the children, told them to be good for their mummy and hurried back to her car. Eve wondered if the woman had expected her to change her mind and want to go back home.

Eve didn't want to but she was apprehensive. However, as Marianne looked like a force of nature, she wouldn't have dared voice any anxiety.

She was an East Ender, a big woman on the wrong side of fifty with enormous saggy breasts, purple hair and dressed in what looked like jumble-sale clothes, all different colours and layers thrown on recklessly. Aside from her initial greeting when she shot questions at Eve like gunfire and dismissed Martha briskly, once inside the house she became warm. Eve wondered if she'd learned to appear hostile when at the front door to repel troublemakers.

Her smile was a wide, joyous one, and she held out her arms to Olly and Tabby, embracing them with the kind of hug that said she genuinely loved children.

'I've put you in what I call the honeymoon suite

for now,' she said to Eve. 'It's got an en suite and you'll have it all to yourselves for a couple of days until you've settled in. But I will have to move you into one of the dormitories to share with others after that. Sadly, we are always full to bursting here. But, first, a cup of tea and some cake.'

The tea and cake were served in the kitchen, a big room with surprisingly modern blue units. There was just one woman in there sitting at the central table preparing vegetables. She had a plaster cast on one leg, and a very raw-looking scar down her cheek.

Marianne introduced Eve and the children. 'This is Fiona. The other women have all gone out, but Fiona is finding her crutches a bit difficult to manage. But do sit down. I'll pop the kettle on. Would you kids like some squash?'

Marianne did pull Fiona into the conversation from time to time as she explained the rota for jobs, according to ability, and other house rules. But it was clear Fiona was shy, though she did say she came from Paisley in Scotland and that her two children were with the other women and had gone to the beach.

Marianne suggested Tabby and Olly went out to explore the back garden. 'It's not much to look at, but it's big,' she said.

'We find the children adapt quite well to staying here,' she said once the children were out of earshot.

'They are happy to be somewhere where they and their mother are safe and to have friends to play with. All the mothers muck in with the cooking and cleaning. At the moment we have eight mums and fourteen children.'

Eve had many questions, but her eyes kept being drawn to the scar on Fiona's cheek and she got the idea she was going to hear in the coming week about men who were even more violent than Don. So she only nodded and smiled.

The honeymoon suite was right at the top of the house but bore little resemblance to its name. It had a double bed that sagged in the middle and bunk beds for the children. All the furniture was battle-scarred, and the blind at the window was torn. But Olly and Tabby didn't appear to notice; they said there was a climbing frame and swing in the garden, and they wondered what the food would be like.

'I want you to try and eat whatever comes,' Eve warned them. 'We are lucky to be here by the sea, and I'm sure you'll have fun with the other children. But please remember this isn't forever. The solicitor who arranged this is going to try and get your dad out of the old house so we can go back there.'

'He won't like that,' Olly said, looking anxious.

'No, he won't, but it will all be done legally, and he'll have to accept it,' Eve explained. 'In time we'll move away from Grove Park so we can forget the bad stuff and start again. As long as we're together, we can put up with roughing it for a bit, can't we?'

There were times in the following two weeks when Eve wanted to run away from the refuge. Not only were her broken ribs and her leg hurting, but eight women and fourteen children made a lot of noise, and some of the women were very rough. There were many arguments, fights even, not just between the women but the children too. But Marianne had a knack of calming everyone down, and it could go from a full-on fight, with punches thrown and abuse shouted, to laughter in half an hour.

After the first two days, Eve was moved to a room with four other women and the children were in the dormitories, one for boys and one for girls. There was another room shared by two women who had small babies, and yet another room where the three youngest children slept. Eve was surprised by how easily the children adapted; they didn't complain that they had no toys of their own, quite happily rummaging through the box of tattered books and comics to find something to read or playing board games in the playroom when bad weather stopped them playing outside. She didn't like that some of the children used very bad language, as did their mothers, but she kept that to herself.

It was the lack of privacy Eve hated most. She

couldn't use the loo or bathroom without someone banging on the door, and there was no such thing as having an early night, as her room-mates would go on talking till the early hours. Annie, a loud peroxide blonde, helped herself to Eve's pink T-shirt one afternoon and when Eve challenged her she called her a selfish bitch. Fortunately, Marianne heard what was going on and intervened, making Annie take it off and apologize.

As time went on, though, Eve found her own way of coping. She had always been good with children, and she was happy to read or play games with them. She was also a good cook, and her spaghetti Bolognese was voted the best they'd tasted. Bit by bit the other women opened up about how they had come to be there, and their stories were awful. Yet most had run away a couple of times and then gone back to more of the same. Marianne told Eve that on average most women leave seven times before finally giving up on the relationship.

As the weather grew warmer at the end of May, some of the women and their children would go down to the beach. It wasn't warm enough for swimming yet, but the kids paddled, and it was lovely to lie in the sun with company. Eve noticed Olly and Tabby were getting a suntan – they looked the picture of health – but she was worried they were missing out on school. She tried to get them to do some writing and arithmetic each day, but Marianne claimed it didn't matter as it was only six weeks or so till the end of term, and that they'd soon catch up in September.

One evening soon after the evening meal, when most of the women were still in the kitchen and the children in the playroom, someone came hammering on the front door. All the woman blanched and looked at one another. No one came to the house after six and the strength of the knock suggested it wasn't a Jehovah's Witness or the Avon lady but an angry man looking for his woman.

Marianne got up, closing the kitchen door behind her. They heard her put the chain on the door before she opened it.

'Can I help you?' she said.

Eve was fairly certain it wouldn't be Don. He would never imagine she'd go so far away from London, and how would he have found out about this place?

'Open the fucking door or I'll kick it in.'

The loud aggression made each of the women, including Eve, reach out for their neighbour.

'It's Alf,' Dianne, a quiet mouse of a woman from Bexley Heath, whispered. She shook with fright, her eyes darting around the room as if looking for somewhere to hide.

Annie the peroxide blonde took charge, picked up the phone and rang the police. There was a special number for incidents like this.

But Alf put his shoulder to the door and with a loud crack and the wood splintering he knocked it in.

'Go down into the cellar,' one of the women hastily suggested to Dianne. 'He won't know we've even got one.'

'I can't! My kids are in the garden,' said Dianne. 'He'll take them.'

But it was too late to do anything. Alf charged into the kitchen and caught hold of his wife by her shoulders.

He was a very big man, at least six three, and perhaps eighteen stone. His tattooed forearms were like tree trunks and beneath his black T-shirt muscles stood out the size of bowling balls.

'You are my wife, and they are my kids, and you belong with me!' he shouted at her, pushing his face right up against hers.

Dianne was so terrified she lost control of her bladder and began to scream hysterically.

Eve was trapped between this giant of a man clutching his wife and the range cooker. She was glancing around, looking for the best way out, when she saw the heavy cast-iron frying pan. Without stopping to think, she snatched it up, leaped up on to her chair and brought it down on the man's head with all the force she could muster.

He just collapsed, sinking to his knees, then on to the floor, ironically his face landing in his wife's urine.

The women cheered. 'Well done, Eve!' they shouted. 'Let's hope he stays out till the police get here.'

Eve liked being the hero of the moment, but her ribs hurt from the exertion. Most of the time she was able to forget what Don had done to her, but then she'd stretch too far, move awkwardly and the pain came back.

The police arrived shortly afterwards, handcuffed him and led him away. He was still stunned and thankfully silent.

'I'll have to get you moved,' Marianne said to Dianne, who was shaking with fear. 'Go on upstairs and get changed before the children see you.'

Dianne scuttled away, Annie mopped the floor and everyone else kept remarking on Eve's presence of mind to hit Alf.

Marianne clapped her hands for silence. 'Before I call the children in, I want to know who let it slip Dianne was here? I don't think anyone did it intentionally but there is a small network of men in Sidmouth who know what this house is, and they chat women up for names and then pass on what they've found out. Have any men spoken to you on the beach in the last couple of days?'

'Only the deckchair men,' Ruth, one of the youngest women, offered. 'But they were nice, treating us like queens.'

'And they asked your names?'

Marianne looked anxious, as Ruth admitted she'd given her name, Dianne's and Annie's.

'But surely just our first names wouldn't matter?' she asked. 'I mean, Dianne comes from Southampton, doesn't she? How would they know her husband?'

'I don't know exactly, but it seems to me there's a network for men to find missing wives, as this isn't the first time we've had an irate man turn up and kick the door in. Deckchair men, park-keepers, funfairs, any place where women go with a group of other women and children. Also, in small towns like Sidmouth it doesn't take much to leak there's a women's refuge here.'

Eve felt a bit sick at that. She had felt certain Don could never find her. What if he turned up?

The children came in then and all the mothers changed the subject, while Marianne phoned an emergency carpenter to fix the front door.

'Did you ever clobber your husband over the head with a pan?' Annie whispered to Eve.

'No, I would never have dared,' Eve replied. 'But now I've found I can do it, I'll bear it in mind if I ever get bullied again.'

4

It was a whole new experience for Eve to find herself admired. Suddenly the other women were seeking her advice about things, asking if she wanted to go for a walk with them or just coming out in the garden with a cup of tea for her. She admitted to Marianne she hadn't expected hitting a man over the head with a frying pan would raise her status in the refuge.

Marianne laughed. 'They've all become so cowed by the men in their lives so they see you as a woman who can stand up for herself.'

'But I can't stand up for myself. He was just so ferocious; I saw the pan and suddenly I did it. I wasn't brave at all.'

'The bravest deeds are always to protect another,' Marianne said. 'Now I heard you mention to Annie that you used to make curtains. Is that right?'

Eve said it was. 'Why, do you need some?'

'I do indeed,' Marianne said. 'The ones in the playroom are threadbare, and when the light is on you can see right through them. Not a good idea here. I bought a length of material some time ago, the lining and the header tape too, but as so often happens here the person who had said she'd do them left suddenly without any notice. Could you run them up for me? There's a sewing machine in the playroom cupboard.'

Eve was delighted to be given a job she knew she'd shine at. The coral-coloured fabric Marianne had bought was very attractive too and it would transform the playroom. She worked on the curtains in the evenings when the children had gone to bed. There was a table in there with leaves to pull out, which was ideal for sewing by hand.

They were completed in three evenings, and once Eve had pressed them and hung them, she was delighted with how they looked and called Marianne in to see.

'Oh my goodness!' she exclaimed, clapping her hands. 'They look wonderful! A really professional job. In winter this room is going to be so much cosier.'

Eve had grown to like Marianne and was reminded of her own grandmother who had died when she was six. Granny was in her sixties, stout, a blue rinse in her white hair and a well-powdered face. Like Marianne she always helped people. Had she known any beaten wives, she'd probably have taken them in too.

'How did you get them to hang so perfectly?' Marianne asked, running her fingers down the edges. 'I tried to make curtains once and the lining puckered up the whole thing and they looked a mess.'

'You have to hand-sew the lining to the curtain fabric,' Eve said. 'It was lucky for me you had this big table; the secret is to lay them out on something large.'

'I do hope you didn't hurt your broken ribs again?' Marianne looked concerned.

'I was careful with the lifting and stretching, and Mavis hung them with help from Jenny.'

Mavis and Jenny were another two of the inmates, as they jokingly called themselves. Jenny was leaving with her two children the following week for a flat in Brighton. Mavis was a hard-faced East Ender, with closely cropped hair, tattoos and, at her own admission, had been a drug addict and served time in prison. There was something very likeable about Mavis: she told the funniest stories, she was generous with her time and often bought cakes for everyone out of the little money she had.

'So how much do I owe you?' Marianne asked.

'Nothing. It was my pleasure to do it, and you've helped me so much by letting us stay here.'

'Hannah was right about you; she said you were a good woman,' Marianne said. 'She's rarely wrong about people, and when I chatted to Tabby and Olly I could sense they'd been well brought up. We're lucky at the moment all our ladies are wholesome. It isn't always the way. We've had some monsters in the past, with equally nasty children.'

Eve giggled. She wondered what one had to do to get the label of 'wholesome'; it was the sort of thing her grandmother used to say.

She had learned that Marianne had started to take in women at risk when she had been widowed over twenty years ago. She had worked for the Citizens Advice Bureau, so she had come across women who needed temporary help in her work. But she was known to be fussy about who she would take, insisting that the go-betweens, solicitors and social workers vet the women for drink, drugs or a criminal record. If she didn't like the look of them when they arrived, she refused them. But it appeared that Marianne's system didn't always work; there were upper-class women she'd accepted that were absolute horrors, liars, thieves, refusing to help with the housework, fighting and expecting the other women to mind their kids. Marianne had to take a step back and take the women in most urgent need.

'Perhaps I could ask you to give me a reference when I leave here, so I can get a job?' Eve said hopefully. 'I mean, for my sewing skills. I haven't worked since I got married, though I make Tabby's dresses.'

'Was your husband the kind that wanted his woman barefoot and pregnant in the kitchen?' Marianne asked.

Eve was amused at the old-fashioned statement and had a job not to laugh. 'Yes, I suppose he was.

Though I thought it was sweet at first that he wanted me at home.'

'It's very difficult to know how a man will be once you're married to him,' Marianne said thoughtfully. 'My Percy was old-fashioned. He didn't do a hand's turn around the house, but I didn't expect him to. Our generation of women were programmed to serve. But Percy was kind and loving and shared all he had with me, that's what's important. It will give me pleasure to give you a reference, my dear, and I hope it helps you move on to a happier life.'

That night Eve thought on Marianne's words and realized that in the three weeks she'd been in the refuge she had grown. Firstly, she'd stopped being scared. When she'd arrived, she was not only scared of Don but almost everything: meeting new people, any form of change, being disapproved of, even strangers in the street. That had vanished, perhaps because she'd been forced to change. As a result, her bond with Olly and Tabby had become much stronger. They were laughing again, relaxed, eating and sleeping well, the three of them really liking being together. She knew whatever happened she wasn't ever going to subject them again to any man's bad temper and violence.

By talking to the other women here and learning about the benefits system which she had been completely ignorant about, she felt more confident about

the next step. If Don refused to pay her maintenance, which was likely, she would need that.

But perhaps the best thing of all, and rather surprising to her, was that all the other mothers looked
up to her. It wasn't just her quick thinking in bashing
the frying pan on Alf's head. One woman had said it
was the quiet way she spoke and her calm air. Having
always described herself as timid and dull, it was
wonderful to hear she didn't come across that way.

She was, of course, in the same boat as the others.
Each of them had picked a violent man, but though
Eve had the excuse that she was young and unworldly
when she had met Don, she soon learned from the
other women that some had been involved with dangerous men all their lives. Mavis warned her that
falling for dangerous men could be addictive, as she
knew to her cost. She said she'd known women that
had escaped from one toxic relationship and then
run straight into another. She said they always
claimed, 'I couldn't help myself.'

Eve had no intention of forming any relationship
until she'd got her life back on track, made a new
home and had work. But however anxious she was to
get started on that, she knew soon she would have to
leave here. Hannah had said three or four weeks, and
that was nearly up.

She didn't want to leave. Olly and Tabby loved it,
and she would miss the camaraderie with the other

women. Despite having lost just about everything, they were all incredibly open and friendly, and they shared so much laughter and banter. She'd never really experienced that before. One hot afternoon everyone, mothers and children, went to the beach together and it was about the most fun Eve could ever remember having. They'd all dug into a box of donated things to find swimming costumes. Some were really old, others huge or tiny, some just bizarre, the kind someone might have bought in a sale then regretted. But they all managed to find something to fit. Eve's was bright orange, the sort of vivid colour she'd never have worn normally, and like all the others she didn't really care what she looked like. It just gave them more to laugh about.

Someone said how good it would be if they could all share one big house instead of all going their separate ways. They spoke of having no need for babysitters, always having company, sharing the children and so on. Eve knew that in the real world it would never work, but it had felt good to think these women who just a couple of weeks ago were total strangers now didn't want to part company with her.

When Hannah arrived on Friday morning, Eve knew immediately her days here were numbered.

Hannah's best asset was being straightforward; she came right out with stuff and was realistic.

'You knew this was just a stopgap,' she said, as Eve took her into the sitting room away from the other women in the kitchen. 'It's given you a chance to heal, to consider what direction you want to go in next. You said you felt you had to go back to the Grove Park area because of the children's school. Well, I haven't managed to wangle you a flat, but I've had an offer from someone I know well. She has offered to let you and your children have three rooms upstairs in her lovely house.'

Eve thought that sounded loaded with problems. Perhaps Hannah read her mind because she smiled.

'Sylvia, like Marianne, is a widow with a background of nursing and social work. Just occasionally she'll take a mother and her children in if I feel the family will fit in with her. It's walking distance to the children's school, near St Mildred's Church, which I'm sure you know, and social services will support you financially until such time as the court has made a decision about the house. The downside is that although you will have your own bathroom, you will share the kitchen with Sylvia. But you've got used to that here, so I don't think you'll find that a problem. I hear you're a good cook, and I'm sure Sylvia will be happy for you to take over that role. She claims she can't boil an egg.'

Eve's first thought was that she was going to be very lonely. Again, Hannah must have read her mind.

'If all goes well with Sylvia, I know she'd be happy to keep an eye on the children if you want to get a little job. They can walk home from school quite safely. You can, if you wish, claim Sylvia is an aunt and that you're just staying with her until you get your house back. She won't mind at all, and by working you'll make some new friends.'

'Will I be able to get our stuff from Briar Road?' Eve asked.

'Yes, I'll sort that with your husband's solicitor. My plan is that on Monday Martha will come down here to get you. She'll take you straight to Briar Road and meet our van driver. Donald will have been told he mustn't be there. Should he turn up the driver knows to call the police. I'll also contact the court to ask them to push your divorce through quickly and explain that you are virtually homeless. That is one huge advantage of this arrangement. Had I managed to get you a flat, they'd be in no hurry to sort the property and assets out. This way they'll see you as a priority.'

Eve smiled weakly. For the first time since settling here, she was scared. It was a big step living alone with the children, and under another woman's house rules. What if Sylvia was a strict disciplinarian and didn't like the children making a noise? What if she wanted a servant not a lodger? Was she old, infirm? She had so many questions, but it seemed too rude to ask them when Hannah had arranged all this for the right reasons. She was going to miss the other women here so much. But being alone was how it was going to be for the foreseeable future, and she would just have to get used to it.

Eve made her famous spaghetti Bolognese for everyone on Sunday night, and she bought two bottles of cheap white wine and a couple of bottles of lemonade for the children, plus several sticks of French bread. She wanted to create a bit of a party atmosphere, however sad she was to be leaving. Marianne had also bought some wine, and Annie had made a vast trifle which Marianne claimed would feed the whole of Sidmouth.

Once they'd all squeezed around the kitchen table, the children on a separate folding one, as normally they had a couple of sittings, Mavis filled the glasses with wine. Each of the mothers had bought Eve something: lipstick, nail varnish, fish earrings to remind her of Sidmouth, and from Annie a little address book with everyone's address in it. 'Not necessarily a real home address,' she said, 'but somewhere we can be contacted. We all hope we can meet up again one day.'

Mavis stood up and clinked her glass for attention. 'We all want to wish you well, Eve. We're going to miss you more than you know. Just don't let any man push you around again, and if you do decide to marry again, make sure he's rich. But let's try and arrange a reunion. The end of July 1999, next year. I'm sure we can all squeeze into B&Bs somewhere here for the weekend. But as you are the organized, brainy one, Eve, we'll expect you to write and remind us . . . and also find a venue.'

There was a burst of laughter at that.

'If you've found a rich husband, we'll come and dump ourselves on you,' Annie said.

Marianne had the last word after all the food and wine was finished.

'It's always sad to say goodbye to someone we've grown fond of, and the story of Eve whacking Alf with the frying pan will be passed on to all new mothers who come here. But please don't let me open the door to any of you again to find you with battered faces and misery in your eyes. Whatever you do when you leave here, please don't find a brute to do it with. Now, how about three cheers for Eve, Olly and Tabby, and happiness in the future?'

Eve could still hear the cheers ringing in her ears as Martha drove them away back to London the next morning. It was the first day of the school summer holidays and already very warm at nine in the morning. As they drove along the Esplanade to leave the town, Eve noticed Olly and Tabby looking enviously at children going off to the beach carrying buckets, spades and inflatables. She knew they felt the same as her and wished they weren't leaving.

*

Alan, the man with the van, was already parked out-side the house in Briar Road when Eve, Martha and the children arrived.

Eve felt a tremor of fear as she got out of the car. Her old house looked no different to when she'd left it, except that Don hadn't cut the grass in the front garden. There was no reason she should be afraid; Don wasn't going to come here. But it was as if she'd stepped back four weeks to being the mouse who took the beatings and was somehow convinced she'd earned them.

'You'll be fine with Sylvia; she's a good woman,' Martha said, picking up on Eve's anxiety. 'This is the start of a new life. It won't be perfect for a while yet. But you know it will be before long.'

Hannah had said that Don hadn't once asked his solicitor about seeing his children, not even to ask if arrangements should be made. He had never been much of a father. He never went to school events, always putting his work first. He never took the chil-dren to the park and she couldn't remember when they last had a family day out. Indoors he said board games were tedious and he never read to the chil-dren at bedtime. In fact, Eve had always felt that once he realized children made a noise, demands on him and were expensive, he'd have preferred not to have any. Yet, for all that, Eve was surprised he hadn't asked for custody of them, even if just to spite her. Hannah had said he might very well do that still, once he realized he hadn't got the whip hand any longer. But she didn't think any judge would take him seriously.

Could he have another woman? The kitchen didn't look as if he'd cooked anything in it since she left. It was messy with unwashed cups and takeaway food containers, but she got the impression he'd only spent a few nights here. So where had he been?

There was a time when it would've broken her heart to discover he had someone else. Now she hoped he had, as it would make him far less likely to stall on divorcing her, and with luck he might forget he had children. They wouldn't care if they never saw him; they'd seen too much of his nastiness to care about him.

Alan got a couple of big suitcases and a few boxes for toys from the attic, and they all set to work.

The children sorted the toys and books, mentioning to Alan they'd like their bikes from the garage, but they didn't seem to want to take much. As for clothes, Eve had to supervise that, or they'd have no warm coats in the autumn or stouter shoes.

Eve took only the clothes and shoes she liked the best; in the past few weeks she'd got used to having little choice of what to wear, and she'd found it liberating. She was more concerned with taking her sewing machine and her boxes of threads, bias binding, buttons and all the other equipment she needed for dress- and curtain-making.

Finally the van was packed, and they set off from Briar Road to 64 St Mildred's Road, just a five-minute drive. Martha said Alan would drive her back to get her car after they'd unpacked.

Eve knew St Mildred's Road well as she'd helped make curtains for two families in the road, back before she married Don. Her boss had taken her to help hang them when they were finished, she remembered, noting the similarity of the forties-built semi-detached houses with leaded windows to her parents' home in Eltham.

It was a short distance between the two houses — too short really, as Eve had to face up to the fact that soon she'd be in a house with a strange woman and Martha would be gone.

Alan set to work unloading the van and Martha marched purposefully up to the front door and rang the bell. Eve and the children followed her.

The door was opened by a slender woman with white neatly permed hair, wearing a pink print dress. She had cornflower-blue eyes and her smile was a wide one. 'Come on in, Eve, I'm Sylvia, as no doubt you realize.' She looked at Alan who was carrying the two big cases. 'The big bedroom at the front,' she said. She then looked at Olly and Tabby and held out her hands.

'And you two must be Oliver and Tabitha. I'm so pleased you're coming to stay for a while. In a minute, when you've got all your stuff upstairs, we'll have some tea and cake. And we can start to get to know one another.'

It didn't take Alan long to carry everything upstairs, and then Martha said she must go.

Eve stood in the hall, moving from one foot to the other with nervousness. 'Can I phone you sometimes?' she asked in a small voice. As quiet as Martha was, she had a feeling they could be friends.

'Of course you can,' she replied, then, looking at the two children, she held out her arms. 'Big hugs, please. I'm going to miss you two, and mind you're good to your mum.'

The children let Martha embrace them and told her they were going to miss her too. Martha turned to Eve then and enveloped her in her arms. 'Stay strong for those lovely kids, and for yourself,' she said quietly to Eve. 'You can be happy here. Sylvia is a good woman. Keep in touch.'

'You've been so lovely,' Eve said, trying hard not to cry. 'One day, when I've got my own house back, you must come to dinner. But go now, before I frighten the kids by crying.'

5

'Now, remember you don't have to tell anyone at school why you left Briar Road. You can just say we've had a holiday and now we're living with my aunt Sylvia,' Eve said to the children as they put their blazers on ready for the first day back at school in September. 'I'm coming with you this morning as I'm going in to see Miss Edwards to explain what's been happening.'

Eve knew Miss Edwards the headmistress was the soul of discretion, and she would be a great ally should Don ever go to the school to try to get the children.

The summer holiday had been blessed with fine weather and the children had made new friends locally. It was a quiet street with little traffic, and it had been good to see them joining in games of rounders, hopscotch and chase as if they'd grown up here. Northbrook Park was very close and most afternoons they went there and had a little picnic. One thing Eve had noted was that children from older, more traditional homes, were kinder, more welcoming. The children in Briar Road had been very uppity sometimes, boasting about foreign holidays, their fathers' cars and a great deal more.

Living in Sylvia's house was so much better than Eve had imagined. She was easy-going, generous with her time, and affectionate to the children. She'd had a problem with her hips a few years earlier so she'd had the ground floor of her house renovated and extended into the big garden so she wouldn't need to go upstairs. What had been her sitting room at the front was now her bedroom, the dining room behind was now a spacious modern kitchen with French doors on to the garden, and the old kitchen a very smart bathroom. She told Eve she hadn't been upstairs for at least eight years, but she got her cleaning lady to clean it once a fortnight.

Before they got here, Eve had imagined one of those primitive dark and ancient kitchens like she remembered from her grandmother's, so it had been a nice surprise to find a house with all modern conveniences, like a dishwasher, fridge and freezer. She was only too happy to cook for Sylvia and do the shopping, and they had come to an amicable financial arrangement where Eve paid three-quarters of the food costs and Sylvia one quarter. Only Sylvia didn't stick to it; she bought fresh fruit, fish and vegetables from a mobile shop that called each week, and refused to say how much she had spent.

Eve liked cooking for Sylvia as she appreciated it

and was always happy to try something new. Often the children would disappear while Eve was cooking, and she'd find them snuggled up with Sylvia on the sofa watching the children's programmes on her television. It was a happy relationship for them all. Eve weeded the garden and cut the grass, something she loved, while Sylvia took the washing out of the machine, hung it on the line, and often had it ironed before Eve had time to remember it.

Just last night Sylvia had said she was going to miss the children now they were going back to school, but that if Eve wanted to find a job, she would happily mind the children after school. On the strength of that Eve had decided that later this week she would go up to Blackheath and see if her old employer still had her shop there, as maybe she'd take her on again. But today, after leaving the children at school, she was going to give their rooms a spring clean.

Eve left the school at ten. She'd had a good chat with Miss Edwards and put her in the picture. Along with cleaning the children's rooms thoroughly she had to finish some curtains she'd made for a neighbour. She'd put a little advert in the local shop window for curtain-making services and she'd had some response, though the curtains tended to be very basic unlined ones, not the kind of hand-finished work she liked to do.

Eve was feeling happy. The children had been glad

to go back to school, even though Tabby had to start at the nearby senior school and leave Olly in the old juniors. Although money was tight, she was coping and feeling optimistic about the future.

Suddenly she recognized the sound of a car engine coming up behind her and her blood ran cold. If it was Don, and she was certain of that by the sound of the engine, she didn't want him to know she'd seen him, so she bent down as if to retie her trainer laces and surreptitiously glanced behind her.

It was Don. She might have known he'd come to the school today just to unnerve her. Possibly he'd seen her go into the school building and guessed she was putting the headmistress in the picture about the separation, then waited for her to emerge, intending to follow her to see where she was living.

'Right, you bastard,' she muttered to herself. 'Good job I've got time for a wild goose chase.'

She teased him by going right back to their old house, nipped up an alley and then led him down back streets the long way towards Lee. He was still on her tail right up until she came to Lee station. She darted in and ran up the stairs. There was a point on the platform where she could look over the fence down on to the road. There he was, just across the street on a double yellow line. She went into the ladies' until a train came, and after it had gone, she came out to look over the fence again. He had gone; he clearly believed she'd got on the train to Lewisham.

She rang Hannah then to report him. Then, after carefully checking the street again and making absolutely sure he wasn't lurking somewhere nearby, she went home. It had been a very long walk and she felt exhausted, but her delight that she'd got the better of him perked her up. But he might be at the school again at three thirty.

'Don't worry,' Miss Edwards said when she phoned to explain what had happened. 'I'll keep Olly here for the after-school club and get someone to bring Tabby here too. I'll personally check your husband isn't outside. If he is, I'll call the police. If not, I'll take the children home myself.'

In the weeks that followed, Eve often felt she was some kind of special agent, constantly vigilant to keep her children safe. They walked to school alone, but she followed them, just to check he wasn't lying in wait. At home time she did the same in reverse, getting to the school early and taking up a position where she could monitor the cars arriving. Miss Edwards was supportive; she appointed someone each day to take Olly and Tabby to the school gates after the bulk of the children had left. At that point Eve would come forward and take over. After three weeks with no sighting of their father, Eve felt he'd lost interest and finally Olly and Tabby could walk to and from school alone.

When she first moved in with Sylvia, she had thought making curtains there would be impossible as there was no big table and little spare space. She had her sewing machine on a small side table in her bedroom but trying to cut curtains on the bed or floor was a recipe for disaster. Then Sylvia said she thought there was a folding table in the garden shed and she should go and look.

Sylvia was right, there was a sturdy white plastic one, and while nowhere near big enough there was also a large piece of wood, some three feet wide and eight feet long which she could balance on top of the table. She carried them up to her room and tried it out. It certainly wasn't perfect, but she could slot the wood against the wall at the side of her bed until she needed it.

When she looked at a finished batch of curtains draped over a chair, awaiting delivery, she felt God was helping her. That made her laugh as she'd abandoned any belief in such things at eight when she'd prayed to God to make her hair curly. But nowadays she was prepared to believe in anyone who appeared to be on her side.

By the end of September, Eve stopped thinking Don might do it again. She could see that the new peaceful life showed in her face; she felt she looked five years younger. Olly and Tabby were happy. Sylvia was like a grandmother to them, and they were eating and sleeping well. They never mentioned their father, and rarely even the old house, though they did talk about the house in Sidmouth and the fun they had had there. Sometimes the three of them would look at pictures of houses in estate agents' windows and pick the one they'd buy if they had the money. Eve daydreamed about that a great deal. She thought that if the courts decided the house must be sold, she would move down to Devon and start a new life.

She was lost in one of those daydreams late one evening as she was pressing some curtains she'd just finished sewing. There was a sudden sharp crack, quickly followed by the sound of glass breaking and a thud as a brick landed on the floor inches away from her.

'Good God!' she exclaimed, and began to shake with fright. She knew immediately this was Don's work. But she wasn't going to look out of the window in case that was what he was hoping for.

She wondered how he'd found out where she lived, and how he could be sure that the children weren't in there with her. What if the brick had hit one of them?

Sylvia had gone to bed and must have been too deeply asleep to hear the glass breaking, so Eve didn't wake her. Olly had the other front bedroom, and he hadn't woken either. She rang the police to report it, but they didn't offer to come immediately, saying only that they'd call to take her statement in the morning.

It was impossible to fall asleep. She lay there trembling with fright, all the past hurts and cruelty running through her mind. If he was still angry enough with her to do this, months after she'd left him, what next?

Sylvia was shocked when Eve told her what had happened the next morning, and even more shocked when it transpired to be a waste of time calling the police. When they came at ten, they showed little interest or any sympathy. They said they would speak to her husband, but pointed out there was no proof it was him; it could've been done by someone on their way home from the pub.

However, when Eve phoned Hannah to tell her, she was concerned. She said she thought it was because Don had been told that their decree nisi would be going through in a matter of days and then the court would decide how the assets would be divided. 'He's running scared,' she said. 'He knows that he'll be lucky to even get a third of the value of your house, and he'll be ordered to pay maintenance. The brick thing was probably just to put the wind up you. But two can play at that game. I'm going to put in a claim that you wish to go back to Briar Road because you're staying with a friend under cramped conditions, which isn't ideal.'

'But won't that make things worse?' Eve asked.

'For him it will. Trust me, Eve, we must never let him think he's winning. He's trying to bully you and intimidate you. We have to show that those tactics are not going to work.'

Eve got the window mended, telling the children she thought it was just a hooligan who had done it. Even after everything she didn't want them to think their father would do something that might hurt them.

A few weeks later the decree nisi was granted, and just another week after that Hannah arrived at Sylvia's with a big smile on her face. 'You can go back home,' she said.

She handed Eve the letter she had received from the family court. The first part was legal stuff for Hannah, but then it moved on.

We understand that Mrs Hathaway and the two children are living temporarily in a friend's home, and therefore it is in the interests of Oliver and Tabitha Hathaway's security and well-being that they are not subjected to another disrupting move. It is the court's opinion that they should be living in the family home at Briar Road in Grove Park. It has been reported to us that Mr Hathaway has not been living there since Mrs Hathaway moved out, and so we recommend she moves herself and her children back there forthwith.

'I am really surprised they've done a complete turnaround,' Hannah said, smiling broadly. 'This was what I wanted for you when I first agreed to act as your solicitor, because it's the ideal solution. But they said back then that due to your husband's volatile nature it was better for the house to be sold and the proceeds divided. However, your ex-husband is living with a divorced woman in Catford. He told his solicitor he wished to marry her, with the probable intention of moving her into Briar Road. That would be a real miscarriage of justice, when his ex-wife and children might be left without a permanent home. But quite honestly, Eve, I think he's lost interest in you.'

'That's the best news ever. I mean, him losing interest in me,' Eve said stoutly, even though she didn't really believe it. Don didn't like to be thwarted; even now he was probably dreaming up some kind of revenge. 'You can't imagine how often I've daydreamed of my spacious pretty home. I know I've got everything I need at Sylvia's – she's a darling – but it's not my house filled with my things. One thing worries me, though. Don might have lost interest in me, but he certainly won't have lost interest in the money he stood to get if the house was sold.'

She knew her curtain-making business could be more profitable in Grove Park; she'd have more space to work in, and the house itself was almost a showcase to her design abilities. Had it not been for making curtains she would've been struggling to make ends meet on the benefits she received, as so far not a penny had come from Don. When the CSA finally nabbed him, he was going to blow a fuse. But maybe she'd soon be in a position to support herself without any money from him.

'So does this mean I can sell the house if I want to?' she asked. She had, after all, wanted to move away and put the bad memories behind her.

'No, you can't sell without his permission as it was bought in both your names,' Hannah said.

Eve's face fell. Don wouldn't give his permission; she knew that.

'Don't get upset, Eve,' Hannah said. 'At that point I expect Don's solicitors will agree to the sale providing he has a share of the sale price. As there was no mortgage and the money to buy it came from your father's estate, I would anticipate they'd only ask for the profit made on it since you bought it, and any money Don spent on improvements to the house.'

'He didn't make any improvements except his garden shed.' Eve smirked, remembering what a big child he'd been about it, saying no one was allowed in there but him. He spent hours out there, smoking and drinking beer. 'He's welcome to take that and the profit,' she added.

'If you are happy to go along with this, I'll set the

wheels in motion. But Sylvia is going to miss you once you've gone home.'

Eve didn't want to think about that, all three of them were going to miss her. But perhaps they could have a regular day when they visited.

'What if Don does threaten me, though?' Eve asked, and she could hear her voice quavering. 'Somehow I can't see him taking this lying down.'

Hannah put her hands on her hips and looked determined. 'You, Eve, have the full force of the law behind you,' she said firmly. 'His solicitor will spell out to him what will happen if he does make a nuisance of himself. But I don't think he will, Eve. He hasn't demanded access to the children. That one day of going to the school was most probably a blip when he was feeling sentimental. He hasn't been there since. I'm not entirely convinced it was him who threw the brick. How would he know you were there? For your own good, Eve, you must try to forget him.'

To Eve's delight, Don agreed via his solicitors to pack and remove his belongings within two weeks, and also to pay up what was owed for utilities. They did point out that they would be putting in a claim for a share of the value if she decided to sell the house. Eve had opened her own bank account soon after moving in with Sylvia, and as she'd never attempted to withdraw any money from the old joint account, he couldn't demand anything else back.

Child support was the only thing that hadn't been brought up. Doubtless he'd told his solicitor that as she'd left him, he saw no reason he should pay anything. She could almost hear him saying that. However, as she had made a claim for social security, they would get the CSA on board whether she or Don liked it or not.

Knowing that if Don was pushed too hard, he'd dig his heels in, when a child support officer rang her, she informed him that her ex-husband was a violent man. Hannah had told her they never liked to put a woman and children in jeopardy, and she hoped saying that would make them back off.

As she'd managed so far without money from Don, she wasn't anxious to start now and give him something to hold over her. Of course, she hoped that in time he would help out financially of his own free will, and then she'd be happy to allow him to see the children. But she certainly couldn't bank on that.

Alan, the man with the van, came back again to move her. The only difference was that this time she had to pay him. But it was good to see him again and he was delighted she was going home. 'You and the kids belong in your old house,' he said, ruffling the children's hair affectionately. 'I hope your life has turned a corner now and you can learn to be happy again.'

When they arrived at Briar Road the first thing he

did was change the locks on both the front and back door. He also suggested she always put the burglar alarm on.

One early Sunday evening, two days after moving back in, Eve stood at the back door gazing happily at the garden. Despite the uncut grass and a great many weeds, the late-summer flowering plants she'd put in over the years blazed with colour. She knew that in a few weeks the Indian summer they were having would be gone and that autumn would set in. Tomorrow after the children had gone to school, she would get the mower out of the garage and cut the grass. That was a job she'd always loved. For now it was enough to just look and be happy. But she was a little concerned as to why Don hadn't done anything with his shed. It was locked so she couldn't get in, but she'd stood on tiptoe to look in the window and it didn't look as if he'd taken anything. All his tools were still there, and the old wicker chair in which he liked to sit and have a beer was still in place.

Perhaps his new lady didn't have room at her place for a shed and didn't want his tools cluttering up her home. Yet he'd taken things from inside the house that she hadn't expected, like a lovely bone china dinner service her father had bought them, two oil paintings they'd bought on their honeymoon, and the twin bedside lamps in their old bedroom that they'd bought in a ridiculously expensive shop in

York when they'd had a few days' holiday there. If his new lady didn't appreciate his tools, why would she find room for things that were clearly a reminder of his marriage?

Eve knew this was Don being spiteful. He had targeted the things he believed she cared about most. But it was laughable how wrong he was. The washing machine, the hoover and the dishwasher were more valuable to her; she certainly didn't want to hold on to things they'd bought together. They were just reminders of how bad it had become.

He had left the house messy and grubby, but she had expected that and worse. For now she was happy to see her children's delight to have their own rooms again. She was looking forward to adding new little touches to the house that Don would never have liked, and as soon as she had a bit of spare money, she was going to have some driving lessons and buy a little car. Her father had been teaching her when she was in her twenties and had said she was good enough to put in for the test. But then he'd died, and Don had pooh-poohed her passing. But she wouldn't let anyone put her off now; she had become a new woman.

6

Eve stood for a little while at the French windows before drawing the curtains, looking out into the garden. It was just half past five in the evening, but already it was getting dark. Recent heavy rain had brought lushness back to the grass; it had looked dead after she had cut it when they had returned here. The leaves on the trees were turning gold and yellow, some already beginning to fall. She had almost forgotten how lovely the fiery red Acer looked in early autumn, and she reminded herself that she must get out there soon and plant some more spring bulbs under the bushes and trees.

'What's for tea, Mum?' Tabby yelled from upstairs.

Eve sighed. She was always telling her and Olly to come down if they wanted to know something, not shout like fishwives from upstairs. She smiled at herself – that had been something her mother had always said. Like so many of the things that her mother had said when Eve was a child, she found herself saying exactly the same. *Do you have to wear that? I've just ironed it.* Or: *Pull faces at me and the wind will change, and you'll stay like it.*

As a teenager she'd thought such remarks completely nonsensical. Well, perhaps she still thought the one about the wind changing was ridiculous, but she did sometimes despair about the amount of washing and ironing she had to do.

'So what's for tea?' Tabby repeated, this time at the door of the sitting room.

'Chicken casserole,' Eve said. 'I've made some apple crumble too. If you haven't got any homework to do afterwards, I thought perhaps we could play a board game?'

Tabby's face lit up. Both she and Olly loved playing games but quite often Eve had too much work making curtains to play with them. It was fantastic how well her little business was growing, and many of her clients asked for her advice on wallpaper too. She was toying with the idea of doing an interior design course, with the long-term plan of maybe opening a shop. But tonight she wanted to play with her children. She knew before long they would say they were too old for board games.

It was a really good evening. Olly and Tabby were their usual competitive selves, arguing about who was the best at the game. Eve felt she was lucky having two children who actually liked one another. 'It's so good to be back home,' Olly said at one point. 'I liked being with Auntie Sylvia, and I miss her, but it's nice to have all our old stuff around us.'

'Speaking of Auntie Sylvia, I must ring her tomorrow and suggest we go down and see her on Saturday. I'd like to ask her here for the day, but she can't walk that far.'

At nine Eve packed them off to bed with hot chocolate, then did a bit of sewing by hand.

She had only been in bed with the light turned off for perhaps twenty minutes when Eve heard a click. It wasn't loud, but she recognized it as the latch on the gate at the side of the house.

Alan had noted there was no lock on the gate when he had changed the other locks, but she'd told him not to worry because Don had to get his stuff from the shed.

She got out of bed and went over to the window to look out. To her dismay she saw Don making his way to the shed.

Judging by his unsteady gait, he was drunk. Had he forgotten he didn't live here any longer? Surely not! But occasionally in the past when he'd been very drunk, he'd gone in his shed and fallen asleep. She wasn't going to call the police unless he did something to upset her.

As she watched he unlocked the shed, went in and lit the Tilley camping lamp he had in there and opened the window a little way. Then, slumping down in his chair, he lit a cigarette.

Eve watched him for a while, feeling oddly sorry

for him. She wondered if his relationship with the woman in Catford had turned sour. She had plenty of grievances with Don, but she had hoped he could be happy with this woman. As he wasn't doing her any harm, she decided to leave him there.

He was gone the next morning, and Eve thought no more about it.

Two weeks passed and the same thing happened again. Don came in through the side gate, unlocked the shed and fell asleep in the chair. Once again, he was gone in the morning. But this time Eve felt she should do something about it. She didn't like the idea of him coming every two weeks forever. Besides, that shed really belonged to the house and she should have a key to it. He might want to collect his tools, and that was fine, but it would be far more convenient to her to keep the lawnmower and garden tools and chairs in the shed.

She wrote a very polite letter to Don's solicitor, saying that the shed and its contents belonged to her ex-husband, but she wasn't happy about him turning up drunk to sleep in it. She offered to buy the shed from him for a hundred pounds. However, if he did want it and his tools, she asked that he make an appointment to take them away.

His solicitor acknowledged her letter and said he would pass on the content to his client.

A week passed, and when Don didn't telephone or come to the house, Eve assumed he'd accepted what she'd said and that he'd make an appointment to sort out the shed. But about ten days after she'd written the letter, he was out in the street on a Saturday night, screaming abuse at her.

She looked out of the window to see him in a loud black-and-white-checked jacket and jeans. As he was standing under a lamp post, she could see his face clearly and it was contorted with rage.

'You had to put the boot in, didn't you, bitch?' he shouted, and waved his arms like a madman. 'I only dossed there for the night, but they say I've infringed the fucking rules. What do you want? To see me put in prison?'

She knew there was no point in going out to try to talk to him. So she ignored him, hoping he'd just stop and go home.

But he became more vocal and abusive, turning on a neighbour who came out to try to reason with him. Then the police arrived and Don ran off like a rocket. One police car pursued him and the other one remained and an officer spoke to the neighbour who was outside and then came and knocked on Eve's door.

She explained how he'd slept in the shed a couple of times and about the letter she'd sent to his solicitor. 'Then tonight he just turned up ranting and raving,' she explained. 'I didn't go out because I was afraid he'd hit me. He often did in the past.'

'I expect your letter to his solicitor wound him up,' the older policeman said. 'We will give him a warning and that will probably be the end of it. But should he return, tonight or any night, give us a ring.'

After that evening, Eve found herself jumping at every little sound and constantly peering around the curtains to see if he was in the shed. She was irritated that he still hadn't made arrangements about it, and she resented having it hanging over her head, never knowing when he might turn up again.

Two weeks later Eve found a curt note from Don pushed through the letter box.

I will be collecting the shed and tools next Sunday morning, she read. He hadn't even signed it.

It was dry the following Sunday, but Don didn't turn up. The Sunday after there was a little drizzle, but still he didn't come.

Eve became really angry then. She knew it was his way of winding her up, and he was succeeding. On Tuesday morning the post brought her decree absolute, confirming she was finally divorced from him. That made her feel braver. She decided she'd wait for one last Sunday. If he didn't come then, she'd break into the shed, pack up his tools and sell them.

Joanne Monday, a neighbour in Briar Road, invited Eve and the children to a birthday and fireworks party on a Friday night in late November. Sam her son was going to be twelve that day and he had become Olly's best friend since they moved back.

It had turned wintery the day before, and when Eve ran into Joanne at the supermarket, she joked that she wished she'd never agreed to it.

'I've always hated fireworks,' she said. 'But Sam went with Greg to buy the damn things back in October, and then, as you probably remember, it tipped down for three solid days around Guy Fawkes Night. I don't like them lying around in the garage, and I thought Sam's birthday was a good time to let them off. I must've needed my head examined.'

'It'll be fun,' Eve said. 'You and I can stay in the kitchen to organize the party food and Greg can be with all the kids outside. Men like fireworks; they'll all come in as soon as the fireworks are gone and if it gets cold.'

Joanne laughed. 'Good idea, Eve. We'll open a bottle or two and pretend we're really busy.'

Eve had loved Guy Fawkes Night as a child; her father always took great pleasure in making a guy for the fire and a great display of fireworks. They always invited lots of children, and her mother made hot dogs and toffee apples.

But those good memories had been wiped out three years ago. Don had thought it was great fun to light firecrackers, a kind of firework Eve thought had been banned years before. Once lit and thrown on

69

the ground, they jumped and banged completely randomly. Obviously they were very dangerous, especially around young children. Don took no notice of her warning and threw a lit one down. It almost hit Tabby's leg, and when Eve dared to scream at him, Don hit her and swung her around into a wall, fracturing her arm. She'd had to get a taxi to the hospital to get it X-rayed and set in plaster. The A & E department had been full of people with firework or bonfire injuries. She was there in agony for almost eight hours, a night she would never forget.

She had only taken Olly and Tabby to organized firework displays since then, and never considered having a party at home. The pain she felt that night and the gruesome sights she had seen in A & E were enough to put her off fireworks for life. However, Greg, Joanne's husband, was a kind, organized man, not the type to allow any child near fireworks or to get in a rage with Joanne. So Eve had promised to make some chocolate-covered flapjacks and the children would be happy with her just being there with them.

The party was fun. Joanne had invited Colin and Eileen Tolworth who had only recently moved to Briar Road. They had three children, all similar ages to Tabby and Olly. Eve felt that five adults and seven children was the perfect number of people to get to know. She had half expected someone would remark on the scene Don had made a couple of weeks earlier when the police had been called, but fortunately they didn't.

It was nearly ten when Eve took the children home. By eleven they were in bed and Eve turned off the lights downstairs to go to bed herself.

She was at the foot of the stairs when she heard the side gate click and her blood ran cold, afraid that Don had once again called to make a scene. She went upstairs without putting any lights on. There was a faint glow from the night light in Tabby's room but that was all.

She went to the bedroom window to peep out and, as she had expected, Don was there and to her disgust he had dropped his trousers and was defecating on the lawn. Rage welled up inside her. This was the final straw, completely wiping out the joyous evening she'd had with her children and neighbours.

He stood up and fastened his trousers, and the way he fumbled at them was proof he was very drunk. He had a job to unlock the shed, dropping the key on the ground twice. But finally he was in, locking the door behind him, and as before he lit the Tilley lamp and settled down in his chair for a cigarette.

She thought of phoning the police, but it would be hours before they came, and then suddenly an idea came to her.

The window was open, the Tilley lamp just inches

from it. If she waited until he fell asleep, she could creep down there and, using a stick, push it over. That would teach him a lesson about coming round here, shitting on her lawn and making a nuisance of himself. With luck he might even get a bit burnt before he got out.

7

As Eve made her way to the kitchen door in the dark her heart was thumping so loudly she was afraid they'd hear it next door. She had waited patiently for Don to fall asleep in the shed, getting into her night-clothes so that should a neighbour spot her she could claim she'd just heard a noise in the garden and gone out to investigate. It seemed like an hour she waited, but, in fact, it was less than fifteen minutes. She was armed with a wooden spoon to push the Tilley lamp over, her plan being to put it in the dish-washer afterwards, which conveniently was almost full.

The sky was clear and quiet now; by morning there might be frost. Could she really do this? Teach that brute of an ex-husband once and for all that she wasn't one to be pushed around any more?

Yes, you can, she said in her head. *A good fright is what he needs.*

She stayed on the path to the shed. She wasn't going on the grass for fear of stepping in the disgusting addition he'd left on the lawn, but she hoped he'd step in it himself when he came running out.

The small shed window was just above her face level. But by standing on tiptoe she could see the Tilley lamp and his head lolling on the back of the wicker chair. He was snoring loudly, something she'd managed to forget he did in the past months. Taking the wooden spoon firmly in her fist, she lunged at the lamp and it fell. There was no crash and she thought it must have landed on his coat.

Time to turn tail and run, lock the door and get into bed.

As she got into the dark kitchen and locked the door, it struck her that if the fire brigade was called, they might wonder why she'd started the dishwasher up around the same time the fire started. So she ran the hot tap, gave the wooden spoon a scrub and put it in the dishwasher with the dirty things. Then she ran swiftly up the stairs.

She was just nodding off when she heard a whoosh, something like the rockets she'd seen and heard earlier. She leaped out of bed and went to the window. To her horror, the scene before her was one from a disaster movie. The whole shed was ablaze – not just the small fire she'd envisaged, but a roaring, crackling fire eating everything in its path.

He'll have got out, she told herself as she dialled 999. 'My shed is on fire,' she blurted out after asking for the fire service. 'Please come quickly – it might set the house alight.'

She gave the operator the address and was told they would be there immediately.

Back at the window she saw the fire was licking up the Leylandii tree on their neighbour's side of the fence. Another time she might have been glad of that – they were ugly and kept the sun from the garden – but her thoughts were all with Don. Unless he had got out just after the lamp had fallen and she didn't see him as she washed the spoon, then he might still be in there. There was a crack as the window glass broke, and another bang which could be the fire igniting stuff like white spirit or even petrol he'd kept for his strimmer. She shuddered at the thought of him being in there still. If he was, he'd be dead. Despite all the horrible, hurtful things he'd done to her, she'd never wished him dead. Only to give him a good scare.

You've got to keep your head, she told herself, pulling her fluffy pink dressing gown on. *You have two children who need you.*

As the fire engine tore into the road, siren wailing, Eve went out by the front door.

'There's a gate at the side,' she said, pointing it out, her voice strident with fear. 'Why did it catch alight? Should I wake my children up and get them out?'

'Calm down.' One of the burly firemen put his arm comfortingly on her shoulder. 'We'll just investigate and if we think you should leave the house, we'll come and tell you.'

'OK,' she agreed. 'Is there anything I can do to help?'

He smiled a smile that said this was men's work. 'Go indoors into the warm.'

Suddenly the drive and the road beyond was full of frantic activity as firefighters pulled out their hoses. Lights came on all down the road, and people began coming out of their houses to look. Just then a police car arrived. She thought the police would come straight to her, but they didn't and disappeared round the side of the house. Eve went back inside so she could see what was happening.

The water was turned on and two men held the hose directing it on to the shed roof, letting the water run down it. Almost immediately the fierce blaze slowed right down and one of the firemen kicked the door in.

From the angle she was watching from, Eve couldn't see what was inside the shed. But there was still a red glow through the window on the side.

When she heard a fireman with the hose shout and point inside, she knew Don had not got out. Eve felt sick then. Her head reeled, but she knew she had to control herself until they came and asked who could've been in the shed. She must look baffled and deny that she knew anyone had gone in there.

Eve wasn't a natural liar. Even at school one straight question from her teacher about wrongdoing and she admitted it. But she had to remember what was at stake now. Her children's security. If she went to prison, they would be taken into care. Don had hurt her in so many ways, not only physically but mentally too. She couldn't allow him to hurt her and the children now.

All too soon two grave-faced police officers came to the door. 'We're sorry to tell you this, Mrs Hathaway, but we found a man in your shed. He's dead, I'm afraid. Have you any idea who he could be?'

'Oh no, how awful,' she gasped, clutching on to the door frame as her knees buckled. She didn't need to act; having it confirmed was truly shocking. After a few seconds she pulled herself together to ask them to come in as it was so cold outside. They smelled of bonfire, a smell she'd always liked but now it made her stomach churn.

'Could I get you a hot drink?' she asked, her voice shaking.

'No, thank you. Why don't you sit down? Now, have you any idea who the man could be?'

She began to cry. 'It might be my ex-husband Donald. He's been a real nuisance in the past weeks, coming round here and shouting abuse, also just going in there and sleeping. Just a week or so ago his solicitor told him he was to come and collect the shed and its contents, as it was his. But you need to speak to his solicitor about it.'

'We will, Mrs Hathaway,' the older police officer, who had introduced himself as Sergeant Withers, said. 'Now, can you tell us what you did this evening?'

Eve told them where they'd been to a birthday party and how they came home about ten and the children went straight to bed. 'I stayed up for a little while, doing some odd jobs. Then I went to bed. It must've been nearly eleven, I think. Though I didn't look at the clock.'

'Did you hear anything that might suggest some-one had come in and got into the shed?'

'No. Not a thing. I was asleep and woken up by a whooshing sound, and it became bright even with heavy curtains drawn. Like someone had turned on lights in the garden. I got up, looked out, saw the shed on fire and that's when I rang 999.'

'Do you have a key to the shed?' he asked.

'No, Don refused to give me one. He said he didn't want me or the kids poking about in there. It was his hidey-hole. He used to go in there, lock himself in and sit in his chair to read papers or smoke a cigarette.'

'I'm sorry to bring this up, Mrs Hathaway, but it's on record that you reported him for physical abuse several times during your marriage.'

It hadn't occurred to her that they would check her and Don out so soon. That threw her. But she reminded herself that they were bound to find out about her injuries.

'Yes, I did. He was a violent bully, that's why I divorced him.'

'We understand the courts made him leave this house so you could come back here. Did that make you feel he could still be a danger to you and your children?'

'I certainly wasn't anxious to run into him,' she admitted. 'I fled from here to a women's refuge. But it was only right I should have the house; you see we bought it with money I inherited from my father. So it was mine by rights.'

'So how did he react when he had to leave?'

'I didn't see him then. I was told he was living with another woman in Catford. He hadn't been staying here. But I was nervous because he was very unpredictable. The first night he came to get into the shed I was really scared about what that might lead to, but I couldn't bring myself to go out there and have it out with him. I decided that I would eventually sell the house, give some of the money to him and move away from London.'

The sergeant's questions went on and on, about who Don's friends were, who might know he was in the habit of coming here. Whether he saw his children regularly and if he paid her maintenance.

Eve thought her head might explode; it was quite obvious to her that she was the prime suspect. 'Can we do this in the morning?' she pleaded eventually.

'It's been very upsetting and surely it must have been a careless accident.'

'Maybe, but we'll know more when the scene is examined by forensics. They'll be here at first light. Why didn't you keep the side gate locked, Mrs Hathaway?'

'It used to be,' she said. 'When I came back here, a man changed the front and back locks, and he asked me about the side gate because the bolt part had rusted and fallen out. I said I needed to leave it for the time being as Don was supposed to come and get the shed and his tools, and he was unlikely to tell me when he was coming.'

They left then and she locked the door behind them and went upstairs. She was trembling all over. She was shocked to the core at what she had done. It was supposed to have been to teach him a lesson, not to kill him.

'You murdered him,' she said to herself as she stared at her reflection in the bedroom mirror. She looked pale and hollow-eyed, her hair lank and dull. She guessed that she would be questioned over and over again in the next few days. They'd interview the neighbours too. Perhaps even go to the children's school. And how was she going to tell the children?

8

Eve felt nauseous. She had barely slept at all and got up at first light. She sat at the kitchen table, her head in her hands, deeply regretting her actions.

It was just four weeks to Christmas, she had dozens of things to do, and yet somehow she had to tell her children that their father had died in a fire in his own shed. How did you tell children something like that? Especially when she was responsible. Last evening both Olly and Tabby had been so joyful. She had even dared to feel proud of herself for leaving their father because it was having such a good effect on them, especially Olly.

They had woken fleetingly at the noise of the fire engines and men shouting, and called out to her. They were both still in bed and accepted her story that the shed had caught fire, perhaps started by a stray rocket. Olly got up and looked out of his bedroom window for a second or two but went straight back to bed. She had expected them both to insist on coming downstairs and to feed on the drama that came with a fire, but they didn't. There weren't even any further questions. Just two sleepyheads wanting the warmth of their beds.

Today, however, would be the day of reckoning. They'd be getting up soon, excited because she'd promised to take them to Bromley to do a bit of Christmas shopping and get a few new decorations as the old ones looked a bit sad. But once she told them their father was dead, all that excitement would vanish and there would be tears and questions. Eve didn't know how she was going to get through it.

At eight the police and a senior fire investigator knocked at the door, wanting to look in daylight at the burnt-down shed. The children didn't even respond to the doorbell and remained in bed.

Eve was still in her pyjamas and dressing gown, but she went out with the police to look properly. There was little left of the shed. Two blackened upright posts were on their side by the neighbour's fence, the floor planks had mostly burned right through and there was a heap of metal on the ground below from spades, forks and such like, the wooden handles gone. There were also tins of old paint and piles of screws, nuts and nails, their cardboard boxes destroyed.

The worst thing to Eve was to see the legs of Don's chair and even part of the back and his cushion had survived. She supposed his burning body had sheltered them. She told herself that at least that meant he died without waking or he would've been on the floor. But that was no comfort and guilt washed over her like a tsunami.

She scuttled back indoors then, not just because it was cold but because she was afraid she'd blurt out what she'd done. The senior officer said he would be back to speak to her after the inspection. The smell of smoke still hung in the frosty air. She also noticed Don's excrement was still in the middle of the lawn. No one had stepped in it.

Sighing, she made her way upstairs to take a quick shower and get dressed, then she'd wake the children.

'Dad's dead?' Olly frowned, looking incredulous. 'He was in the shed and burned with it?'

Tabby was sitting beside him on his bed, both still in their pyjamas. Her eyes were wide with astonishment at what they'd been told.

Eve had told them as gently as possible, but her own eyes filled with tears as she told them she thought he must've knocked over his lamp.

'You said you thought it was a rocket last night,' Tabby said accusingly.

Eve had forgotten she'd said that, and was surprised Tabby even remembered as she'd been so sleepy. 'I know, I did,' she agreed. 'I said that on the spur of the moment as it was the only thing I could think of that might have started a fire. Of course, I had no idea he was in the shed then.'

'But you're glad he's dead, aren't you?' Tabby said petulantly.

Eve's stomach lurched. 'No, of course not,' she snapped. 'He was horrible to me but that doesn't mean I'm glad he's dead.'

Then the police were banging on the back door, so Eve told the children to get dressed and she would let the police in.

Sergeant Withers, the man who'd spoken to her the previous night, was with Detective Inspector Radcliffe, a tall bony-faced older man with piercing dark eyes that unnerved her.

'Will you run through the sequence of events last night for me?' Radcliffe said. 'I believe you went to a birthday party along the road.'

'Yes, that's right, at number twelve. They had fireworks they hadn't used at Guy Fawkes because it was raining that night, so they decided to use them for Sam's birthday. Sam's their son, my Oliver's best friend. We were there till about ten and then came home. The children went straight to bed. I went in their rooms to tuck them in and kiss them goodnight and I wasn't long in following them to bed.'

'So what woke you and what time was it?'

'I was woken by a whooshing noise. I thought I was dreaming about a rocket for a moment or two, then I noticed there was light coming through the curtains, so I got up and looked out of the window. That's when I saw the shed was on fire. I didn't think about what time it was – I just ran downstairs to the phone and rang 999.'

'How did you imagine the fire had started?'

'I didn't know. I had that thought about a rocket, but it surely wouldn't make a shed go up like that. Besides, all the fireworks had been let off at the party long before we came home. It did cross my mind Don might have lit it to scare me. He has been coming back here sometimes, drunk as a lord, and going in there, continuing to drink and smoke until he fell asleep. The last time he came here I called the police because he was shouting abuse at me out in the street. But it never occurred to me when I saw the fire last night that he might be in there.'

'But you considered he might have started it to frighten or upset you?' Sergeant Withers took up the questioning, looking at her intently.

'Well, yes, but I was too panicked by how fierce the blaze was to think of anything much except whether it would spread to my house or next door. Their tree was already alight.'

'We found human excrement on your lawn,' Sergeant Withers said. 'Have you any idea who did that?'

Eve forced herself to gasp and look horrified. 'Really? How disgusting. It could only have been

Don. He would know that such a thing would make me very upset and angry.'

'We will, of course, be taking a sample away to be analysed. Now the door was locked from the inside. Do you have a key to it?' Withers asked.

Eve shook her head. 'No, he said when he put the shed up that he didn't want me poking around in there. He never let me or the children go in there.'

'Sounds like quite a charmer?'

'He was to other people, but he had become very nasty to me and put me through more misery than I can describe. But he's my children's father and it's horrible he should die that way. Do you know how the fire started?'

'It looks like an old camping lamp was the culprit. Maybe it was knocked over.'

Her blood ran cold at that. Had they worked out she could've knocked it over?

She tried hard not to let them rattle her, just kept crying and saying how awful it was. There were more questions about why she and Don had separated and where she had been when she was away. She explained all that and about how she'd only recently been able to come back to the house.

'He must have been angry about that,' the sergeant said.

'I'm sure he was. He got angry very easily. But I hadn't seen him since I went away to Devon with a badly injured leg and broken ribs. I've had no contact with him at all until he came round here shouting and calling me a bitch.'

'Do you have life insurance?' Radcliffe gave her an intense look, as if he could see right down to her soul.

But Eve was genuinely surprised by his question. 'I don't know –' she hesitated, trying to remember – 'I think Don took some out when Tabby was born, but I don't know if he carried on paying it.'

'Surely you'd see payments for such things on your bank statements?'

'I couldn't look at his bank statements. He said financial things were his job.'

'You didn't have a joint bank account?' Withers asked, and he sounded like he didn't believe her.

Eve felt foolish. Hannah had been shocked by that and made her open one of her own. 'Don wasn't what they call "a new man",' she said by way of explanation. 'He had old-fashioned ideas about men's and women's jobs. He was the breadwinner, the master of the house, and sorted the bills and finances. I cooked, cleaned and looked after the children.'

The two men nodded. She suspected they had the same values.

'I only got my own account when I came back here to live,' she went on. 'He may well have cancelled the insurance, and there were no bank statements here in the house when I came back; he wouldn't have left them here for me to look at. Anyway, to be honest, the only thing I thought about was putting the utilities in my name and about the buildings and contents insurance. But I still haven't got around to checking about that insurance; I must do it.'

Withers asked a great many more questions about Don's work, his friends and what she knew about the woman she'd been told he was living with.

'I know nothing about her,' she said truthfully. 'Not her name, how old she is or even her address. But his solicitor would know. I have his address. I don't know much about Don's work any more, or friends either, because in the year before I left he rarely spoke to me about anything. We didn't go anywhere together. He was hitting me more often, and maybe that was because he was worried about his business, but if he was, he didn't tell me.'

'So you won't be grieving for him?'

Although that question was said in a gentle manner, she felt it was a test.

'Not weeping endlessly,' she said tartly. 'But I did love him once, and he is my children's father. I wouldn't wish such a horrible death on anyone, least of all Don. But he got in that shed to wind me up. That's how nasty he could be, so, no, I won't be playing the grieving widow, but nevertheless it is terribly sad.'

'Quite so,' Withers said. 'But his post-mortem will give us more information about whether he'd been drinking or using drugs. I suppose under the circumstances you won't feel comfortable with contacting his parents. We could do that for you.'

'I don't know them,' she said.

The detective inspector had been standing silently by the French window for some time, allowing the sergeant to do most of the questioning. She had the idea that he wanted to study her. She had noticed his eyes widen at her response to the question about Don's parents.

She hadn't once thought of them. Did that make her a bad person? Should she tell these men they'd never shown any interest in her or the children?

'I'd be grateful if you could contact them. Don didn't have much to do with them, and they didn't bother with me or the children,' she admitted, 'but all the same it's a terrible thing to lose your son, and I don't think I could tell them that.'

'Quite so, Mrs Hathaway,' the detective inspector said. 'Do you know where they live, have an address for them?'

'I think they live in Ongar in Essex,' she said. 'But I've never had their address.'

'We can find them,' he said.

'So what happens now?' Eve asked.

'Well, given the time of year, that a post-mortem will be needed and more investigation and forensic evidence will need to be collected, I can't see us being able to release the body until January,' Radcliffe said.

Eve thought it was awful that it wouldn't be over before Christmas, but she bit that back for fear of sounding heartless. 'Who's supposed to arrange his funeral now we're divorced?' she asked.

'As you are the mother of his children, I'd say you,' Radcliffe said with a frown. 'But that seems unfair, all things considered, and maybe his parents will want to deal with it. Or even his girlfriend.'

'They aren't likely to get in touch with me, but could you tell me how his parents react?'

'I'll give them your address and telephone number, and say they need to liaise with you. I hope that won't cause further headaches for you. Now, if you'll excuse us, Mrs Hathaway, we have to speak to your neighbours. Do be prepared for other people coming to look at the site. And obviously you and your children must not touch anything in there.'

'Why can't we touch anything?' Tabby's voice piped up from the hallway. She came into the kitchen, her fair hair tousled and unbrushed and her face a curious mixture of suspicion and naivety.

Radcliffe leaned down to her level to answer. 'Because, my dear, when we investigate accidents like this we don't want anyone who isn't involved, like you and your brother, leaving fingerprints which might confuse us.'

'Daddy never let us go into his shed,' Tabby said. 'Olly and I used to wonder what was hidden in there.'

'I don't expect there was anything hidden,' Eve said. 'Sometimes grown-ups just like having a place to go that's all their own.'

'Your mummy's right.' Radcliffe smiled at Tabby. 'I've got a shed too, and I really don't like other people going into it. Especially when they think they're tidying it up for my own good.'

Eve was touched that Radcliffe was being so nice to her daughter, but she wanted him gone so she could get on with the day. 'It's time for breakfast now,' she said. 'Call Olly and I'll make some scrambled eggs.'

'We'll be off now,' Radcliffe said. 'Goodbye, Mrs Hathaway. I'll be in touch as soon as I have something to tell you.'

The sergeant said his goodbyes too and they went out through the kitchen door, and she saw them stop to speak to the two men still checking the shed.

Olly came into the kitchen then. 'Are we still going to Bromley today?' he asked as if nothing had happened.

'If you two still want to,' Eve said calmly. 'It's up to you.'

'I want to go,' Tabby said, twisting a lock of hair round her fingers. 'And what will we do for Christmas now?'

Eve wondered if they'd both taken in what had happened. They were behaving as if it was just any old Saturday morning. She didn't want them to be crying or asking endless questions, but it was very odd that there was no reaction.

'What would you like to do?' she asked.

In past years, various people on the road had invited them in for drinks, some in the morning, some in the afternoon. Don had always been keen to go, and she'd gone along with it to please him. 'I expect some of the neighbours will feel awkward asking us after what's happened, so perhaps today we could look for some good games to play.'

'I wish we could go back to the house in Sidmouth,' Tabby said. 'They'll all be jolly, and we wouldn't have to pretend about anything.'

'Why do you think we have to pretend here?' Eve asked as she whisked up the eggs.

'Because that's just the way it is.' Tabby shrugged. 'Olly said he's glad Daddy's dead. He said he hated him. You feel that way too, Mummy, don't you? But neither of you will say it to the neighbours, will you?'

'"Hate" is too strong a word,' Eve said gently. 'I'm not glad your father has died, and I'm sure Olly isn't either. But Olly and I won't miss the man who bullied us. That isn't hate; it's just being honest and realistic. Now, how about inviting Sylvia for Christmas dinner? She'll have to get a taxi here, but you both like her and it's sad for her to be all on her own.'

9

London, 1999

Patricia and Ernest Hathaway, Don's parents, or Patty and Ernie, as they liked to be called, came to Sunday lunch with Eve and the children at the end of March.

It was their first visit since Don's funeral back in January, though they had kept in touch by telephone. Eve had been astounded by Patty and Ernie when they rang her after the police had informed them of their son's death. There was no reproach, no sharp remarks; they were genuinely concerned for her and the children, asking what they could do to help. It soon came to light that it was Don who had turned his back on his parents, not the other way round. To Eve's further shock Don hadn't seen them in years, so when he had said he was going to see them in Essex, he had been lying and going somewhere else.

The couple immediately volunteered to help with funeral costs, but as Eve had found the life assurance had been kept up, and she was told all funeral costs would be paid, she thanked them and said it was covered.

Eve met them for the first time at the funeral at Hither Green Crematorium. It was a bitterly cold grey day and she found them just as she'd imagined from the phone calls, kind, gentle people, who had been hurt badly by their son's indifference to them.

Patty was short and chubby with tightly permed hair and a blue rinse. Ernest was tall like Don, his hair snow-white and his shoulders stooped. They were only in their early seventies but in their black clothes they had looked old and careworn. Yet they had been so happy to greet the grandchildren they'd never met before. In fact, Patty had held their hands throughout the service and the tears in her eyes when she looked down at them spoke volumes about how sad she was that she'd missed out on so many years and milestones with them.

Today Ernest had volunteered to take Tabby and Olly to Northbrook Park before lunch, perhaps knowing his wife had things to say to Eve that she didn't want the children to hear.

'He was the worst kind of son,' Patty blurted out almost as soon as the door closed behind them. 'Always trouble. There were times when he was a teenager when I wanted to throttle him. But how could he have kept you and our grandchildren from us? Was he ashamed of us?'

It was that cruelty to his parents that helped Eve

feel less guilty about his death. Almost everything Don had told her about them was lies. He had claimed they refused to meet Eve because they had wanted him to marry a previous girlfriend. Over the years Eve had given him many photos of the children to send to them, even written letters for him to enclose with the letters he said he was going to write. But he didn't write, or send them; she supposed he'd just thrown them away.

Some of Don's friends and customers had approached Patty and Ernie after the funeral service to offer condolences, saying what a good man he was, how reliable and hard-working, and how terrible it was that he had died in a fire. Yet Don had clearly bad-mouthed Eve because none of them offered her any sympathy or even acknowledged her as the widow. She was tempted to tell them a few home truths about the man they were praising, but she was neither bold nor brave enough for that. If it hadn't been for Patty and Ernie's support and that of her neighbours, she felt she might have broken down.

Since then Patty had told Eve on the phone many things about her son. A couple of years before he met Eve he'd borrowed money from them to set up his plumbing business. It was a large sum which they could ill afford, and he never repaid a penny of it. They wrote many letters asking for repayment, but he ignored them. When the house in Lewisham was sold and Don and Eve moved to Briar Road, Ernie and Patty had been unable to find the address or phone number. Eve was blissfully ignorant about this. It had made her so happy to hear the joy in their voices when she had invited them here. Perhaps they thought that after Don's funeral she would distance herself from them.

Now sitting with Patty, drinking coffee in front of the gas fire, Eve felt a great sense of comfort and growing affection. 'Why did you think Don was so mean to you?' Eve asked, feeling she had to get to the bottom of it.

Patty sighed. 'When he was about eight, he got in with some boys at the junior school who had parents who were better off than us. We lived in Lewisham then and Ernie worked for the railways, and he didn't earn that much. Anyway, Don got invited back to these other boys' homes, mostly in Eltham, and suddenly we and our home weren't good enough for him.'

Eve could imagine that. Don had always been impressed by wealth. In his work he would rush out to do jobs for the chosen few who had big houses and smart cars; a couple of pensioners with a leak in their kitchen or bathroom had to wait until it suited him.

'Ernie's father died when Don was twenty-four. He left his house in Ongar, the same one we still live in, to us. We decided to move into it as Ernie was retiring, and because we were at our wits' end with Don. He was still living with us, verbally abusing us, treating it like a hotel and refusing to give us anything for his keep. He said it was a son's right to live in his family home. He was very messy, came home drunk all the time and played loud music half the night at weekends. So, to make sure he didn't try to move in with us at Ongar, we gave him our old house in Shipley Lane in Lewisham.'

'That house was yours?' Eve was really shocked; Don had told her he had to work night and day to get the money for it. 'That's where we lived when we got married. Both the children were born there.'

'An old neighbour I ran into told us that, but we were always too scared of Don to go there and confront him. In fact, we imagined he'd sell it. By the time we knew you and the children had been there all along it was too late for us to go over there and have it out with him. Mind you, I doubt we'd have been brave enough.'

Eve didn't know what to say. It was appalling he would lie about a gift from his parents. But then she ought to have guessed when he had commandeered the money from her parents and bought the house he wanted.

'It could all have been so different if he'd had a heart,' Patty said sorrowfully. 'It hurt us still more to find he took your inheritance to buy this place, and

97

with the money from our old house he bought himself a flashy car. He even bragged about it to the neighbours.'

Eve moved closer to the older lady and put her arm round her. She could see how upset Patty was to admit all this about her only son.

'We gave him everything we could.' Patty sighed. 'Ernie took him to football, swimming and anything else he wanted to do – endless weekends where we went out of our way to please him. I cooked the meals he liked, struggled to buy him nice clothes, a bike, roller skates, whatever the latest craze was. Maybe that's where we went wrong?'

'I always tried to please him too,' Eve admitted. 'But except from some odd times when he seemed happy, like after we moved here, he was impossible.' She showed Patty the scar on her shin, some three inches long and the marks of stitches showing clearly. 'That was the last beating, the one that made me run away with the children.'

Patty patted Eve's arm in understanding. 'You know, as we drove back home after his funeral, I was glad he'd gone. God forgive me for saying that, but it's true. When the police said he'd died in a fire in his shed here, when he shouldn't have been on the property, I guessed he had come round to try and hurt you. Thank goodness he didn't succeed.'

Eve had been pleased to see they looked so much

younger today than they had at the funeral. She felt it was probably the relief of the pressure they'd lived under for so long. Patty wore a two-piece pale blue outfit that made her cheeks look rosy and matched her blue eyes. Ernie wore a tweed jacket and cavalry twill trousers. His shoes were highly polished, which made her think of her father. Don's looks obviously came from his father's side: dark eyes and tall with broad shoulders. Olly had the dark hair and eyes too, but Eve and Tabby both had fair hair and blue eyes.

Eve got up as she remembered the lunch. 'I'd better get the veg on; they'll be home any time now. But thank you, Patty, for telling me all this; everything slips into place now.'

'And what are your plans now?' Patty asked, following Eve into the kitchen area.

Eve was getting a bunch of carrots from the fridge door. 'I can't make any plans until probate has been settled. Since I found out about the big insurance policy I did get to wondering if Don intended to kill me.' She laughed nervously. 'To my surprise it was for a quarter of a million!'

'Really! I tell you, he might have been my son, but I wouldn't have put it past him. Coming back here to frighten you. That was plain nasty and maybe the start of something worse.'

The police knew before Eve did about the size of the potential insurance payout and her heart skipped

99

a beat when they told her, expecting that would further convince them that she had set the fire. Since his death they'd come again and again with more questions and dug into her background too, so it was obvious she was the only real suspect. But it transpired Don had upped the insurance premium just two years before, and possibly that put Eve in the clear as she'd known nothing about it.

'So when that's all sorted, any chance you could move nearer to us?'

If Eve had known the Hathaways all her married life, she would probably have been delighted to move nearer them, but she'd set her heart on moving to Devon now. Maybe not Sidmouth, but somewhere along that stretch of coast.

'Think how nice it will be for you to come and have holidays with us at the seaside,' she said to Patty. 'I can probably get a higher price for this house than it will cost to buy a similar-sized one in Devon.'

Ernie and the children came back in then. 'We saw daffodils out in people's gardens,' Olly said excitedly. 'Does that mean it's spring?'

'Almost,' Eve said and smiled at her son. He was a ray of sunshine, sensitive, kind and he loved nature. He noticed leaves unfurling, sunsets, rainbows, jotted down all the different birds he saw in the garden, wanted a dog and he was even patient with Tabby when she got in one of her moods. He might look like Don, but he was as opposite in nature as it was possible to be. He went out of his way to make friends with the kids at school that others rejected. He didn't want stuff, not computer games or expensive toys; give him some paper and a pencil and he'd draw for hours.

'I need some new trainers,' Tabby said, looking down at her feet in disgust. 'These are so last year. No one wears this brand any more.'

'You bullied me to have those, and it was only last November,' Eve said jovially, not wanting her daughter to throw one of her strops. 'Let's see after Easter.'

This was typical of Tabby. Whether it was being twelve and going on eighteen, or her father's influence, Eve didn't know. But nothing seemed to please her except fashionable new clothes and sleepovers at other kids' houses. It was like she didn't want to be part of her own family any more. Eve dreaded to think what she'd be like at thirteen or fourteen.

During a lengthy roast beef dinner and apple crumble, Eve was able to catch up with what Patty and Ernie had been through over the years. Ernie had been in the army during the war and was wounded in 1944. He was sent to a convalescent home in Tunbridge Wells and Patty told an amusing story of the first time she had travelled down on the train to see him. The station names were blacked out, and she'd got off at the wrong station; it had taken two hours to get back to Tunbridge Wells, by which time she was frozen solid and wished she'd dressed for warmth rather than glamour.

All too soon, though, Patty and Ernie said they must go home, as Ernie didn't like driving in the dark.

'It's been such a lovely day,' Patty said, hugging Eve and then the children. 'You've made us feel we've got a family now.'

Later Eve was to think perhaps she shouldn't have been so quick to tell them she wanted them as family too; they would, after all, be a constant reminder of Don. But she needed their love and affection as much as they needed hers, and she resolved that when she got the insurance money she would pay back the money that Don had borrowed from them.

10

London, 2000

The young woman who stepped on to the drive and into a bright red Mercedes at Briar Road and drove away confidently at speed, looked very different from the drab, careworn Eve Hathaway of fifteen months earlier.

Last year people were saying that the approaching millennium would have far-reaching results for everyone. Whether it was universal, or just Eve finding new determination and direction, she didn't know, but she had achieved a great deal. Eye-catching in an emerald-green velvet jacket, which set off her newly coloured and bobbed strawberry-blonde hair, and jeans tucked into long green boots, she had the air of a woman who now knew what she was worth. Probate had finally been settled, and she had rung the estate agent's today to put the house on the market. The insurance had paid out months earlier, but she had wanted to wait until everything was sorted, including her own mind, before jumping into moving away.

She had booked the five-star Victoria Hotel in Sidmouth for her, Tabby and Olly for the two weeks of the Easter holidays. It was right on the Esplanade, with parking, a swimming pool to keep the children happy should it pour down, and from there it would be very easy to get to Exeter, Lyme Regis and many other places where she felt she might find the perfect new home. Patty and Ernest were coming down to stay for the Easter weekend too, so they could all go to some of the local attractions.

Eve had reverted to her maiden name Taylor and changed the children's names too, and the changes didn't end there or with the stylish hair and clothes. They had come about after she finished an interior design course last year in Chelsea. She realized that to make people want her to come into their homes and design their decor, she had to look the part.

The design course had stimulated her creativity, challenged and amused her. Most of the other students hadn't a clue how to make curtains or sew anything. They were Sloane Rangers who thought their privileged background also gave them superb taste, which it didn't. They also wanted to head a business but get other people to do the real work. Eve was not just good at making curtains, she could wallpaper and paint too. She knew that once her business was under way, she would need to take on staff, but she intended to be the kind of employer who led by experience in all the different facets of interior design.

Her tutor, a very upper-crust woman called Hester Carmichael, had actually offered her a job as her junior designer. It was flattering to be asked, and tempting too as Hester was often on television, so she'd be getting plum jobs, but Eve had set her heart on leaving London. It would be a brand-new start so she could finally put Don out of her mind.

'You have the eye, darling,' Hester had said. 'And that, along with your practical knowledge of decorating and soft furnishing, puts you well in front of most would-be interior designers.'

Eve intended to keep in touch with Hester, and buoyed up by new confidence in her abilities she booked an intensive course of driving lessons, which took seven days, with the test at the end of it. She was astounded she passed, and that boosted her confidence still more, so she bought the red Mercedes immediately. Yet throughout all this, making curtains, cooking, cleaning and all the rest of the motherly chores, her mind was constantly on the house of her dreams.

It needed to have either a big ground-floor room, or better still an annexe built on to the house, which would be her workroom-cum-studio, large enough for a vast cutting-out table, sofas for clients to relax and discuss their ideas, plus shelves and work surfaces to hold the books of fabric and wallpaper samples her clients could browse through.

Money was not a problem; after the house was sold, she could buy the right property in cash if she wanted. And afford any necessary renovations. But she had to think of schools for Tabby and Olly, a place which would be easy for clients to reach, and she would need to set aside funds for advertising her business.

Today Eve was popping down to visit Sylvia, hoping she might like to go out to lunch in Blackheath. She could hardly wait to see her reaction to her change of image.

'Goodness me, your hair is absolutely fabulous!' Sylvia gasped when she opened the door. 'Come on in. What do Olly and Tabby think of it?'

Eve closed the door behind her. 'Olly loves it, but Tabby was a bit odd about it. She kept asking me why I'd had it done. Sort of disapproving. Now, do you fancy going out to lunch?'

They had a cup of coffee first, and Sylvia said how she'd noticed at Christmas that Tabby was very critical.

Eve sighed. 'She's been like it ever since Don's death. I got a man in to clear the site of the old shed back last spring and she made such a fuss about it. I would've thought she'd prefer not to be reminded of his death. She questions me about where I've been during the day when they're at school, and when I bought the new car, she accused me of being a spendthrift and asked why I didn't keep Don's old one. I couldn't even if I wanted to, as his girlfriend had it.'

'She's at that funny age,' Sylvia said with a wry smile. 'Mostly it doesn't start till fourteen or so, but everything seems to start earlier these days. How are they about moving away?'

'That at least seems to please her,' Eve grinned. 'I suspect she wants to reinvent herself in a new place. She's accused me of that too.'

Sylvia laughed. 'Well, you have rather. I hardly recognize you from the Eve who came to stay here. Going on a course, driving, moving, new hair and clothes. But I see it as all good. You do need to put the bad stuff behind you and move on.'

Later in the afternoon Eve drove home in time for the children returning from school. She and Sylvia had enjoyed lunching in a new little bistro and catching up with each other, and afterwards they'd browsed Blackheath's antique shops.

'When we've moved you must come for a visit,' Eve said as she drove Sylvia back home. 'I'm going to miss seeing you.'

For one reason or another she hadn't seen Sylvia since Christmas, but they had chatted on the phone most weeks. She owed Sylvia a great deal for helping her out when she'd most needed someone and she valued her friendship, and she thought she'd like to come and see the new house, when she found it. But even as she asked, she wondered if Sylvia could manage the journey. She had seemed quite spritely today but walking around shops in a place you know well was very different to getting on trains and the Underground.

'You mustn't worry about me,' Sylvia said as Eve dropped her home. Once again she was tapping into Eve's thoughts. 'A phone call now and then is fine with me; I don't need to travel to see you. To be honest, I like my home. I don't really want to go anywhere else.'

Eve's house was sold for the asking price within three days. There had been a great deal of interest and constant viewings, but the couple who wanted it were ready to proceed, having already sold their house. The estate agent told Eve they were very complimentary about the decor and curtains she was including in the sale and said they wouldn't change a thing and hoped to complete a month after Easter.

Eve had planned to contact lots of estate agents in Exeter and all the way along the coast to Lyme Regis and make viewing appointments for during their holiday down there. But she hadn't expected anyone to agree to buy Briar Road quite so quickly. Now she thought she might need to find a temporary house to rent down there and put her furniture in storage until she'd found the perfect place to live. All this made it a bit scary. She would have to pack her stuff, arrange new schools for the children and find the perfect house all on her own.

Because Eve felt anxious, she rushed down to Sylvia to discuss it. As she expected, Sylvia had some sound advice.

'You don't need to search everywhere yourself to find your home,' she said airily. 'Just call the most prestigious estate agents in the area. Explain what you're looking for. A smart area but not remote, near good schools, room for a workshop and studio. Tell them you don't have time to wade through dozens of totally unsuitable properties and ask if they will do the leg work for you and select the best properties for your approval.'

Eve loved the idea, but she didn't think an estate agent would agree to it. 'They'll send me packing,' she said.

'They won't. You've got a big budget, and remember they get several thousand in commission for selling you a house. Just don't tell them you had an insurance payout; let them think you're a successful interior designer already. Bet they'll find a house for you to rent too.'

Eve laughed at the idea of portraying herself as some kind of doyenne of the design world. 'Where on earth did this idea come from?'

'Magazines I read,' Sylvia said with a knowing grin. 'You don't suppose that the likes of Madonna or Julia Roberts go house-hunting, do you? No, they use personal assistants to research the market, take pictures, etc. They only get back to the boss when they've struck gold. And don't tell me estate agents won't do it. They will if they think it's worth their while. And how about pointing out all their other clients will need new curtains, wallpaper and carpets when they move, and if they send them your way, you'll give them a cut.'

Suddenly Eve saw what Sylvia intended. This was advance publicity, getting her name about. While Eve wasn't convinced that she was capable of portraying herself as a rich, successful interior designer, it would be fun to try.

'I'd better get some arty, posh cards printed then,' she said and giggled. 'What will I call my business?'

'Well, in my humble opinion using your own name always sounds confident and classy rather than a made-up name like "Beautiful Homes" or "Elegant Living". "Eve Taylor, Interior Designer" strikes exactly the right note.'

Eve thought on that for a moment. 'Gold print. maybe on a fuchsia-pink background,' she suggested.

'That sounds glamorous,' Sylvia said. 'Now just remember you have to project yourself as the woman you want to be. Do that and you'll get there. Before you speak to any estate agent convince yourself that you're doing them a big favour, which you are, of course. And don't doubt yourself.'

Eve laughed nervously. 'Easier said than done.'

Sylvia looked at her appraisingly. 'Less than two years ago you arrived here like a scared little mouse; you looked like you thought I was going to bite your head off. But you made curtains to get some money and became brave enough to follow your solicitor's advice and got your home back. When Don died in that fire it must have been harrowing for you, but you coped superbly. So I know you can handle anything now.'

Just the day after visiting Sylvia, a woman came to the door at Briar Road. 'Mrs Hathaway?'

Eve immediately felt uneasy. The woman was in her mid-thirties, smartly dressed in a dark suit, but she had a thin foxy face, large dark-rimmed glasses with scraped-back dark hair, and her overall appearance made Eve think of Keyhole Kate in *The Dandy*.

'I'm Ms Taylor now. And you are?' Eve asked.

'Dawn Button, freelance journalist. As I understand it, your husband died in a fire some eighteen months ago, and I've been compiling an article about how wives cope in the aftermath of such a tragedy.'

'We were divorced at the time of his death,' Eve said crisply. 'And I wouldn't be interested in being part of such an article. I assume that's why you're doorstepping me?'

'I like to think I can help people who have suffered such a loss, especially those with children,' the journalist responded with a touch of indignation in her voice. She had a faint Liverpool accent, but she spoke in a clipped manner as if trying to hide it. 'Please let me come in so we can talk.'

Alarm bells were clanging in Eve's head. She'd had a couple of local journalists call on her soon after the fire, hoping for a more in-depth story rather than the bare bones which had come to them via the police. They had both been perfectly pleasant people, but she had just said she didn't wish to add anything more to what they already knew. But Dawn Button was different. Not just her off-putting appearance and accent, or her cold grey eyes, but an underlying aggression Eve could feel as keenly as a cold wind.

'I'm sorry, but I'm very busy just now preparing for a holiday.'

'But –'

Eve cut her short. 'I'm sorry. I don't mean to be rude, but I have moved on in every way since that fire. I don't wish to talk to anyone about it, so thank you for calling but goodbye. I have work to do.'

Eve shut the door quickly and went into her kitchen. But she was shaken. She had believed that questions about the fire and Don's death had all been asked. The police had been back to her dozens of times in the aftermath, and that had been scary as she felt they didn't believe her. But she had a feeling this woman had found out something which had piqued her interest, perhaps that Eve had been beaten by him, or that she'd had a big insurance payout. Or just local gossip that intrigued her. It was quite bizarre that she'd been reminded of Keyhole Kate, but she was a character who spied on people. It was also a well-known fact that journalists dug for dirt.

She just had to hope Dawn Button was gone for good.

On the last day of their glorious fortnight's stay in Sidmouth, during which Eve must have looked in every estate agent's window, not only in Sidmouth but Exeter, Lyme Regis and other small towns, she'd collected some thirty or so details of properties for sale, but now she thought she'd finally cracked it.

She was standing outside an empty rundown builders' yard and office waiting for George Mulberry the estate agent to join her, but even without going inside she knew this place was for her.

It was in the Mill Lane area, not the most prestigious of spots – there were car parks, a few offices, backs of shops and the council swimming pool – but this property at number one was just around the corner from the busy high street, the Esplanade and the sea. It had been empty for a while but it had enormous potential. Not only the yard for parking, but the reception area/office at the front looked vast. Judging by the five windows upstairs there were plenty of rooms, and as the children had loved Sidmouth more than ever on this visit she knew they would be enthusiastic.

'Ms Taylor, I assume?' Eve turned to see a tall dark-haired man in a beautifully cut grey suit coming towards her. 'George Mulberry. Sorry if I've kept you waiting, I had trouble locating the keys.'

'It's fine.' Eve knew she mustn't look too keen, but it was hard not to grin like the Cheshire Cat. 'It certainly will need a lot of renovating.'

'That's a fair statement, but it is structurally sound; a new roof was put on just four years ago. It's got the parking space you needed, plus a variety of rooms downstairs which are ideal for your plans. It's a short cut to the high street from the car parks, so there's a big footfall past the door. There's even a small garden at the back. I also imagined an interior designer would want a blank canvas to work on, rather than a move-in-ready house.'

'Maybe,' she said, even though she had already decided an attractive veranda along the front and a wall of glass where the two poky office windows were would be superb.

She'd spoken to this man, the owner of Mulberry Estate Agency, on the phone several times before she'd arrived here in Sidmouth. While other estate agents seemed only to have rather unimaginative staff, or ones that gushed so much she wanted to put the phone down on them, George seemed intelligent, resourceful and determined to find her a property. Other companies had sent her details of small ter-raced houses, flats, a farm and various other places so far removed from her remit that she was often speechless at their stupidity and felt annoyed by them wasting her time.

Over the phone a couple of days ago, George had said he thought most people would run away when they saw this place, unable to see the potential, but he had a feeling she was the kind who would love a project and could see beyond the messy frontage and the uninviting area. Maybe he was using reverse psychology and conning her, but, in fact, he had got her bang to rights.

An hour later Eve drove away smiling to herself, with the name of a builder George had recommended and the knowledge that as soon as this builder had inspected the property and given her a rough idea of the cost involved for the renovations she needed, she would be making an offer.

Inside she'd observed that the six upstairs rooms only needed decorating. Two were very large, one would make her bedroom with an en suite put in, the second the family sitting room. The present kitchen was hideous, broken-down and fit only for ripping out. But it was a great space, and she could make it a fabulous kitchen-cum-dining room. It opened out on to what George had optimistically called a garden, which was actually a tiny weed-covered rubbish dump. The front offices and the big storeroom behind were perfect for her studio needs, and even the toilet/washroom on the ground floor, which was disgusting, could make a perfect cloakroom for her clients to use. She left the property buzzing with excitement and drove to see Marianne at the refuge.

Marianne opened the door and looked blankly at her.

'It's me, Eve! Remember? Tabby and Olly, eighteen months ago?'

Marianne's eyes lit up. 'Well, I never!' she exclaimed. 'You look so different. Come on in. I take it you aren't on the run from the old man, not looking like that?'

Eve laughed as she walked in. 'No indeed. Sadly, or not so sadly, he's dead and I'm going to come and live down here.'

Marianne was agog to hear the news and took Eve into her private sitting room.

'I feel I will have to give up soon,' Marianne said,

with real sorrow in her eyes. 'Just lately I've had some real horrors here. It's exhausting when they won't cooperate, fight with the other women and cause trouble. I'm too old for it now. But seeing you looking so good might give me back my old enthusiasm.'

Eve hadn't entirely forgotten the backbiting and petty jealousies during her stay, so for Marianne to speak of giving up it had to be far worse than that. 'Don't these women realize how lucky they are?'

'Come on then, tell me,' Marianne said a little later after describing some awful scenes. 'How did he die and what brings you back here? And I want to know all about Olly and Tabby.'

Eve stayed for an hour and told Marianne how her life had turned around.

'You sure you didn't start the fire?' Marianne joked. 'I would've.'

Eve laughed. That was one story she wasn't prepared to tell. But seeing Marianne again energized her even more. From time to time there were angry outbursts from the women in the kitchen and children squabbling. She supposed it must've been the same when she was here, yet she only had good memories of it. She remembered how she and the other women had pledged to keep in touch and to meet up here again. She'd meant to, but as time went on she realized they would have little in common after all this time.

She had to leave and get back to the children; she'd promised she would take them to Bridport in the afternoon – one last excursion before going home.

'I'll be back in Sidmouth in a few weeks,' she told Marianne, as she was going out of the front door. 'Maybe I can take you out for a meal and convince you what a good job you're doing.'

'When I look at the difference in you now, I do feel a sense of pride,' the older woman admitted. 'You were very broken when you first arrived, but you did heal here. But then you always did have a bit of gumption. Remember whacking that man with the frying pan?'

Eve laughed and hugged Marianne. 'You're great at what you do. Tell the women they'd better be nice, or you'll get someone you know to clobber them.'

As Eve drove away, she glanced back at Marianne in the doorway. She looked worn out. That wasn't right when she had spent most of her life helping others.

11

Eve found it hard to settle into a routine when she got back to London after the Easter holidays. Before she left Sidmouth, leaving the children at the beach, she had returned to the property to meet Tom Bolton, the builder recommended to her. After letting him inspect the place for problems she hadn't seen, she ran through her ideas of what she wanted.

She liked Tom Bolton on sight. He had a portfolio of properties he'd worked on to show her, all of which were impressive. He was late thirties, with blue eyes, a freckled sunny face, fair curly hair and a great sense of humour. But more importantly he appeared to understand what her vision was, and clearly wanted the job as it would be a prestigious one for him and a local shop window for his talents. He said that there was a great deal of work to do, but the building itself was sound, the location ideal and the price pitched perfectly.

As soon as Eve had got back to London, she rang George Mulberry with a cheeky low offer. He came back within the hour with a counter-offer of just three thousand more. She accepted that cheerfully, asked that he took the property off the market immediately and pushed for a quick sale. She had never felt prouder of herself for being dynamic. She just hoped she could keep it up.

Four days later a folder arrived with Tom's sketches, details of the work involved and an estimate of cost. She hadn't expected for one moment that Tom would have taken on board all the ideas she'd mentioned. Neither had she anticipated he would be able to draw the ideas so well. Looking at his drawings she saw he shared her vision and knew how to bring it to fruition. She was thrilled and excited, anxious for the sale to be completed and work to start.

George Mulberry had agreed to find her a house to rent while the property was renovated, but with all these plans being somewhat up in the air, she felt fidgety and unsettled. It was just as well she had eight sets of curtains to complete, so she threw herself into that instead of daydreaming. Then, just when she'd almost forgotten her, she saw Dawn Button in the road. She appeared to have just come out of a house across the street. Eve hardly knew the family who lived there. She believed the wife was a schoolteacher and her husband a graphic designer. Their three children were younger than Tabby and Olly and went to a private school, so there was no direct line of communication. But Don had installed a new bathroom for them when they first moved in, about nine years ago, and done smaller plumbing jobs since. He had never introduced them to Eve, almost certainly because he'd sucked up to them as they were rich and told them a few tall stories about her.

Eve wasn't one to believe in coincidence. Dawn was digging for dirt, and as Glenn and Martha Onslow were two of the people who had come to Don's funeral and blanked her, they were likely to pass on anything they could about her. They couldn't know anything about the fire because Don's shed wasn't visible from their house, but they had witnessed Don shouting abuse at her in the street and probably heard other rows.

The thought of this Button woman digging into Eve's life made her shudder. While she hoped the police no longer suspected her of causing her ex-husband's death, almost every day in the newspapers there were reports of new evidence coming to light about old crimes. Eve had sensed that Dawn Button was a human jackal, and, as such, more than likely to keep chewing the bone and collecting further evidence to write a scurrilous article about Eve.

Nervousness about Dawn Button stopped Eve from talking about the new property to Tabby and Olly. She hadn't taken them to see it when they were in Sidmouth, knowing they'd hate it, because they wouldn't be able to imagine it as she could. Now she also didn't want them telling anyone where they were going either. However, when Tom's sketches arrived, she relented enough to show his sketches to them. They were enthusiastic about them, delighted to see how close the property was to the sea and shops, and impressed that they would have large bedrooms. Strangely neither of them showed any reluctance to leave London and their friends behind. They both said a new start was exciting and that Sidmouth was wonderful and agreed they would just say they were moving to the south coast.

Although the solicitors couldn't give Eve a definite date for completion, they had promised to push the present owners hard. Tom had said he had about a month's work to complete with his team before he could start on her job, but he promised that once he began on it, he would work solidly there with a view to it being finished by September.

One afternoon Eve was doing the final stitching by hand on a set of very heavy curtains when Tabby came in looking red-eyed and troubled. Olly had stayed on at school at a chess club and would be home later.

For a moment Eve thought Dawn Button had collared her.

'What on earth's the matter?' she said to her daughter, putting her arms around her. 'You've been crying! Has someone said something to you?'

Tabby mostly thought she was too old for hugs or cuddles now and usually went as stiff as a plank, but not this time. She leaned right into Eve, burying her face in her mother's neck.

'Abigail said we were glad Dad died, and she reckoned you'd started the fire so we could have the insurance money.'

Eve's stomach lurched. Abigail lived five doors down and had always been a spiteful girl. She got it from her parents who, like Martha and Glenn, were social climbers and only interested in making the acquaintance of rich and influential people. So Eve felt Abigail had probably repeated something her parents had said. Was it just guesswork or did they know something? Had Dawn Button spoken to them too? If so, Eve had no doubt they would have slandered her.

'Do you believe that?' Eve asked her daughter.

'No. But you were different after he died. And now we're moving and selling this house, and with you going on and on about your interior design business it does look as if you didn't ever care about him.'

Eve cuddled Tabby tighter, feeling ashamed that she hadn't considered how the plans she'd made might seem callous to both her children. 'My darling, I used to love your dad dearly, but you can't have forgotten how often he hit me. Each time it happened the love I felt for him got chipped away. In the end he gave me no choice but to take you two and leave for the refuge. Anyone's heart would harden towards someone who put them through all that,' she said, tears starting up in her eyes.

Eve took a moment to compose herself, and to think what she was going to say next. 'When we got this house back your dad tried to annoy or scare me by getting in the shed at night. I didn't tell you every time he did it. But you'll remember that night when he was out in the street shouting abuse at me?'

Tabby nodded. 'Yes, he was nasty. Olly and I were scared.'

'I didn't hear him go into the shed the night he died. I woke to a bright light coming through the bedroom curtains. I looked out, saw the shed was alight and thought he'd done it to frighten me, but I didn't know he was inside it.' She paused and tilted Tabby's face up so she could see her properly and try to make her feel better.

'After I knew he'd died in there it would've been a whole lot easier for me to behave like the helpless tragic widow. I could've got people running around for me and lapped up the sympathy. But all the hurt he'd given me kind of galvanized me into being stronger. I wanted to show he hadn't beaten me down. I can't claim to miss him, Tabby – he was too mean to me to say that – but I'm not glad he's dead. As for the life insurance, I didn't even know he'd taken any out until after he was gone. You shouldn't listen to nasty people like Abigail.'

'She's spread it around the school,' Tabby said, and more tears came.

Eve sighed. She wasn't telling the whole truth about what happened that night, of course, but in her defence it was true she'd never intended to kill him, only to scare him, the way he'd so often scared her. She also knew that she would probably be tortured by what she'd done for the rest of her life. That was her punishment.

However, right or wrong, she was reconciled now that Don's death had been for the greater good. To her mind her job was to love and protect her children. To be the best mother she could be and build a good life for them all.

'Tabby, if what Abigail said was true, I'd be in prison now, not here holding you in my arms. We'll be leaving here very soon, and if you don't want to hear things like that again, you can leave school now if you like. But I think it's better for you and Olly if you do these last few weeks with your noses in the air, ignoring spiteful gossip.'

Tabby's tears turned to just a sniffle, and she let go of Eve. 'But you have changed, Mummy. Why is that?'

Eve felt saddened that her daughter couldn't applaud her new decisiveness, when she knew just how badly she'd been treated. It was true that Eve had changed; almost as soon as Don's funeral was over, she was making plans to do an interior design course and looking at her whole life and her appearance in a different way. But was that wrong?

Maybe she had become a bit obsessed with moving, and during the past year as she waited for probate to come through, the children might have felt they were in a waiting room because she was always saying, 'When we leave here' or 'In the new house maybe we'll have this or that'. But she had thought both Tabby and Oliver understood what she was doing.

'I had to change, Tabby. For years I've been that meek little woman who got beaten by her husband and was too scared to stand up to him. Would you have wanted me to stay that way? Or are you just looking at me changing my hair and clothes?'

'Yes, why did you?' Tabby's lip stuck out the way it always did when she disapproved of something. 'Olly and I liked you the way you were.'

Eve tried not to get irritated at her daughter's selfishness. 'I liked you two when you were toddlers, but I didn't expect you to stay that way. I want to become a successful interior designer for me to feel I've achieved something, and so you'll be proud of me. But for that I need to look the part. Being all mumsy in jeans and a baggy jumper wouldn't really do it.'

'But now you look so nice you might get married again and the new man might not like me or Olly.'

Eve felt like shouting 'hallelujah' because she real-ized that at long last Tabby had come out with her real worry. This was one thing she could be totally honest about.

'You two are the most important people in my life,' she said firmly. 'And it will be a long while before I trust any man again. Even if Leonardo DiCaprio were to ask me out, I'd make sure he liked you two before I took him seriously.' She smiled at Tabby. They had just recently watched *Titanic* together, and they both adored Leonardo. 'But in a few years' time you and Olly will want to make lives of your own, perhaps go to university or share a flat with friends. You'll be happier to go your own way if I have a friend I want to be with. Don't you think it would be incredibly selfish if you wanted me to stay alone forever?'

'Abigail said if we got a stepfather, he'll be evil to us.'

Eve laughed then. 'She has a crystal ball, does she? Tabby, right now, I can't possibly imagine a time might come when I would want to share my home and family with a man again. But I can promise you that in the unlikely event I meet someone, if I ever saw him being unfair to you and Olly, I'd give him his marching orders immediately. But, my darling, the bad stuff we went through is over. We have a new exciting life ahead of us, so let's all be happy about the future and not look for problems.'

Tabby kissed Eve's cheek. 'OK, and I'll go back to school until we move.'

Just a few days later George Mulberry asked Eve to come and view a house he'd found for them to rent. Eve arranged for the children to go to a friend's house after school, as it was a long drive to Sidmouth and she would probably be late getting home.

As it happened she made good time and arrived in Sidmouth just after twelve. She parked her car close to George Mulberry's office, as he'd said he'd take her to the house in his car. He'd already told her it was a detached Edwardian house in a very good part of town, but when he pulled up outside it, she gasped.

It wasn't the best kept house in Manor Road, most of the others were perfection, the kind of family homes she'd seen in glossy magazines with immaculate front gardens, flower-filled borders, trimmed hedges and lush lawns. Yet like all the houses in the road, number seven was big, designed for very well-off people; she wouldn't have been surprised to see a tennis court in some of the back gardens, and top-of-the-range cars in the double garages.

'It's very grand here,' she said in a small voice, thinking it was too grand and big for her and her children.

'That's why they asked me to hand-pick a tenant,' he said. 'They wanted someone who would respect their home and look after it for them. I knew you were that person. But let's go in, Eve. It really is a family house.'

George was right. Despite its size and outward appearance, inside the interior was homely. The furniture was big and old, not antique-shop old but stylish and in good taste and lovely muted colours.

'The owners have gone over to Spain to check a property being built for them and they'll be happy to let this on a month-by-month arrangement,' George explained. 'I thought of you because when you said you needed space to cut out and sew large curtains, I thought you might need to start making some here before your studio is ready.'

'I will if I start getting orders,' she said, looking into the large dining room with an oval table designed to seat ten. 'That table would be perfect for cutting out.'

She did feel the house was far too large for them, but the farmhouse-style kitchen with a big central table was gorgeous. And they'd be here just for the summer, so she didn't need to worry about heating costs. The kids would love the big bedrooms and there was a spare one if they wanted a friend to come for a holiday.

'I've got you the names of two removal companies that also do storage,' George said, handing her a couple of cards. 'It's cheaper if you use a Devon firm rather than a London one. When you're ready to move in to the new property, they'll do that too. But ring them quickly to get a quote. They tend to get busier in the summer months.'

Eve tried out one of the two huge sage-green sofas in the sitting room. 'This is bliss,' she said, leaning back and grinning at George. 'Sign me up.'

'When you've finished looking around and maybe taken some pictures, perhaps I could take you to lunch before you go home?'

Eve wondered if that was a thing he often did with new clients, or did he fancy her? She had never been very good at picking up signals. 'That would be lovely,' she said, taking her camera out of her bag. 'And we must talk about completion dates and when I start the tenancy here.'

Half an hour later they were in a little bistro on the Esplanade. They ordered ham, egg and chips. Don had always said it was the choice of common people, but George said he loved it, and no one could call him common – he was ex-public school and had a real BBC voice – so Eve felt vindicated in liking it too.

She was finding George more attractive by the minute. He was divorced and had a ten-year-old boy he saw infrequently as his ex-wife had moved to Eastbourne. The estate agency belonged to him, he had a flat above it, and he was something of a film buff.

'I go to the cinema every week, sometimes twice. If you like the cinema, I hope you might come with me sometimes,' he said, his dark eyes looking right into hers.

'I haven't had much opportunity to go out in the evening since having my kids,' she said, feeling as if she was under close surveillance. 'I found it hard to get a babysitter.'

She got out a couple of photographs of Olly and Tabby to show him and he remarked on what attractive children they were. 'But when you move here, you'll have to get someone to keep an eye on them,' he said with a knowing grin. 'I mean, you'll have to go to clients' homes in the evenings, won't you?'

'I suppose I will, for measuring up and checking what their style is. I hadn't really considered that. I suppose I thought they'd just come to the showroom.'

'You wouldn't buy a house just by looking at the estate agent's pictures,' he said teasingly. 'But you must have gone to clients' houses in London?'

'Well, yes,' she admitted reluctantly, realizing she'd been caught out. 'But I always arrange daytime viewings, when the kids are at school. But then I've mostly been doing curtains and blinds. Now that I'll be doing the whole design thing it's bound to be a bit different.'

'You can be honest with me,' he said, dark eyes twinkling. 'I know and applaud an ambitious lady, and I know you can carry off the whole interior-designer thing.'

Eve blushed. 'I've been doing soft furnishings for years and always had a flair for design. Plus, I did a design course, but maybe I did big myself up a bit.'

He put one hand over hers on the table. 'I have to big myself up constantly,' he admitted. 'I once worked in a shoe shop. But let's keep our secrets between ourselves.'

His hand over hers felt good, and his dark eyes were making her feel weak. She hadn't expected to feel desire for any man, but she knew that was what was coming. But she had to resist. It was far too soon; she had to get a grip.

'We can be friends, go to the cinema together and tell each other our secrets,' she said, making herself look right into those come-to-bed eyes of his. 'But I'm not looking for anything more, George. I've been through too much recently and the scars haven't healed yet.'

'OK, I get that,' he said, pulling a sad face that made her smile. 'How old are your children anyway?'

'Tabby is twelve, nearly thirteen now and very prickly about almost everything. Olly is just eleven and mostly a delight, but I suppose that's likely to change very soon.'

Eve found George a pleasure to talk to, interested but not nosy, volunteering information about himself and his son Noah, but not too much. He was keen to hear about her plans for the property she was buying, and he didn't use the old 'You don't want to do that' put-down thing that so many men did when women talked about building work.

'I've never been much good at DIY,' he admitted. 'I leave such things to experts and admire their skill. But you seem very knowledgeable about building work. Where has that come from?'

'Well, my late ex-husband was a plumber and his friends were carpenters, electricians and plasterers, so I picked up some of it from listening to them. But I've always been interested in houses and everything that goes into them. I read magazines, watch TV programmes about restoration and stuff. It's a bit of a passion.'

'I know someone who's just starting to convert three terraced houses into apartments. He's intending to have a show flat. Would you like me to put your name forward as the interior designer?'

Eve's heart leaped at the thought of that. 'Yes, please, George, that's my idea of a dream job. I could even source the furniture for him. I have to admit viewing show homes is like a hobby to me. I've seen some fantastic ones, and some horrors too.'

'I like them too,' George admitted. 'Luckily now I'm an estate agent it's not considered a weird thing for a man to like. I'm hoping he'll put the apartments with me to sell.'

After another half-hour in which they discussed

the start of the tenancy at the house and the possible date for the exchange of contracts, Eve said she needed to leave as it was a long drive home.

'I'll ring you as soon as I have dates for you,' George said. 'I could post the tenancy agreement for you to sign, but I'd like it if you came down here to sign it so we could do this again.'

'I'll see,' she said with a smile, knowing full well she wouldn't be able to resist meeting up with him again.

12

When George rang to say he had the tenancy agreement ready for her to sign, and the solicitors were ready to exchange contracts on the Mill Lane property too, Eve wanted to jump with joy. She told herself she was only excited to go back to Sidmouth because it was a momentous day. But the truth was she wanted to see George again, and she'd chosen her outfit for his benefit.

She was up and ready at seven in the morning. She was more than happy with her hair; she'd had a cut and blow-dry the day before and the roots touched up. It was shining like a new penny and it enhanced her golden tan. Her cream linen dress was new, and a very sexy pair of mock-snakeskin high-heeled sandals finished off the look.

She woke the children and reminded them she was going to Sidmouth so they must get their own breakfast and that she'd left pizza for their tea in the fridge. She caught a glimpse of herself in the hall mirror as she was leaving, and a sudden pang of guilt caught her by surprise. She looked like a woman who was out to impress a man. And she'd promised Tabby she wasn't interested in such things!

George jumped out of his chair as he saw Eve and flung open the door of his agency. 'Come in. I must say you are looking very lovely. Coffee before I take you up to Manor Road? You must need one after such a long drive?'

'Yes, please,' she said. It was now nearly noon, and the drive had seemed endless this time. Her appointment to see the solicitor to sign the exchange of contracts on the property and to pay a deposit wasn't until three, but she hoped George was going to take her to lunch again.

After coffee, George drove her to Manor Road. 'The owners have left it spotless,' he said as he unlocked the front door, standing back for her to go in first. 'They've removed all their personal belongings, so we just need to go through their inventory and sign it if you agree that everything they've listed, you've seen.'

After a few minutes of George reading the inventory and pointing to each entry: 'Two sofas, four patterned cushions in shades of blue and green, one dark green footstool, one marble-topped coffee table', then going on to rugs, curtains and even waste-paper baskets, Eve was bored to tears. She wanted to say she'd just sign without checking, but she supposed that would just make her look foolish, so she paid attention and occasionally asked a question so George knew she was on the ball.

The house looked even better than she remembered. The children had a whole eight weeks here before they had to start at their new schools in September and it was well situated for them to easily explore their new hometown and go to the beach.

'That's the end of it,' he said as he finally locked the garden shed after showing her the lawnmower and a couple of sunbeds. 'Are you happy to sign now?'

'Very happy,' she said with a wide smile. 'And the tenancy will start from next week as we arranged?'

'Indeed, I think the solicitor will be able to arrange completion on Mill Lane the same day,' he said, 'so I can pass over both sets of keys then. Now lunch, and as it's such a lovely day and you look so gorgeous let's go to the seafront!'

George flirted with her throughout a fish and chip lunch on the Esplanade. Eve knew she was on dangerous ground, but she couldn't help responding. He was gorgeous, his soft brown eyes like a puppy, and a dimple in his chin; as for his lips, they were made for kissing. But she managed to act as though unaware of how attractive he was and steered the conversation away from personal subjects.

He walked her round to the solicitor's office after lunch, and she told him she would be going straight home after her appointment.

'Can't I tempt you to stay later?' he pleaded. 'I could take you into Lyme Regis. I know a lovely little wine bar with a sea view.'

'That sounds lovely, but it's a long drive home and I have to start packing in earnest now. The removal firm you put me in touch with are delivering boxes first thing in the morning. I have to separate things we need for the rental house from the stuff for storage, so it's not a quick job. Not with two kids arguing about what they need and complaining if I dare suggest they do their own packing.'

'Fair enough,' he sighed. 'So, it's *au revoir* till you come to pick up the keys.'

He sounded disappointed, and on an impulse she moved nearer to kiss him on the cheek. But to her surprise he caught her in his arms and kissed her on the lips. It wasn't a real smoochy kiss, but a taste of what a lingering one would be like.

Eve scooted quickly into the solicitor's office, a little shaken. She hadn't meant things to get that far.

'Well, Eve, all packed and ready to go.' Gino the very friendly removal man grinned broadly at her.

It was a week since she had signed the inventory on the rental house. Packing up had been hard. She was ruthless and took masses of stuff to a charity shop, and lots more went in the dustbin, yet they still appeared to have far too many belongings for just three people.

'I can't believe it's all gone in there,' Eve laughed, looking into the back of the removal van and seeing it packed tight.

Gino smiled. 'We can always get a gallon in a pint pot,' he said. 'But, just to be clear, all the things for the storage unit are right at the back of the van. We pick up the keys from Mulberry's and start unloading at Manor Road, just as far as the red blanket we've put up to mark stuff for storage. Tomorrow that lot will be locked away until you want it out again. Is that correct?'

'Yes, it is, Gino, and you've been marvellous so far. I'll see you in about three to four hours' time at Manor Road.'

It was just after twelve and once the removal van had left Eve quickly hoovered round, put bleach down the loos and swept up the garage too. Tabby and Olly were due back any minute. They had left their schools the previous day, but today they'd popped round to say goodbye to a few people, including Sylvia.

She was just putting the hoover in the boot of her car when they arrived back. 'That's it,' she said with a smile. 'All done and dusted. Do you want to go in one last time to say goodbye?'

'No,' they said firmly in unison, as if they'd rehearsed it. 'We're glad to be going.'

'And so am I,' Eve said, putting an arm round each of them and kissing their foreheads. 'I think we are going to be very happy in Sidmouth. On the way there, you must tell me how Sylvia was about you saying goodbye.'

Tabby and Olly were in high spirits. They had sung along to the radio, told Eve lame jokes from a little book Olly loved, and opened the sandwich box she'd prepared at six that morning, for once totally happy with her choice of fillings. Surprisingly they didn't even complain about how long the journey was, and thankfully the traffic was light. They stopped briefly at Taunton Deane services to go to the loo and get a cold drink. Then, within the hour, they were in Sidmouth and walking up the drive past the removal van.

'Gosh, Mum.' Tabby sounded a bit taken aback. 'I didn't expect it to be so huge and lovely. It's a rich person's house!'

'We're only borrowing it,' Eve reminded her. 'And we have to be careful with it too.'

'Wow,' Olly called out from the top of the stairs. 'It's like a palace. Which is my room?'

'One is very boyish,' Eve shouted back. 'That will be your one.' She turned to her daughter then. 'Want to go and find yours? The other two are very pretty. You choose or go wherever the men have put your stuff for now. But the big room at the front is mine.'

Although Tabby had been happy on the way here, she spoke about Sylvia as if they were abandoning her. As Tabby rarely thought about anyone but herself it was strange. Eve told her how much Sylvia loved her own home and explained how she'd reacted when she'd asked her if she'd like to come to stay in Sidmouth.

'Older people don't really like going to other people's homes,' Eve said. 'They like what they know, and she's got lots of friends close by. We can phone her weekly, and if we go to London, we can pop in to see her. She told me we weren't to worry about her. But I'm glad to see that you can care about an old lady, Tabby.'

'She's nice,' Tabby said with a shrug. 'I felt a bit weepy when we said goodbye to her.'

Eve had smiled to herself at that. Perhaps Tabby was finally growing a heart.

'What will we have for dinner?' Olly yelled again.

'Nothing if you yell like that,' Eve said tartly.

'There's a good Chinese takeaway not far away,' Gino said as he walked past carrying a box of Eve's clothes. 'We'll be out of your hair in half an hour.'

'I'll make you all tea,' she said, grinning at Gino and his two assistants. 'I'm so organized I have a box in my car with all the tea-making stuff. I've even got some special cream cakes for us all to share.'

'Now you're talking,' Gino laughed. 'We do like

moving organized people. And ones that offer cream cakes are even better.'

Later, when everything had been brought in and the men were leaving, Eve gave Gino and his men twenty pounds as a tip and said she'd ring them to bring the rest of her stuff out of storage when the other property was ready. 'And, of course, everything you brought in here today,' she added. 'But at least you won't have a long drive then too.'

'It was a pleasure working for you. I hope the kids enjoy the summer here,' Gino said. 'We all hope you'll be very happy here.'

The men had only just driven away when George arrived, looking as dashing as ever, carrying a huge bouquet of pink and white flowers and a bottle of champagne.

'Just came to say the other property sale was completed an hour ago, when the money transferred. I came to give you the keys, and these, with my best wishes for a happy future,' he said, handing her the flowers and champagne. 'Now can I do anything to help?'

'Well, thank you, kind sir,' Eve giggled. 'As the champagne is cold, perhaps you could open it. I'll find a vase for these gorgeous flowers.'

She found champagne flutes in the kitchen and the perfect white vase. 'It's very well equipped,' she remarked. 'When we were doing the inventory, I was impressed at the eight champagne glasses, along with brandy, wine and even port glasses. But after tonight I'll tuck them well behind my Tesco ordinary ones so none of hers get broken.'

George just stood there smiling at her.

'What?' she said, as she put the flowers into the vase. 'Have I got cobwebs in my hair or something?'

'Not at all. I was just thinking how good you look in jeans and a T-shirt. I had the idea you were the sort of girl who was always dressed up.'

Eve spluttered with laughter. 'Me, dressed up? Never. I like to do it for special occasions, but the rest of the time I'm like this. Sorry to disappoint.'

'No disappointment,' he said. 'Quite the reverse.'

Tabby came in then and Eve introduced her, showing her the flowers. When George popped the cork on the champagne, Tabby moved closer.

'Can I have some?'

'Just a drop for a toast,' George said. 'That is if Mum doesn't mind?'

Eve was surprised how chatty Tabby was with George; she usually ignored her mother's visitors, sometimes to the point of rudeness. But maybe the half-glass of champagne brought out the best in her.

About an hour later Olly started to ask when they were going to eat. George took that as a signal and said he must go.

'Sleep well tonight, all of you,' he said. 'I hope

this is the start of a wonderful new life for all three of you.'

They waved him off out of the drive. 'Looks like he's after you,' Tabby said as they went back in for Eve to get her jacket and money for the meal.

'Don't talk rubbish,' Eve sniggered. 'He was just being friendly, and why wouldn't he be when I've just bought a property he'll get a big slice of commission on and a fee for finding tenants for his house?'

'I saw the way he looked at you,' Tabby said with a sly look. 'He's got the hots for you.'

'That's a horrible expression,' Eve said tartly. 'He is a bit of a ladies' man. I expect he puts on that face for all his female clients. Now let's go and find this Chinese takeaway. I'm starving.'

13

It took Eve a couple of days to get the house straight, and she was about to go out when Tom Bolton the builder dropped by.

'Hi, Eve,' he said with a wide twinkly-eyed smile. He was in working clothes – dungarees, a grubby T-shirt and serious workman's boots – but with his tousled curly hair and freckles across his nose he made her think of Tom Sawyer. Very cute.

'I'm free to start on the property and wondered if you wanted to come there with me now so I can go over with you what needs to be stripped out. Then I can get the first skip in for tomorrow.'

'That's great,' she said, delighted it was all systems go. She handed him a set of keys. 'You go on. I'll just leave a note for the kids, as they've gone to the beach, and then I'll join you there.'

When she arrived at Mill Lane a little later, he was opening windows to let in some air.

'Upstairs first,' he said, leading the way.

If Eve hadn't seen Tom's detailed plans already she might have been frightened at walls and a staircase being ripped out. But as she walked round with him she could see the logic in everything he was intending to do. By the time he'd gone through the kitchen and out on to the drive, she thought they'd probably need dozens of skips. But it was great that he didn't keep asking what she thought. His ideas were all brilliant. She'd have a bigger family bathroom, an en suite and a walk-in dressing room for her, plus a new, much better staircase, and a fabulous kitchen, plus a vast studio and workshop.

'So we start tomorrow,' he said cheerfully, as he finally finished the tour. 'We'll be here at eight.'

'If you need me, I'll have my phone with me all day,' she said.

He frowned. 'Give us a few days, then come and look,' he said, clearly meaning he didn't want her checking up constantly. 'Soon after that you'll need to start kitchen and bathroom planning. They often have a long lead time. The electrician will need to liaise with you, to plan where the power points and lights will go. I suggest next week. But once you've found the style of kitchen and bathroom, let me see pictures as I can probably source very similar ones cheaper. You need to think too on what you want doing to the car park. Likewise think about the garden. Are you a gardener?'

'Yes, I am, though not very experienced,' she admitted. 'I think just paving and a few raised flower beds.'

'It's walled and south-facing. Shame about all the rubbish out there,' he said, then pulled a dejected face.

'More skips?' She laughed. 'We need a skipper!'

'I know a couple of guys who will clear it and lay a terrace, but we don't want them cluttering up the car park while we've got skips going in and out and building material being delivered.'

He mentioned windows and the veranda, and said he'd text her telephone numbers of companies he'd worked with before.'

'Looks like you've got everything covered,' Eve said.

'Oh, there's always things I've forgotten about, usually the small but crucial ones,' he grinned. 'But your homework is to explore kitchens, bathrooms and windows.'

'I didn't realize there was so much to it,' she admitted. 'My head is reeling.'

'You don't have to do anything more than choose what you want,' he said, putting a hand comfortingly on her shoulder. 'I do all the worrying and planning. You just dream up how lovely it will be.'

As Eve drove home, she thought Tom's words were like music to her ears. Don never consulted her about anything, but blamed her when things went wrong. She could hardly wait to start planning her kitchen and bathrooms.

*

It was just the best of summers; Eve woke up each day feeling happy with so much to look forward to. If it rained, she stayed in and researched stuff for their new home. If the weather was good, she made picnics and took the children exploring Devon and Dorset. Long walks along clifftops and checking out quaint small towns like Lyme Regis and Bridport. Olly picked up tourist pamphlets and local papers and directed them to butterfly farms, pick-your-own fruit farms, a donkey sanctuary and weird little museums. Then there were the blazing-hot days when they stayed on the beach, going for a dip when they got too hot.

Eve hadn't once heard the children say they were bored as they always did in London. If she had to stay in because she had to telephone suppliers of fabric and wallpaper samples, or was ordering a large cutting-out table or tweaking the design for the kitchen, the children were happy doing something up in their rooms or exploring the town on their own. Sidmouth felt completely safe too. Eve didn't worry when they were out without her.

She'd hardly given Don a moment's thought since coming here. Yet at Briar Road he'd jumped into her head all the time, bringing with him an avalanche of guilt and remorse. But it wasn't quite over; sometimes, just as she was falling asleep, she would remember the fire and have a moment of panic. She supposed that was something she would have to live with. Then there was Dawn Button. Eve thought it was unlikely she'd track her down to Sidmouth, but she was wary just in case.

The one thing which stopped her dwelling on the past, and Don, was 1 Mill Lane. Work there was coming on a treat. Windows, electrics, plumbing and tiling were all done. She loved the new staircase of beautiful blond ash, complete with gorgeous hand-turned newel posts at both ends. And her idea of having a veranda across the front of the property was a triumph. The sage-green Victorian-style powder-coated aluminium posts and quarter arches had lifted the flat, bland front of the building and created something rather more New Orleans or Parisian in style. People kept stopping her to tell her how lovely it was. They were waiting now for the kitchen to be fitted, and hardwood floor to be laid throughout downstairs.

Of course, there were still masses of jobs to do. The parking area would be the last thing, but they could move in before that was done. Meanwhile Eve was planning an opening event. She would invite shop and hotel owners, and George had suggested she sent out invitations to all his clients who had bought homes in the area in the last year or two.

George turned up about twice a week, sometimes with a good excuse for calling or he said he was 'just passing'. Sometimes he invited her and the children out to dinner or the cinema. It seemed like he wanted her – he flirted, paid her compliments and took a great deal of interest in how the building work was going, and her plans for her studio – yet he never actually asked her for a date on her own. She wondered why that was? Did he have someone else?

She spoke to Sylvia about it on the phone, and she suggested inviting him round for a meal, but Eve didn't think she could really be bothered to go to that much trouble. She wasn't even sure if she fancied him any more. She thought she would sooner just have him as a friend, and that way she wouldn't be going back on her promise to Tabby.

In the middle of August Eve got a fright when she saw someone she thought was Dawn Button going into Fields the department store on Market Place. She stood across the road and waited for the woman to come out, but whether she was mistaken and it wasn't Button at all, or she had left another way, Eve didn't know. But it worried her, and she found herself constantly looking over her shoulder when in town.

One wet afternoon towards the end of August she decided to walk down to Mill Lane. She had the idea of putting up some brass rails in the studio so she could display a few curtains with different headings, coloured linings and some with fancy braid or beads.

She thought it would give clients inspiration. She couldn't order the rails until she'd decided exactly where they were going to go, and knew how long they needed to be. She'd been cooped up all day, so the exercise would be good. So, putting a notepad and tape measure in her shoulder bag, she shouted what she was doing to the children and left.

There was so much green around Manor Road, beautiful trees, lush lawns, more countryside than seaside, and she liked that contrast between the green of trees and grass, and the sea further down the hill. The rain felt soft on her face, the air was warm and the roads were almost deserted. She was so happy she'd moved to Devon; life had never been like this in London.

She chose to walk along the Esplanade, as always enjoying the view of the red cliffs up ahead and how the sea and sky were almost as one, light grey with no sun. She crossed over into Fore Street, pausing for a moment or two to look in the window of Toto's, the tiny shop specializing in stuff for dogs. The children kept asking if they could have a dog, and she was becoming keen on the idea too. A small fluffy one that didn't shed hair, a dog they could all share.

She was getting close to Mill Lane when she saw a man she'd seen earlier up in Manor Road. She'd noticed him there not just because the roads were deserted but because he wore a long dark raincoat and he had the hood up, concealing his face. He also had a rather odd way of walking, as if his feet hurt. He must have taken the more direct route to town, and Eve wondered if he'd got lost, as she got the impression up on Manor Road that he was unsure of which way to go. But he fell in behind her, so clearly he wasn't going to ask her for directions.

She glanced over her shoulder and felt rather uncomfortable at how close he was to her. She picked up speed, but again when she checked behind her she saw that he had too. But what was more worrying was that she got a glimpse of something in his hand.

Scared, she began to run, turning into the narrow lane that led to her property, but she sensed he was close behind her, running too, and all at once he was right behind her, so close she could hear him panting.

Whack. He struck her so hard on her shoulder she fell. Lying on the ground she screamed, covering her face in case he hit her there, but instead he kicked her hard in her side and snatched her bag from her shoulder.

'That'll teach you,' he snarled, and he loped away down the lane towards the swimming pool and the River Sid.

It was so much like the way Don attacked her that for a second or two she thought it was him. But this man was thinner and lighter on his feet. Then suddenly she heard heavier footsteps and looked up to see Tom running towards her.

'Eve!' he gasped, and reached down to help her up. 'I heard a scream. What happened? Was it that bloke I saw legging it down the road?'

'He hit me and took my bag,' she managed to get out as Tom helped her to her feet. She felt dizzy and disoriented, her shoulder hurt and she was afraid her ribs were broken again.

'We must call the police. Can you walk to the house?' Tom asked, putting his arm around her waist to support her.

The concern in his voice made her cry. Aided by him she managed to walk gingerly home.

Once inside Tom swept sawdust off his builder's bench and lowered her on to it. 'The bastard!' he exclaimed. 'Attacking a woman and in broad daylight too. Did you get a good look at him?'

Eve shook her head. 'I felt he was young – dark hair and a long black raincoat. He had something silver in his hand, that's what he hit me with.'

'A wrench, a spanner?'

'I don't know.' Her tears came faster then. 'He said, "That'll teach you." He was up in Manor Road earlier. That suggests he knows me, doesn't it?'

Tom had the kindest face, usually full of smiles, but right now it was hard and serious. 'Maybe, but perhaps he just saw the smart house you came out of and followed you to rob you. But I'll phone the police,' he said, 'then make you some tea. Or maybe I should take you to hospital?'

'Just a cup of tea,' she said, trying to pull herself together.

She hadn't expected Tom or anyone to still be in the building. They all normally left at five, and it was a quarter to six now. She didn't want to turn this into a drama.

'Look, Tom, I think I'm OK. If he did break my ribs when he kicked me, there's nothing they can do at the hospital. My shoulder hurts, but I don't think there's anything there to break either. Besides, I've left the kids on their own. I need to get back. I'd only come to do some measuring.'

He looked at her for a moment as if considering what she'd said. 'Why don't I take you home and we can ring the police from there then? But just let me look at your shoulder.'

Without asking he slipped her raincoat down over her arm, then dropped the neckline of her T-shirt off too, exposing her shoulder.

'It's red. That's going to be one hell of a bruise,' he said, gently touching it. 'Does that hurt?'

'Only if you press it.'

'Then maybe I'll just kiss it better. My mother always did that, and it seemed to work,' he said, pressing his lips against her shoulder.

The warmth of his lips on her skin, and his gentleness and concern, flared up the most inappropriate feeling of desire. She squashed it immediately. 'I do that to Olly and Tabby,' she said and laughed, but laughing made her ribs hurt. 'Ouch, not a good idea to laugh. That hurt my ribs, and you are definitely not going to kiss them.'

She'd had a shock, her handbag had been taken and, among less important things, her keys, purse and a credit card were gone. Yet here with Tom standing close to her, his hand still on her upper arm, a finger softly caressing it, she felt soothed. Why was that?

When she looked up, he was gazing at her, like he knew he should be making tea, calling the police or even taking her to his van and driving her home. But he didn't want to let her go.

'Maybe we should go,' she said softly, not wanting to break the spell.

With his hand still on her arm, he lifted his other one and put it on her cheek. 'You are very pretty, Eve; I can't bear you being hurt.'

Eve gulped. It felt like the beginning of something, but was it wise to encourage a man who was working for her?

'I'm not badly hurt. A couple of days and it will be all better. It was the shock that made me scream and cry. I'll live.'

He moved a step closer and brought her head up against his chest. He smelled of wood shavings and white spirit, and it was mixed with the lemon liquid soap she'd put in the new downstairs cloakroom.

'We only ever talk business when you come here,' he said, and the hand on her cheek moved down to her neck. 'But I get the feeling you've been badly hurt by a man. Am I right?'

She took a deep breath, which hurt her ribs again. 'Yes, you are, Tom. My ex was a violent bully. But I've begun a new life.'

'Yes, I sensed that and I'm happy for you. But I'd like to be part of that new life,' he said, his voice so low she knew he wasn't in the habit of saying such things to women.

'But you are, Tom. You're making my new home beautiful.'

'I meant something more than that,' he said, and he bent down and kissed her on the lips.

It was a tentative kiss, like he expected to be rebuffed, but his sensitivity touched her, and she lifted her free arm to draw him closer. All at once she felt she was on fire; she wanted him regardless of her sore shoulder and possibly broken ribs too.

The kiss grew deeper and everything around her seemed to vanish; her only thoughts were of his touch, his tongue, lips, her heart beating faster and desire threatening to overcome her.

It was Tom who stopped it. He broke away, but took her hand in his. 'Eve, I want you, but not here with damp plaster and sawdust. We need to call the police and report that man, to check you are all in one piece. And there's your kids.'

'Mr Sensible,' she said, and smiled. 'But it was lovely while it lasted.'

He kneeled down on the floor in front of her. 'Eve, I wanted you from the first time we met. I get excited when I hear your voice as you come in and I put extra care into work because it's for you. I didn't mean to take advantage today.'

She hadn't realized that he had felt that way about her. Don had convinced her that no sane man would want her. But she somehow knew that Tom was sincere; he hadn't meant to use the attack on her for his own ends.

'I know you didn't. I didn't mean to be the way I was either. Maybe we should just forget what happened?'

'I won't be able to,' he said, and cupped her face in his hand. 'Couldn't we just start again? Like, I ask you out, and we see how that goes.'

She could hardly believe this was happening. She'd liked Tom from their first meeting, and her respect for his work had grown daily. But not once had she ever harboured romantic thoughts about him. She didn't know if he had a wife or a girlfriend; she didn't know if he owned his own house, rented it or even who he'd last worked for. Their relationship was all about this building, making it just how she wanted it. But suddenly she saw that he had had strong feelings for her right from the start, and that was why it was so perfect. But should she let that influence her?

'It's difficult with Olly and Tabby,' she said, but her mind was whirring to think how she could arrange it. 'But I'll think on that. But we'd better go now.'

He leaned forward and kissed her lightly again. 'The kitchen is being delivered tomorrow. How about we make that a bit of a celebration? You bring the kids down here, and we have a drink with the other guys and make it fun for Olly and Tabby.'

'So they don't think of you as the Big Bad Wolf?' Eve asked, and laughed when she realized how ridiculous that was.

'Exactly. Good idea?'

'The best.' She grinned, ruffling his already tousled hair. 'I'll come with them about four, with nibbles and wine, or beer.'

The police came as soon as she phoned them when they got back to the house. By then Eve could sense that her injuries were minor, but she had to give them details so they could possibly catch the man. Also, she had to cancel her credit card.

Olly and Tabby were very sweet and adult, concerned for their mother and grateful Tom had looked after her. 'Will you stay and have dinner with us?' Olly asked Tom, when the police had left. 'Mummy got pizzas this morning, but she always gets too much.'

'Maybe Mummy wants to go to bed,' Tom said.

'She doesn't,' Eve said. 'I'm fine. A bit achy, but nothing a pizza wouldn't make better.'

When Eve got into bed later, she thought she couldn't have arranged a better way for her children to meet Tom if she'd racked her brain for weeks. They had met him at Mill Lane a couple of times, but they hadn't engaged with him in any way. Tonight, it had been on their terms – pizza was so informal and they were indebted to Tom as he'd helped their mum. Perhaps they were worried the man would find Eve again and so they welcomed Tom being there.

It was tipping down with rain outside and cosy indoors. After the food Tom suggested they played a game, and to Eve's amazement the kids agreed. It was a game Eve didn't know, but every player had a name stuck on their heads, and then they had to ask the other players for clues to find out who they were. Olly and Tabby were good at it and made it very funny as Eve and Tom hadn't got a clue about it so had no chance of winning.

About nine the children went up to bed, but although this looked like a golden opportunity, Eve knew Tabby would make some excuse to come back down and check what they were doing.

'You must go home,' Eve said, kissing him frantically. 'They already like you, and tomorrow at the new house they'll like you still more. But we have to be careful. It's too soon for them to suspect we might be . . .' She paused, not knowing what to say.

'Falling in love? Having sex?'

Eve blushed. 'Perhaps.'

'Eve, I'm not after a one-night stand,' he said, taking her two arms and looking right into her eyes. 'I've seen you in shorts and wanted to stroke those lovely long tanned legs, I've seen you puzzling over paint charts, and being bored witless by the electrician and irritated by the plumber. I love your enthusiasm; I believe even without seeing one set of curtains you've made that you're the best interior designer in the south-west. So I can wait till the time is right.'

Eve looked into those swimming-pool-blue eyes and was not so sure. 'I don't know that I can wait,' she said.

Tom kissed her on the nose. 'That's music to my ears. If there were no children in the house, I'd take you now on the kitchen table.'

She giggled. 'They do that in films. I always think it must be horribly uncomfortable.'

'I don't think it would be for the man,' he said, and his eyes twinkled. 'We must make a note of that and try it one day.'

She laughed, looking at his sunny, freckled face,

and wishing she dared kiss him a few more times. 'Go now, Tom. You've been wonderful, and our moment will come. I'll see you tomorrow at four.'

She was almost asleep when a thought came to her. She had assumed her attacker was a man; for some reason people always thought violence was done by men. But Dawn Button was tall and thin, and how many men put a hood up on a raincoat? But she would do that to hide her identity. Then there was the odd walk; she'd thought it was sore feet, but it could've been caused by wearing ill-fitting men's shoes.

That'll teach you. Her attacker's remark. Teach her what? To be more careful? To be nicer when questioned? As for the tone of voice, it had been a snarl. Anyone, male or female, could sound that way just by deepening their voice.

If it was Button, she had got herself a lot of information with the bag she'd stolen: a credit card, an address and cheque book, plus some letters, including one from Patty Hathaway and one from Sylvia. She thought the sales details of Number One were still in there too. To an investigative journalist that was probably a gold mine of potential information.

14

The police came at ten in the morning, by which time Eve's bruises, though ugly, weren't giving her any problem and she felt fine in herself – excited about Tom and looking forward to the evening.

She told PC Hawthorne and PC Riley what had happened, and the contents of her stolen handbag, then asked if they thought it possible it was a woman wearing men's clothes.

'What makes you think the mugger could be female?' PC Riley asked.

'Just a feeling,' Eve said, and explained briefly about the journalist who had tried to interview her after her husband's death. 'She was very pushy, quite intimidating really. Maybe I'm just being paranoid. But I saw her a couple of times in my old road in London before we moved here, and the other day I thought I saw her going into Fields, the department store. Plus, how weird is it that a would-be mugger would start out in Manor Road? It isn't likely there would be anyone there to mug. And then he or she nips down to run into me again near my new property.'

PC Hawthorne agreed it was odd and wrote down

the name Dawn Button. 'You have cancelled your credit card and everything else in your bag?' he asked, and then went on to ask her to describe the shoulder bag. 'Sometimes we find bags dumped,' he explained. 'But we will look into Dawn Button and if anything shouts out to us, we'll let you know.'

'Should I dress up to go to the party too?' Tabby asked around four in the afternoon.

Eve felt herself blushing because by washing her hair and putting on a new blue dress she had given Tabby the idea that the little party was something special.

'No, don't bother,' Eve said quickly. 'I'm only wearing this dress because it's nearly the end of summer and I might not get an opportunity to wear it again. It will only be Tom and his two workmates; they just thought you might like to see the latest things they've been doing in our new home.' She wasn't sure that was the right response, but it was the best she could think of.

'Well, I'm wearing shorts,' Olly said. 'It would be mad to wear anything smart there; it will be filthy.'

'I expect the boys will have swept up,' Eve said. 'Now help me put some glasses and other goodies in a box.'

Tabby had disappeared back up the stairs; Eve had no doubt it was to find something more festive to wear.

'I like Tom,' Olly said, as he wrapped kitchen paper round glasses.

'Why's that?' Eve asked. She was putting sausage rolls, small pork pies and sandwiches on to a couple of platters. She added a few bowls to the box for the crisps and peanuts to go in.

'He's just nice; he talks to us like he's really interested in us. Dad never did that.'

Eve thought it best not to ask anything more.

To Eve's surprise, the boys *had* swept up the kitchen area, and, furthermore, the kitchen unit with the butler sink and a couple of cupboards were already assembled and fixed.

'I thought they were only delivering the kitchen today,' Eve said. She could see other units stacked against the back wall, along with all the white goods and cooker. She looked back at Tom; he was wearing clean jeans and a blue-and-white open-necked skirt. Ian the plumber and James the carpenter were looking equally smart too.

'The kitchen came early this morning,' James said. 'So we thought we'd crack on and get the sink in as a surprise for you. Of course, we have to do the whole kitchen before the granite men come in to do the work surfaces. But at least the taps work.'

'And what a lovely surprise.' Eve was so glad she'd chosen glossy dark ink cupboards. People had tried to tell her it was a mistake, but it wasn't; her kitchen was going to be stunning.

Tom came over to her then, his eyes twinkling and trying hard to suppress a huge grin. 'How are the shoulder and ribs?'

'Not so bad,' she said. 'The ribs ache if I move too quickly but the shoulder is OK.' She leaned towards him to whisper, 'One or two more kisses should heal them completely.'

Tabby and Olly were already setting up the nibbles, drinks and glasses on a table which someone had covered with a clean dust sheet. Ian went over to them to open the wine and pour fizzy drinks for the children. Eve heard him suggest that they should go upstairs to see their bedrooms and the new bathroom. Fitted wardrobes had been finished in their bedrooms just a couple of days before, and as they hadn't visited for about ten days, they hadn't seen the bathroom finished either.

They came back downstairs looking very happy. 'Your mum has picked the carpet for everywhere upstairs,' Tom said, and showed them a pale grey sample. 'What do you think?'

'Very smart, but a bit boring,' Tabby said.

'Tabby! It won't be once there's pictures on the walls, curtains and I've put up some wallpaper,' Eve rebuked her. 'But that will all happen once we've moved in.'

James put on some music and got Tabby to dance

with him. Eve was astounded she didn't back away in fright, but James took after his Italian father, and he was a young Adonis with olive skin, dark hair and eyes, and gleaming white teeth. He also had a great deal of charm; the first time Tabby met him she kept talking about him for days.

Olly was busy talking to Ian about the intricacies of plumbing, and Tom came over to Eve and poured her a glass of wine. 'It's going well so far,' he said. 'But do you want to see the kids' wardrobes and the rails I've put up in your dressing room? They might be in the wrong place.'

'I'd love to,' she said, trying to keep a straight face. 'I'll take my wine with me.'

Olly was dancing now too, and Eve just said she had to look at something and wouldn't be long.

As soon as they got into her dressing room Tom began kissing her. 'It's a good job there's no carpet yet; we can hear anyone coming up the stairs,' he murmured between kisses.

Eve had never experienced such a heady sensation from just kissing before; she was in the moment – nothing else mattered. But all too soon they heard footsteps. It was Olly looking for them.

'Yes, I think that one is a bit too high,' Eve said, breaking away from Tom. 'Hi, Olly, we're just decid-ing if the rails are right in here. I think I need a long shelf for storage fixed where the rail is now, and then the rail about four inches beneath it. Will that be OK, Tom?'

'Yes, fine,' he said. 'You haven't noticed we painted all the walls and ceilings up here.'

'So you have,' she remarked, as if seeing it for the first time. 'That greyish-white is so nice on the walls. It's going to set my wallpaper off beautifully. I think I'll come one evening and put that up when you've all gone home.'

Tom smirked, getting her drift immediately. 'We'd better go down now and join the party,' he said. 'Maybe Tabby will dance with me now if she's bored with James.'

'Mum, I was thinking that wallpaper you showed me the other day would look nice in my room,' Olly said excitedly as they left the room. 'You know, the one with seagulls. Only on the wall where my bed is going to be.'

'I think you're right,' she said. 'It would be perfect. I'm so glad you've grown out of wanting Spider-Man or dinosaurs.'

'Mum, I haven't ever wanted Spider-Man. And I was five when I liked dinosaurs,' he said indignantly. He looked round at Tom then. 'Did you know Mum is brilliant at putting up wallpaper?'

'Is she now?' Tom grinned. 'She's going to be very busy when you and Tabby go off to school. It's only a couple of weeks now, isn't it?'

Olly nodded. 'I'll be going to the same school now because I'm nearly twelve.'

It was such a good evening. As Eve drove home, she felt proud that her children could socialize with adults without being tongue-tied and awkward. But the men had made a real effort to entertain them, dancing with them, asking their opinion on things. Almost all the food had gone, only a couple of sandwiches and a few peanuts left.

It was so great to see it all getting close to completion. The cutting-out table had arrived last week and the new industrial sewing machine and pressers she'd ordered would be arriving any day now. A bubble of panic rose in her, suddenly aware of just how much more there was to do. Not just wallpapering but sample curtains to be made and indeed curtains for the children's rooms too. Then there was arranging all her furniture and other belongings when they came out of storage.

'What's up, Mum?' Olly asked as they went into the house in Manor Road. 'You've got that look you used to get on your face when Dad was being nasty.'

'Have I!?' she exclaimed, as she shut and bolted the door. 'I was only thinking how much more there is to do before we can move into Mill Lane. It's a bit overwhelming.'

Olly came up to her and put his arms around her.

'We'll help,' he said, and he looked round for his sister. 'Won't we, Tabby?'

'Of course we will,' she said, coming over and making it a group hug. 'We're a team now. And I expect Tom, James and Ian won't go until everything is straight.'

Tabby was right. Eve knew that Tom and his men wouldn't leave until everything was done. True, she'd be paying them, but she'd met plenty of people who had builders walk out on them, leaving with lots not finished.

On the children's first day at school, Eve got home from driving them there feeling sad and worried. Worried that they would find the new school difficult, that they hadn't any friends to lean on, and sad because she was aware that they'd got to that age when they were needing her less and less.

She made a cup of coffee and sat wrapping her hands around it for warmth. It felt cold in the house; it wasn't really, only because she was alone. But she supposed most of her anxiety was about Tom.

She knew he really loved and wanted her. There was no other woman, and he even had a flat of his own, which so far she hadn't seen, but she couldn't imagine how they could be together. You couldn't say to kids of her children's ages, 'My friend Tom is going to stay over.' They probably didn't really understand about adult relationships, but they knew the word 'sex' came into it. And that was enough reason to fight against it.

The doorbell rang and, assuming it was a parcel delivery, she went to open the door. To her surprise it was Tom, not in his working clothes but looking attractive in a navy-blue sweatshirt and cream chinos.

'Could I spend the day with you? I thought you might be feeling a bit lost without Olly and Tabby. I hoped I might make it better for you.'

'Oh, Tom, how lovely!' she said, throwing her arms around him. 'But won't that shrew of a woman you work for be angry that you aren't there, doing her bidding?'

Tom laughed. 'No, not at all. She came to me in a dream last night and told me to come here this morning and take you to bed. She said she would deduct the time from my wages.'

She caught hold of his sweatshirt and hauled him in, slamming the front door behind him. They had lived on stolen kisses for the past two weeks and she had thought of nothing more than going to bed with him.

With arms around each other they went up the stairs, stopping for ever more passionate kisses. As they got to the landing Tom was unbuttoning her shirt and her hands were under his sweatshirt. Eve's shirt came off before they even got to the bedroom, and Tom was kicking off his shoes. He picked her up in his arms and dropped her on to the bed, then unzipped her jeans and pulled them off.

Eve's only experience of lovemaking was with Don. There had been rare times when it was good, loving and satisfying, but mostly it had been rough and uncaring, growing more angry year by year. It had soon got to the stage that if she couldn't avoid it, she had willed it to be over quickly. But all the bad memories vanished as Tom took it slowly, exploring her body with his fingers and kissing her everywhere. He smelled of lemon soap and toothpaste, not of beer and cigarettes as Don always had. She loved the way he ran his fingers through her hair, kissing her throat, shoulders and all over her torso. He made her feel loved and it was utterly delicious.

'I want you inside me,' she whispered, pulling at his boxer shorts to get them off. His skin was silky and as she ran her fingers up his back there was not one blemish; it was smooth to the touch.

'Are you sure?' he whispered. 'Are you on the pill?'

She hadn't thought of that. She'd stopped taking it when she ran away from Don and had never started again. For a moment she wanted to say yes, because she didn't want to slow things down. But she couldn't lie; it wasn't right.

'No, I'm not,' she admitted.

'Then it's just as well I came prepared,' he said with

a little chuckle and he reached out for his trousers beside the bed.

Although he unwrapped the condom, he didn't attempt to put it on immediately and continued to pleasure her until she felt she might explode with wanting. His penis against her leg was as hard as a rock and holding it firmly she led him towards her.

Finally, when Eve felt like she might burst into flames, she was vaguely aware he was putting the condom on, and then he entered her.

'Was it OK?' he whispered later.

She was hot and sweaty, and still breathless from the intensity of it. 'Not OK. It was wonderful,' she murmured. 'I love you, Tom.'

'I love you too,' he said, smoothing back her hair from her face. 'And you were wonderful too.'

It was after two in the afternoon that they finally got up and showered. Eve didn't want to, but she was afraid Olly and Tabby would see what she'd been up to on her face. She had to be doing something normal like sewing curtains when they got home from school.

But even as Tom went to the door to leave, she was clinging to him for one more kiss, afraid the spell would be broken once he walked out of the door.

'There'll be other times,' he said, holding her face between his hands and kissing her nose. 'I'm not going anywhere. I'm all yours.'

'I'm afraid I won't be able to hide how I feel,' she said. 'Tabby always seems to pick up on everything, and it's too soon. I promised there wouldn't be another man.'

'Stop worrying,' Tom said. 'Kids are all the same. They don't much care what their mum does, as long as it doesn't impact on them. Selfish little sods in the main. I certainly was as a boy. My mum left Dad for another man when I was fifteen. I never stopped to wonder what Dad had done to cause it. I didn't even blame her lover, or Mum for that matter, I just wanted my life to stay the same. So I took myself off to my gran's; she had a track record for always being the same. Mum was forever trying to talk to me about it, reassuring me she loved me. I didn't want to talk. I didn't even want to see her much, just to live my life. Of course, that made me very guilty later when she died of cancer. I wished then I'd spent more time with her. But I'm only telling you to illustrate what self-centred little toads kids can be.'

He had never spoken of his childhood before, and because he seemed so well adjusted, generous and thoughtful, she'd assumed it had been an unremarkable happy one. But she was sure Tom must have been deeply affected by it, whatever he said.

'That's so sad, Tom. Are your dad and gran still around?'

'My gran died a few years back, but my dad is in Exeter, still on his own. I get on well with him now. I make more of an effort with him than I used to.'

'Well, Tabby and Olly haven't got someone else to run off to,' she said, and smiled at Tom. 'So let's just cool it and wait and see how comfortable they get with you.'

To Eve's delight both Tabby and Olly had a good first day at school. They had both been paired up with someone in the same class to show them the ropes, and to introduce them to other children.

'The girls in my class all seemed to think coming from London makes you really cool,' Tabby said, flicking her hair back in a way she'd clearly seen someone she admired doing. 'I told them that wasn't true, but they didn't believe me.'

'And what about you?' Eve asked Olly, who appeared to have forgotten he was nearly twelve and had slunk on to her lap for a cuddle.

'My class were all nice,' he said. 'My teacher, Miss Hooper, made me tell the class what the differences were between living in London and Sidmouth. I was so enthusiastic about Sidmouth and all the good stuff like the sea, the parks and the shops, and they all laughed. Miss Hooper said that was good.'

'Well, I'm very glad you like the school. And we'll soon be moving into the coolest home ever, so I think we ought to celebrate by having a takeaway tonight.'

Just two days before moving, Eve saw Dawn Button again. She had just left Number One, where she had been checking that her new industrial sewing machine was working properly. She also checked that the poles she was going to hang sample curtains on were in the right place, with the drawers and cabinets for hooks, rings, brackets and other pieces of vital equipment for curtains and blinds beneath. Everything was fine and she hurried out at midday with the intention of going back to Manor Road to start packing.

It was as she got into her car on the forecourt that she saw Button. She was talking to another woman down in the car park and pointing in Eve's direction. A chill ran down Eve's spine. The police had not been convinced her mugger was a woman and they hadn't managed to find a journalist of that name either. Eve got the distinct impression they thought she was a fantasist.

She couldn't tell anyone; to show fear about what this woman was looking for was almost a declaration of guilt. She thought the only thing to do was to play this woman at her own game.

Taking a deep breath to calm herself she got out of the car and locked it. Then she walked boldly down to the car park. It was amusing to see Button suddenly rummaging in her boot; the tables had turned and now she was worried.

'Hi, Dawn,' Eve called out when she got within twenty yards of her. 'Fancy seeing you here. I thought Londoners favoured Southend. I assume you're looking for me? I saw you pointing to my place.'

'Eh, no.' She looked very nervous. 'I was directing a lady to the department store.'

'Funnily enough I saw you dart in there the other day,' Eve said. 'And you were up at Manor Road?'

'I wasn't,' Button said far too quickly.

'Yes, you were. Don't tell fibs,' Eve said. 'Now tell me what you're doing here in Sidmouth? If you still want to interview me, then that's fine. What rag are you working for now?' Eve was beginning to enjoy herself; it was fun watching the woman's discomfort.

'I've got relatives here,' Button said defensively.

'Well, when you're ready to interview me, let me know, and I'll get my lawyer to sit in with us. But phone me first. You have the number; there were cards in my bag.'

With that Eve turned and walked away. She was proud of herself for letting the woman know she knew the identity of her mugger. She hoped that was the end of it now and that the woman would crawl back into whatever hole she had come from.

*

Two days later, in pouring rain, Eve and the children moved house. She'd picked a Saturday for the removal from Manor Road so the children could help. Yet when she got up and saw the rain she regretted not asking for the day before, as the sun had been shining then. However, the removal men had taken everything out of storage yesterday and put it into their new home, so that at least had been done in the dry. Eve had supervised it too, so everything had mostly been placed in the right rooms. Last night, with the children's help, she'd managed to unpack and put away most of the kitchen equipment, china and glass. Yet there were still dozens and dozens of other boxes waiting to be unpacked, and she felt exhausted just thinking about it.

Four hours later Eve, Tom and the children were eating fish and chips in the kitchen of their new home. They'd got all their belongings out of the removal van, and Tom had arrived with the fish and chips in time to carry the heavy suitcases and big boxes upstairs.

'This house is so lovely,' Tabby said with a happy sigh. 'I didn't think it was going to be, but I was wrong. You are clever, Mummy.' She gazed around at the dark blue kitchen units, the white marble worktop and illuminated glass-fronted cupboards above. 'But maybe we ought to have some blinds on the window. I don't like people watching me eat.'

Eve and Tom laughed, aware there was something Tabby hadn't seen.

'Pop out on the veranda,' Eve suggested.

Tabby opened the door and Olly joined her to go out.

They both looked a bit stunned when they came back in. 'That's like magic – you can't see in,' Tabby said incredulously. 'But it looks like ordinary glass. I hadn't noticed your sign either. "Eve Taylor Interior Designer". I liked the sort of menu too: curtains, cushions, wallpaper. It looks so classy.'

'I wasn't sure about the special glass at first,' Eve admitted. 'It felt very strange to look out and see everything clearly. I wanted to hide if someone was looking. But I soon got to trust that no one can see in, and so will you. We needed to have a window the same shape and size as the sliding one in the studio, or it would have looked very odd. Next summer, when it's hot, my clients can sit out on the veranda too if they want.'

'Will you be leaving us now it's all finished?' Olly asked Tom.

'You don't get rid of me just yet. There's still the car park to do,' Tom said teasingly. 'Your mum wants some raised beds around the walls for bushes and flowers too, plus there are always little things to be sorted. We call that "snagging".'

'I think you don't want to leave because you like Mum,' Olly said.

Eve blushed but didn't know what to say.

Tom grinned, clearly not concerned by Olly's remark. 'I do like your mum a lot, but we'll still be friends after I move on to another job. At least I hope so. But let's stick the plates in the dishwasher, then go upstairs and put everything straight.'

Tom went up with the children, but Eve sat for a moment reflecting on how she could move things on a bit with Tom. She wanted him to be able to stay the night sometimes, but she was very aware that both her children were at very impressionable ages. Tabby wasn't a little girl any more, but neither was she an adult; she'd witnessed her father hitting both her mother and brother, and humiliating them, and this might have left her hoping there would never be another resident man. Eve felt that however much she wanted to have Tom at the centre of her life, her first duty was to show her children by example that women could be happy and successful, without leaning on a man.

15

Sidmouth, 2002

'How long have we got?' Tom asked, as he took Eve's coat and hung it on the back of his door.

Eve rounded on him; she didn't like his slightly accusative tone. 'What do you mean by that?'

'I can't help noticing that these days you always have a timetable to work to,' he said. 'Seven thirty till nine, fit Tom in for a home visit.'

Assuming he'd just had a tough day, Eve wound her arms around him and kissed him. It was, in fact, true that she'd only allocated an hour and a half to him, as she had to get back to finish some curtains, but she wasn't going to tell him that now.

It was nearly two years since they'd first met. Eighteen months since their affair had begun. Back then loving Tom was the most important thing in the world to her. He was everything she'd ever wanted in a man: kind, sensitive, hard-working, generous and a great lover. But right from the opening party, when she had invited hoteliers, guest-house owners and other influential people in Sidmouth, things had taken off like a rocket, giving her no time to pause and take stock of her life. She was ecstatic about the success, but she'd had to take on a full-time assistant and two homeworkers to help deal with the orders. She knew she was leaving Tom out a bit, but she thought he was all right with it and understood the pressure she was under.

For the first three months it was like being on a roller coaster: thrilling, exciting and sometimes terrifying that it might suddenly go wrong. But Tom seemed to understand perfectly why she was sometimes distracted, overtired and grumpy, and that she was afraid of what Tabby and Olly would say if she moved him in or even had him staying the odd night in her bed.

They made love at his little flat mostly, and she told the children she was seeing a client. They always spent Saturday evening and Sunday at her house, and during the week Tom often came and ate with her and the children. They had days out with the children, and went to the cinema, but they also went out alone too for drinks or a meal, although Eve always went home on her own afterwards.

But gradually Tom began to become impatient with her. 'I don't just want to be with you for sex, or because I think you'll feed me and wash my socks,' he said one day. 'I want to wake up with you, to feel you really are my girl.'

She thought that was sweet, but she still used the same old excuse that the children were not ready yet for accepting she had a lover. But tonight, when she tried to distract him by putting her arms around him, she could feel his body was as taut as a coiled-up spring. She knew he wasn't going to be placated this time with sex; he had his own agenda.

'I resent being slotted in somewhere between changing the sheets on your bed and placing a fabric order with one of your suppliers. I'm beginning to think you're just stringing me along,' he said angrily, his eyes growing darker. 'You said at Christmas you'd talk to the kids, then Easter, but now, almost two years since we met, we're no further forward.'

'Don't take that tone with me,' she snapped. 'I've told you my reasons again and again.'

'Yes, you have,' he said. 'But I've told you again and again too that all we have to do is to talk to them, say we want to be together. For fuck's sake, Eve, I know they like me. I keep them company when you have to go out on a job; we have meals together at least twice a week. Weekends we do stuff together. Don't you think the kids know by now that it's a serious relationship?'

'They may do, but are they ready to find you in my bed in the morning?'

The way he looked at her sent chills down her spine. His eyes were cold, his mouth set in an angry line. 'I'm not prepared to put up with this any longer. It's insulting.' He opened his door and gestured for her to leave. 'Goodbye, Eve. Find some other puppet you can keep on a string.'

Eve left. She'd never seen him like that before and his expression frightened her.

Tom stood there in his small flat, a place he'd smartened up for her benefit, and clenched and unclenched his hands in anger. He was entirely serious about having had enough. He loved Eve but he didn't love her selfishness. When they'd first got together and fell in love, he would've married her then and there. He'd even asked her, thinking that marriage made it OK to sleep in the same bed. She kept saying it was too soon.

So what she was really holding out for he didn't know. A more successful man, a professional one, a prince, an archbishop? She claimed to love him, and the sex was great when she came to his flat, but he didn't want a hole-in-the-corner love affair; he wanted to go to bed with her at night and wake up beside her the next day. It didn't have to be seven nights a week; two or three would make him happy. So what was it with her?

One of the things he'd noticed in the last year was that she was getting far too big for her boots. It was obviously because she'd become very successful. People talked about the house makeovers she'd done, how brilliant she was with colour, how much style she had. All that was true, but she'd been lucky that local papers and magazines had rushed to do features on her and claimed she'd brought big-city panache to Devon and Dorset. Yet it was also a fact that she had no competition. There were several shops in Sidmouth that sold material and they'd make up curtains, but there was no business that did interior design like she did anywhere nearby. Seriously wealthy people who lived in the huge fabulous houses in the two counties tended to get someone down from London, Bath or Southampton and pay through the nose for it. Eve had become a big fish in a little pool. She had no time for small fry like him. He ought to have seen this a year ago.

When Eve got home she stood in the middle of her kitchen stony-faced, furious that he couldn't see it her way and had literally made her leave. He'd said many times that he wanted more than her coming round to his place for a quick shag, then rushing off to measure up a client's windows or walls. He said her attitude cheapened their relationship and he felt he was being used.

Was she using him? Even Sylvia back in Grove Park had warned her that taking someone for granted usually ended badly. Sylvia was a woman who firmly believed in the sanctity of marriage and didn't hold with casual sex, but she'd still said it wasn't fair to keep Tom on a leash, then haul him back when it suited Eve.

Eve didn't believe that was what she was doing. She felt proud that she'd built a successful business through her own hard work and persistence. It had been two years since she had first viewed this eyesore of a building. But she'd had the vision to see that it had the space and the right location to turn it into her dream home and workplace.

The cocktail party in the studio eighteen months ago had been a triumph. Those people had nibbled the bait, ordered a set of curtains, a blind or a few cushions, then Eve had reeled them in afterwards as they called her to design a complete room, sometimes several rooms. The ratio of small jobs turning into larger ones was three to five. At times Eve had been scared she wouldn't get all the work done in time.

In December that year she'd taken on Sophie, an experienced seamstress who also loved interior design and had a flair for it. Soon after she'd found Francine and Petra who were happy to work from home making curtains, blinds and cushions. Plus, she had a couple of decorators she called in as and when needed, and an odd-job man and an upholsterer on hand.

She had always credited Tom with brilliant work-manship and using her ideas to design an amazing property. But maybe she hadn't always given him the credit for all the things he had done to make her business run smoothly? He would put up clients' curtain poles and tracks, and even hang curtains and blinds when Brian the odd-job man wasn't available. Almost every week she had at least one appointment in the evening to go and measure up a client's home and talk them through her ideas for a makeover. The children were old enough to be left alone now, but she liked Tom to be there and eat dinner with them. He often had to leave his job a bit earlier and come in dirty work clothes, but he never complained. He liked being with them and they liked him, and he'd often joked that her shower was better than his. She didn't understand why that wasn't enough for him.

'Back so soon?' Sophie popped her head round the door of the studio. 'Is Tom with you? I hoped he might be able to cut a board for a pelmet for me?'

Eve had liked Sophie on sight, and she was a true asset to the business. She was a stunning forty-year-old brunette with a voluptuous figure and an outrageous taste in clothes and an equally bold personality. Today she was wearing a flowing red linen dress, with an orange and yellow chiffon waistcoat over it, plus a chunky necklace in all three colours. There was nothing quiet and retiring about her, yet she was the one who worked best with clients who wanted traditional decor, and Eve went for contemporary and often really wild designs in both wallpaper and fabrics.

'He chucked me out in a huff,' Eve said. 'Same old thing: when am I going to let him stay with me? He doesn't seem to understand that I can't because of the kids.'

'I'm not surprised he's fed up,' Sophie said, shocking Eve. 'No man, not unless he is a complete doormat, would accept how you treat him. Your kids love him. If you announced you were getting married tomorrow, they'd be thrilled. I think your problem is that you don't trust him to stay as Mr Nice Guy. You imagine that after one night with you he'll wake like Attila the Hun.'

Eve giggled despite her anger. 'I don't.'

'It isn't funny, Eve. You'll lose him if you carry on like this,' Sophie said, and wiggled a finger reprovingly. 'He wants to settle down with you, and quite honestly, Eve, you're the luckiest woman in Sidmouth. Men like Tom don't come along very often.'

Eve bristled. Sophie always said what she thought, and mostly that was good, but she didn't have any children, so how could she know what was right for Tabby and Olly?

'I'll ring Brian and ask him to do your pelmet,' Eve said tartly, as she marched indignantly up the stairs. Then, looking down over the banister, she added, 'I don't think we can count on Tom to help out any more.'

Once in her bedroom she gave way to tears and flung herself down on the chaise longue by the window. Was it true that she was afraid Tom might turn into Don once he was living with her? She didn't think it was – besides, Tom hadn't asked to live with her anyway, only to stay the odd night or weekends. Eve liked going to his cosy little flat after work; it felt illicit and fun. For an hour or so she could forget she was a mother. What if he didn't come back?

Glancing at her watch she saw that the children would be home soon. She wondered what she should say to them.

'Nothing,' she said aloud, and she went into the bathroom to touch up her make-up so they wouldn't know she'd been crying. 'You've done what other people want all your life,' she said as she looked in the mirror. 'So let Tom be the one to apologize.'

She passed his absence off to Tabby and Olly as a little tiff, but she sensed they knew it was something more.

That night Eve couldn't sleep. While she was tempted to put a coat on over her pyjamas and go round to his flat, let herself in and climb into bed with him, she couldn't bring herself to back down like that. Ever since she had got Dawn Button off her back by calling her out, she had got the idea there was only one way in her life, her way. Her staff, children, customers and Tom, they had to accept it.

She lay there dry-eyed and angry with Tom for not seeing it her way. She was proud of what she had achieved through hard work and belief in herself. She knew people in Sidmouth and far beyond this small town believed she was the only person to go to for advice on home decor and soft furnishings. 'He'll come back in a day or two,' she whispered to herself.

But Tom didn't come back. A week passed, then another. Tabby and Olly kept asking about him. Tabby even said she knew Eve had been mean to him; she added that Tom deserved better than being ordered about as if he was her employee. Then school broke up for the summer and still there was no word from Tom.

Eve had gone from anger to sorrow, then back to anger. She pointed out to Sophie that he'd earned a fortune doing the place up and that he owed her.

'That is the most ridiculous statement I've ever heard,' Sophie said scornfully. 'You paid him the going rate for a job he did well. If anything, it's you who owes him! I know for a fact he's done dozens of jobs for you for free. Get real, girl. You've got above yourself and it's not nice.'

It was on the tip of Eve's tongue to tell Sophie to

get out too, but she stopped herself just in time and walked away. But she resented an employee disapproving of her.

The children were utterly bewildered. 'Aren't you worried about him?' Olly asked.

'She doesn't care about anyone but herself,' Tabby said spitefully. 'I hope he's found a new lady who shows him some appreciation and love.'

'I did love him, but we had a disagreement,' Eve snapped. 'He said he felt like a puppet on a string.'

It hurt that neither child offered her any sympathy. She could see now that they'd come to love him. One thing he was right about was that if she'd agreed to tell them he would be staying over sometimes, they wouldn't have minded one bit. But she straightened her back, reminded herself of all she'd been through and decided it was too late for self-recrimination now. She also clung to the idea that Tom couldn't have really loved her or her children, or he would have apologized and come back.

Two months after Tom had walked out, and the children had just gone back to school after the summer holidays, George Mulberry called at the studio. He looked as suave and handsome as she remembered, and he'd brought Eve some flowers.

The last time Eve had seen him was at her opening party. His partner that evening was a glamorous young blonde, wearing a dress that she looked as if she'd been poured into. Eve hadn't looked him up since that night, as whenever she passed his office there was always a rather stern-looking older woman manning the fort. Eve assumed he was busy showing people houses, or with the young blonde.

'What a surprise!' Eve exclaimed. 'I began to think you'd joined the Foreign Legion.'

'Just thought it was high time I dropped by to say hello,' he said, kissing her cheeks and giving her the flowers. 'How are things?'

'Good,' she said. 'New clients coming all the time. A bit too much work sometimes. And how is it for you?'

'Booming,' he said with a smile. 'I get all excited about a new house on my books, and, hey presto, it's sold. I could do with a few more properties to sell, though. If you haven't got anything on tonight, why not come out to dinner with me?'

Because she was bored with her own company and wanted to hear some of the town gossip, she agreed to meet him at seven thirty at the Indian restaurant on the high street.

Eve had forgotten what good company George could be; even before they had chosen what to eat, he was making her laugh. His tales about unreasonable clients who thought their little hovels were palaces were very funny. Then he moved on to telling her about a couple of old established shops in Sidmouth that were closing down.

'The trouble is they haven't moved with the times. The gents' outfitters are set back in the forties; no self-respecting chap under seventy would dream of going in there. But enough of me passing on my opinion on failing businesses, what happened between you and Tom? I hear he's gone.'

'Yes, you're right. Two months ago.'

'I thought you two were made for each other,' George said and frowned. 'I am really sorry, Eve. I might have lost you to him, but I wanted you to be happy.'

He had said exactly what she wanted to hear, and she was touched by it.

She told him some of it but made excuses for herself. Not just her fear of upsetting the children if he stayed over, but her own fear of committing to him because of her violent ex-husband.

'You surely didn't imagine Tom was a bully?' George asked. 'You couldn't find a nicer man. And he did such a wonderful job on your place.'

'I know,' she agreed. 'I wish things hadn't gone wrong, but it's done now.'

'Well, maybe you'll look at me more kindly now,' he said with a smile. 'I'd like to take you out and try to woo you.'

Eve giggled. 'Woo' was such an old-fashioned word, but she liked the idea of it. George was also very presentable, and he could bring more prestigious work her way.

A couple of days later Eve went to visit Marianne. She had only visited her when she had first got to Sidmouth, but she had invited her to the launch party and seen her then, and Marianne had called into the studio back in the spring.

'Come in, darling one,' Marianne said as she opened her door, her smile a very welcoming one. 'I thought you'd got too posh for the likes of me.'

'Never,' Eve said. 'I'm just always so busy.'

The house was silent as the mothers had all gone out.

'I'm giving up,' Marianne announced as she put the kettle on. 'October the fifteenth will be my last day. I'm going to take a holiday in Cyprus with an old pal who has a home out there. I want to get someone to clear out most of the furniture. I'll put the rest in store. Then I'll get someone to give all the rooms a coat of paint while I'm away as it's all so shabby now. And then when I return, I'll find a one-bedroom flat to buy.'

Eve didn't say how sad that was or try to talk her round. She could see Marianne was very tired and a little unsteady on her feet.

'Good for you. You've done more than your share for other people for far too long. Time to put your feet up and enjoy time for yourself.'

Over tea and homemade cake Marianne kept her up to date with some of the women Eve had met here. Two of them had gone back to their violent men again.

'If I had more success, like I had with you, Eve, I'd stay on. But mostly what I do is like putting a plaster over a wound that needs stitching. It's so demoralizing. I know the wound is going to burst open again, and it's the children that suffer. But tell me about your lovely Tom. Can I buy a hat for the wedding?'

'He's gone,' Eve said, and went on to tell her friend the whole story. 'I thought I was doing the right thing, not letting my kids think it's OK to hop into bed with a new partner.'

'He was hardly a new partner,' Marianne said, raising one eyebrow. 'I'm going to say what I think, whether you like it or not. I believe from what I saw in your home and studio that you want to control every aspect of your life now: your children, your business and Tom. It's understandable, as Don didn't allow you any control, but I'd put money on it that Tom felt you wouldn't let him sleep at your house but would go to his place when it suited you, as a way of controlling him.'

'That's ridiculous,' Eve said indignantly.

'Maybe it is. But the last time I saw you I could see

you'd grown harder, laughing less, caring about others less.'

'I didn't come to visit you for a character assassination,' Eve said, and stood up to leave.

'I am, believe it or not, trying to help you,' Marianne said quietly. 'You've made a first-class job of your business; I've met people who you've worked for, and they have nothing but praise for your expertise and talent, but I think you've achieved all that at the expense of your family and Tom. And your own happiness.'

'I am happy,' Eve retorted. 'Why would you say that?'

'Because I got to know you when you stayed here. I saw you happy then. You had nothing but your kids, no real plans or hope for the future, but you became happy when you found you were free.'

'I'm free now.'

'Are you?'

'Yes, of course, as free as a bird.'

Marianne sighed deeply. 'Perhaps I'm just a silly old woman. I hope you're right. But I saw you and Tom together and to me that looked just about as perfect as a new love could be. Something destroyed it. Maybe you ought to think on what that was.'

Eve said she had to go. She pecked the older woman on the cheeks and said she had an appointment. As she reached the front door, she turned back to Marianne. 'Let me know how the move goes, and the address of your new home. I'll send George Mulberry round; he's an excellent agent.'

Marianne's words had disturbed Eve. As she walked home, she told herself that none of it was true and that Tom obviously hadn't really loved her or he would've come back. But she also thought back to the night Don had died and wondered if this lump of sorrow inside her for what might have been with Tom was punishment for starting that fire.

Tabby was almost fifteen now, and Olly almost fourteen. They were happy at school; they'd made lots of friends since moving to Sidmouth and rarely spoke of their old life in London. But now she came to think of it they had become distant. Tabby had always been a little standoffish, but Olly used to run down the stairs when she came in. She hadn't noticed when he stopped doing that. Was it just growing up, or didn't he feel that way about her any more? Both of them either disappeared to their rooms as soon as they'd eaten their dinner or rushed off to meet friends. But then Eve couldn't say much about that because she would go into her workroom to put together a mood board for a client, pick out fabric or wallpaper samples or type up quotations and invoices. She couldn't remember when they'd last played a board game or watched TV together.

When she got home, both children were in the sitting room watching TV, so she called up to see if they wanted anything to drink, and then joined them with two Cokes and a gin and tonic on a tray.

The film was one they'd watched dozens of times. *Overboard* where Goldie Hawn, the spoilt wife of a rich man, falls overboard and is rescued by Kurt Russell. Goldie has lost her memory, so he takes her home to look after his motherless children in a grubby little house. However ridiculous the plot was, it had always made them laugh. But Tabby turned it off soon after Eve joined them, saying it was a stupid film.

Eve told them about Marianne giving up the refuge and her plans to have a holiday in Cyprus before buying herself a little flat.

'Good for her,' Tabby said, not even looking at her mother. 'Those women just used her. Silly cows, letting their husbands hit them.'

Eve looked at her daughter in astonishment. 'Tabby, surely you haven't forgotten how your father hit me and your brother. Am I a silly cow too?'

Tabby stared back at her with cold eyes. 'You should've just called the police the first time he did it and saved us all a lot of misery.'

'Hasn't it occurred to you that I stayed and tried to make it OK with your dad to protect you two? Where was I going to go to with two children? I couldn't even drive then.'

Tabby didn't respond; she just picked up her Game Boy and started playing on it.

Olly looked at Eve and shrugged. That seemed to say he was neutral and keeping out of it.

Eve got up to go downstairs to the workroom. 'I just hope you never find yourself in that position, Tabby,' she said as she got to the door. 'Because then you'll find out how few people will offer any help.'

16

'You look beautiful!' George exclaimed as Eve opened the door to him for their date on Saturday evening. 'Where would you like to go?'

She thought he looked very handsome in a cream linen suit. 'I don't mind going anywhere with someone looking so dapper, so you choose,' she said with a big smile.

'Well, as you're dressed for dancing, and there's a dinner and dance on at the Victoria Hotel tonight, shall we go there?'

Eve's heart soared. She knew her chiffon shocking-pink mid-calf dress was a bit over the top for a Chinese or Indian, but she'd been dying for an occasion to wear it. 'Perfect,' she said.

She was in the mood to sparkle as during the afternoon she'd finally been able to talk to Tabby. She'd come down to the workroom just as Eve was tidying up.

'I'm sorry, Mum. That was a mean thing I said about those women.' She hung her head.

Eve looked at her daughter for a moment, suddenly seeing that she had become beautiful and grown-up almost overnight. Her long blonde hair was tied up in a side ponytail fixed with a bright blue scrunchy and she wore just enough make-up to make her skin look pale gold and her eyes as blue as cornflowers. She was about five foot six now, the same height as Eve, and although slender she was quite busty. In tight jeans, with the legs rolled up a few inches, and an off-the-shoulder T-shirt she looked like a model.

'I expect you had the hump with me,' Eve said. 'I used to say mean things to my mum when I was cross with her. But why were you cross?'

'I suppose it was because George came round with flowers for you. Olly and I think you should have tried harder with Tom, because we loved him. We hoped you'd marry him, you know.'

Eve sighed deeply. 'Perhaps you should've said so. Talk about us being at cross purposes! I kept him at arm's length because I thought it would upset you. But it's too late now. I heard this morning that he's working on a big project in Bath, and he's got a place to live there too. But can we put this aside and start again? I'm going out with George tonight, and I hope you and Olly can be happy for me and behave yourselves while I'm gone.'

Tabby nodded and picked up one of the mood boards Eve had prepared; it had a sample of dark blue wallpaper with gold palm trees. 'This is gorgeous,' she said. 'And I think the lighter blue material with its tiny gold motif will be perfect with it. But isn't the dark blue paint a bit much?'

Delighted that Tabby was taking an interest, Eve explained that it was for a drawing room in a hotel. 'The room is enormous, so it needs a fabulous big design on one wall, and there's a big white-marble fireplace, so I was thinking of painting that wall dark blue. As for around the big windows and the third wall, they'll be a goldy cream. The owner has already got two huge decadent gold sofas. Then I'll bring in some warmer colour with cushions and a rug.'

'I think I'd like to go to art school and design wall-paper or fabric,' Tabby said, picking up other mood boards and looking at them.

'What a great plan, and if you get famous, we could work together – you supplying the paper and fabric, and me putting it all together.' Eve laughed. 'Now, let's make sure you and Olly have a good night. There's some lasagne in the fridge and ice cream in the freezer.'

Eve had forgotten how nice George could be. Never stuffy, he talked to people easily, had a great sense of humour, and it transpired he was a good dancer too. The dinner was superb and they had agreed to share a table with two other couples, which could've been a disaster, but turned out to be far from that. The time flew by with great conversation and a lot of laughter. One of the couples were Londoners; they had come down to find a house they could retire to. George was very diplomatic, offering to help, but he didn't pursue the subject, just handed them a card and suggested they telephoned him or came to his office on Monday. The other couple from Stratford-upon-Avon were on holiday; they said they came every year at the same time as they loved Devon. All four of them were interested in Eve's business, and George made her blush by saying how incredibly talented she was.

When the band started to play, George took her hand and led her out on to the dance floor. Eve had always loved dancing; as a young girl she'd taken part in ballroom competitions, but Don's only interest in dancing was a late-night drunken shuffle around the floor. George could waltz, quickstep and tango, along with disco dancing too. He was light on his feet and Eve felt as if she was being transported to a dream world in his arms.

Even walking home along the seafront was fun. It was a mild night with a full moon, which cut a silver swathe across the calm sea. At one point George put his arms around her to kiss her. 'I was so proud to be with you tonight,' he said. 'You looked beautiful and danced so well – I must have been the envy of every other man there. Please say you'll be my girl?'

Eve thought that was sweetly old-fashioned and she liked it. He was such a gentleman, and she wondered if that was why he'd never taken their relationship any further two years ago. Maybe he thought she just wasn't ready for it after being recently widowed?

'I'd love to be,' she said.

'I'm not around now as much as I used to be because I've opened a branch in Exeter,' he said. 'I know you're very busy too, but there's always weekends.'

'Yes, I am,' she said. 'Weekends sound fine to me.'

'But may I take you, Olly and Tabby out for lunch tomorrow?'

He kissed her lingeringly at her front door, not asking to come in. He said he'd ring in the morning to arrange the lunch, and Eve watched him walking back up the narrow lane to Fore Street and smiled because his straight back and brisk walk made her think of a guardsman.

The next day George took them to a pub further along the coast towards Lyme Regis. The sun was shining, and the traditional Sunday roast was delicious. Eve felt she might burst if she ate another thing.

George was great with Tabby. He asked her about school and what she wanted to do when she left.

'I'd like to go to art college,' she said. 'Learn about textiles and stuff. But I sort of change my mind like the wind. A week ago I wanted to be a vet. Well, at least until I found out it takes seven years. Before that I thought an air hostess would be good.'

'Sounds like you need to get a Saturday job to broaden your mind to the opportunities out there,' George said. 'I could do with a Saturday girl myself, not that giving people details of houses for sale actually broadens your mind.' He laughed.

'I think I'd like that.' Tabby's eyes sparkled. 'Would I make appointments and even get to see the houses myself?'

'I could certainly train you to make appointments,' he grinned. 'And make tea and coffee, file correspondence and maybe in time get to see the odd new property so you can tell prospective buyers about it.'

'Are you seriously offering her a Saturday job?' Eve asked. She wondered if he was just teasing.

'Yes, I am. I need someone to mind the shop if I have to nip out with a client. Tabby's a bright girl. I doubt I could do better.'

'So what would the pay be?' Tabby asked.

'Tabby!' Eve was shocked she'd dared ask that.

'How does twenty pounds sound?'

Tabby looked gleeful. 'Pretty good. Could I start next Saturday?'

'I'll be lonely without you,' Olly said, and his face was so doleful that Eve reached across the table and tweaked his nose.

'Your sister needs a job, and we'll do something together,' she said.

Much later that evening, when Eve was in bed, she felt happier than she had in a long time. George's kisses after the children had gone to bed had been lovely and tender, but at no time did she feel he was about to push her into taking things further. She liked that he respected the children were just along the landing, and today he had behaved as if he really wanted to get to know them properly. Offering Tabby a Saturday job was marvellous. She'd wanted one for ages but despite asking in many shops no one had a vacancy.

Eve believed that a Saturday job was the first step in finding a career for all teenagers. She'd worked in a hardware shop when she was Tabby's age and had learned quite a few tips on DIY and which tools did what job, all of which had proved very useful. Working in an estate agent's would teach Tabby office and people skills. Yet, perhaps more important than earning some money of her own, she would be adjusting into the adult world, where you had to work even when you didn't feel like it, keep good time and be polite at all times. Tabby wasn't very good at the last two.

Eve soon found that George wasn't one for phoning for a chat, or to check she was in so he could call round. He had told her he was 'old school', making arrangements for the next meeting at the last minute. And he wouldn't dream of dropping by without an invitation. He claimed it was because he was from the generation who had to find a public telephone to make calls and it had made him a technophobe. Eve quite liked not being interrupted at work and feeling like she didn't have to be dressed up all the time in case he came by.

Yet for weekends George always had a plan, and as late summer slipped into autumn with chilly winds, on a Saturday night he would often suggest the cinema or a DVD to watch with Olly and Tabby, plus a Chinese takeaway. On Sundays he liked a brisk clifftop walk, bacon sandwiches from a mobile cafe he knew or lunch in Bridport, Exmouth or some other small town nearby. Once they all went out mackerel fishing, and they came back with so many fish Eve spent the whole afternoon gutting and filleting them to put in the freezer. She thought she'd die of cold out on the choppy sea so hoped he wouldn't suggest it again in a hurry. But then, as the year grew closer to Christmas, they went to the theatre in Exeter or there were other dinner and dances. Often these were connected to his work or charities he was involved in. When he had nothing organized on a Sunday, Eve tended to breathe a sigh of relief, as in the pre-Christmas period people always wanted new curtains or even whole rooms revamped. She and Sophie were working flat out, with both their outworkers stretched too.

Yet for all this weekend togetherness, they still were not lovers. George kissed her a great deal; he'd even said he loved her one night at a dinner dance, but appeared to want nothing physical. George didn't talk about his marriage either: not little memories, a place they went to, a holiday or when Noah his son was born. She asked him once if he'd like to have a Sunday lunch at her place and bring Noah, but George said it would be 'difficult'. Whether that was because Eastbourne was a long way away or that his ex-wife didn't let the boy go away with him, she didn't know. Or maybe he didn't want to upset her by talking about his past?

There was a certain irony that she'd married a brute, then found a man who wanted nothing more than to share her bed, but that the next one wasn't interested in that. But if that was how he felt, it didn't matter – she loved being with George. He was a gentleman, kind, thoughtful and fun. And he liked Tabby and Olly. She was content with how it was, but she wished he would tell her how he felt; she didn't want it coming between them.

About ten days before Christmas George turned up with a real seven-foot tree, which he put up in the dining-room part of the kitchen as it was the biggest space. They all started decorating it together, but George was ridiculously fussy about how it should be done. The lights had to be just so, then he supervised how the baubles were hung, practically measuring the distance between them was all the same. Eve and Olly found this a bit tiresome and went upstairs.

'Do you remember last Christmas, Mum?' Olly asked as he flopped down on the sofa. 'When Tom came back with those two branches, and he said we were going to have a competition to decorate them.'

Eve laughed. 'He sprayed them white, then stuck them in two little red buckets full of sand.'

'Our team, you and me, did ours best,' Olly said laughingly. 'We used just gold and silver. But Tom and Tabby didn't have a colour scheme; they just chucked everything, regardless of colour, on theirs.'

'Remember what Tom said about it?' Eve giggled. '"Ours deserves to win for the most audacious, taste-less, eye-popping blast of Christmas colour."'

She lapsed into a daydream of how much laughter there had been last year. Tom had got them silly jokey presents but wrapped each one beautifully. She was jolted out of this happy memory by noting that Olly had gone very quiet and looked sad. 'What is it?'

'I wonder what he'll do this Christmas. Do you think he's happy?'

Tears sprang into Eve's eyes, not just because of

what her son had said but her own little memory. She thought about Tom often, and always wished she'd handled things better. Looking back, she wondered if Tom had felt she hadn't wanted to settle down with a tradesman. Nothing could be further from the truth, of course. She had never been a snob, and she had no intention of becoming one. If anything, she would always prize a man who could build a house, lay a floor, tile a kitchen or any other job that required skill, rather than a pen-pushing out-of-the-top-drawer man who could barely put an electric plug on.

Thinking about such things jolted her into remembering about Don's death. He hadn't crossed her mind in months, but suddenly it was there again, and with it the guilt. Would that ever go away? Or was it a kind of retribution that the man she'd found who she could've been happy forever with was gone, and that possibly she'd always miss him.

'Come and look!' George called out from downstairs, startling both Olly and Eve into remembering they had intended to have pizza for supper after the tree was done.

Eve gasped with delight when she saw the tree. It was absolutely beautiful: the twinkling lights reflecting on red and silver baubles, plus some dark blue ones Eve hadn't seen before. Obviously George had bought them as a surprise to tie in with the kitchen decor. But not just those – there had to be at least twenty white roses tipped with silver nestling into the fir tree's branches. It was perfection, and Eve threw her arms round George to thank him.

'Tabby thought you might not like it because you've always been a "throw everything at the tree" kind of person,' George said, grinning broadly.

'In my defence, for donkey's years we always had to put on all the decorations Olly and Tabby made for the tree, and, if I'm honest, they weren't the best of things from which to produce a work of art. Also, I was always too rushed off my feet getting curtains finished to have spare time to ponce around with the tree.' She laughed as she said this, because it was true. Also, it was Tabby who suggested they binned all the homemade stuff when they were packing up in Grove Park. 'But if this splendid tree is the new benchmark, then next year I promise I will surpass it.'

'That's a challenge, is it?' George asked.

'I've put the pizza in the oven,' Olly said. Always the peacemaker, he was clearly worried a challenge might make his mother cross. 'I'll lay the table. Will you be having wine?'

Eve ruffled her son's hair affectionately. She hadn't been best pleased to hear what Tabby had told George – sometimes she could be very two-faced – but Olly could always be relied on to stand by her.

*

Later that evening Eve suggested to George that they shouldn't see each other again before Christmas Eve, when he was coming to stay for two days. 'You said you've got to go to work in Exeter anyway, and I've got a huge house where I have to supervise the decoration, hang curtains and blinds and dress the whole downstairs. And finish off the rest of the outstanding orders with Sophie, plus all the Christmas shopping, present buying and wrapping.'

'Fair enough,' George said. 'Though if I can do anything to help, just ask. But can Tabby help out at the office? Maybe just ten till four.'

Eve looked at Tabby to get her reaction. 'I'd love to,' she said. 'And if you need any shopping, Mum, I can always get it on the way home for you.'

When George gave Eve a goodnight kiss as he was leaving, she wondered if his staying in the spare room here for Christmas would change things. If he was ever intending to make love to her, surely that would be the right time.

17

Christmas Day was almost perfect. Eve got up at six to turn on the oven where the prepared turkey was waiting, then she laid the dining table, with the special hand-embroidered tablecloth and napkins her mother had made years ago. With red chargers instead of table mats, and red candles sitting in a circle of frosted greenery, plus the kept-for-best silver-plated cutlery, crystal wine glasses and the reindeer cruet set, she smiled to see everything was as it should be. Then finally there were the crackers at each place.

She remembered one Christmas how after she'd spent ages laying the table to look inviting, in a sudden fit of anger Don had swept everything off the table, screaming, 'I hate all this poncey stuff.' Tabby and Olly were seven and six at the time and white with terror. Once their father had stormed off to the pub, they helped Eve pick everything up, but after that Christmas she didn't attempt to lay the table properly again – just putting on a red-paper cloth and the everyday glasses and cutlery. One of the reindeer had broken antlers but she had painstakingly glued them back together a few days later and wrapped them in tissue paper. Last Christmas with Tom was the first time she'd used them since, and the children had cheered to see them.

Despite her hopes George hadn't suggested coming into her bed last night. He made an excuse that the children might come into the bedroom on Christmas morning with their stockings to open. She couldn't bring herself to tell him they hadn't done that since they were tiny, as Don had screamed at them once to get back to their beds. Even last year, when Tom wasn't even there in the early morning, they still didn't come in to her.

'George wasn't to know any of that,' she murmured to herself, as she laid some breakfast things on a tray to take up to the sitting room for later. 'He was just being cautious.'

Before anyone got up, Eve showered and put on the dress she'd bought for Christmas. It was cream lightweight wool and very elegant with her light tan boots. She added some emerald-green earrings and fixed her hair up on top of her head with a glamorous and large matching hair clip.

It was a lovely day. George said she looked beautiful, and the children were delighted with their stockings. They had a walk along the seafront after breakfast to work up an appetite for lunch. The turkey was a triumph, moist and perfect, and the shop-bought sticky toffee pudding with ice cream a crowd-pleaser, as no one really liked Christmas pud. Then, full to bursting, they went up to the sitting room to open the remaining presents and watch a James Bond film, during which Eve fell asleep.

She woke to find Olly and Tabby had popped out to visit a friend. George said they'd be home around eight and kissed her. 'We could seize the moment and go to bed,' she whispered in his ear.

George chuckled, took her hand and led her along to her room, then laughingly threw her on the bed.

It was lovely to finally feel his naked body against hers. He was a gentle and sensitive lover, but she sensed a hesitancy in him and a lack of real passion which was a little unnerving. But as they snuggled together afterwards, she silently told herself that the first time with a new partner was likely to be a bit scary, a sort of trial-and-error thing. She wasn't going to compare it to the first time with Tom, which was all fireworks and wonder. George's posh background probably made him a bit inhibited, and he would improve with practice.

Clearly, he didn't want any further practice that day as he sidled off to the guest room around ten thirty. They had played a game of Scrabble when the children got home and watched some TV, then the children disappeared to their rooms too, and Eve went down to the kitchen, poured herself a large gin and tonic and finished tidying up from lunch.

Tomorrow they were going to see *The Two Towers* in Exeter, as both the children were huge *Lord of the Rings* fans. Eve got the distinct impression George wasn't keen to see it. As he pointed out, 'creatures of Middle Earth' weren't his thing. But he hid his lack of enthusiasm well. He even said he really enjoyed it afterwards.

For New Year's Eve George and Eve were back at the Victoria Hotel for a dinner dance, and he booked a room for them too. This was partly because Patty and Ernest Hathaway had driven down from Essex to see the children and to stay for a three-day break. Eve had given them her bedroom. George said seeing 2003 in at a hotel was more fun: no chilly walk home when they were tiddly and a swimming pool to go in on New Year's Day. He was right and Eve thoroughly enjoyed it, but she was a bit disappointed that soon after a swim and a wonderful breakfast he said he would be going off to Exeter in the late afternoon as he had work to catch up with in his office.

It didn't seem to matter once she got home to Patty and Ernest. They thought the new home and studio were fantastic, and Patty said that the night before she'd left the children watching a film with Ernest and spent ages looking at all the pattern books in the studio. She said it had convinced her that her home needed a makeover with something more up to date.

When Eve asked Patty and Ernie what they wanted to do, they said it was too cold for anything more than a short brisk walk, and anyway she and Ernest just wanted to sit about and chat to her if that was OK with Eve.

'So, tell me, Eve,' Patty said as they were getting supper ready. They were having cold turkey and salad, plus some chips. George had left about an hour earlier to go to Exeter and Ernest was upstairs in the sitting room with the children. 'Is this serious with George?'

'I'm not sure,' Eve said. She looked at the gold bangle on her wrist that he'd bought her for Christmas. 'I always imagined when a man spent this much money on a woman, he must be serious about her. He says he loves me too, but it feels like there's something missing. What do you think, Patty?'

'I'd say he's crazy about you. He can't keep his eyes off you. How do you feel about him?'

'I feel like I love him, but I'm nervous. When I got involved with Tom it was like a wonderful whirlwind. I felt so close to him. But that went pear-shaped, so I'm no judge, and perhaps I'm scared of getting hurt again.'

Patty poured two glasses of wine for them. 'You never said what went wrong with you and Tom.'

Eve took a big glug of her wine. 'I was afraid to let him stay the night because I was worried it gave the wrong message to the kids,' she admitted. 'He kept telling me I should talk to them and say we just wanted to be together. But I wouldn't.'

'Oh dear,' Patty said. 'Of course, when I was young it was considered wrong to sleep with someone before marriage. But that's all changed now. I know we never met Tom, but he sounded so nice.'

'He was. I was an idiot. I see that now, but it's over and that's that. I can't turn George into a Tom; he's a different animal.'

'A very well-bred one with impeccable manners, dress sense, handsome and, from what I understand, a good businessman. As my mother would've said, "A good catch".'

'Yes, he's all that,' Eve sighed. 'But a man considering taking on a woman with two children would have to be very careful. Maybe he's holding back because of that?'

'Maybe. But you don't want to jump into anything serious yet, darling. Look what you've been through. Enjoy yourself, take some holidays, have fun.'

Eve smiled. Patty was a very soothing sort of person and she thought she should take her advice and not analyse George – just enjoy the romance for what it was.

*

The studio was busy all through January because Eve had offered a discount on any orders for curtains or blinds placed by the end of the month.

One afternoon just as it was getting dark, to her astonishment Eve saw Dawn Button outside the workshop, looking at the window display. She was shaken because she was on her own. Sophie hadn't come in today as she had a cold and the children were at after-school activities. It was several months since she had last seen Button and she had believed she would never see her again.

Eve felt she should be angry that the woman had turned up again, but for some inexplicable reason she felt sorry for her. Her hair was loose and needed a wash, and her red coat was much too big for her. She looked thin and uncared for. However, Eve wasn't going to take a chance on the woman storming into the studio, so she decided to go out and see what her game was.

'If you've come to make further trouble, I'll call the police,' Eve said as she stepped out on to the veranda.

'I haven't,' Button said, backing away and fluttering her hands as if to say she meant no harm. 'I came to apologize to you. I don't know what I was thinking attacking you. I've been told you're a very nice person.'

It took a few moments for Eve to think on that.

'Come in and have a coffee. It's too cold to talk out here.'

It was clear Button was scared, but that could be an act to get sympathy, so she thought she'd play along with it. 'So who told you I was nice?' she asked.

'Marianne. She runs a refuge here in Sidmouth. I was staying there at the time. I confided in her about what I'd done; it never crossed my mind she would know you. But she got angry with me and said that what I did was inexcusable. I'm surprised she didn't report me to the police.'

It was extremely odd that Marianne hadn't told Eve this. She hadn't even telephoned to check she was all right. But then maybe she knew Button needed help rather than punishment. 'So you were abused then?' Eve asked as she filled the kettle.

'Yes, the last time I was hospitalized for three weeks and Josie my daughter was taken into care. That's how I came to be sent to the refuge here. But with hindsight I should've told you that my husband beat me when I came to your house in Grove Park, then you might have talked to me.'

'It would've made more sense to me,' Eve said.

Button put her hands over her eyes as if ashamed. 'You see I was desperate to get back into journalism, and to get away from him. I read about the fire that killed your ex-husband in the local paper and guessed he'd been turning up to cause trouble for you. I suspected he'd beaten you. I thought I could do a good sympathetic piece about it. I wasn't trying to dish dirt, but I guess that's what you believed.'

Eve thought for a moment before responding. Either this woman wasn't the full shilling or she was genuine and she'd reacted badly out of frustration. The thing was, Eve couldn't tell which.

'Explain how you came to find me again,' Eve said.

'One of your old neighbours said you'd moved to Devon, but I didn't know where. It was pure coincidence that I found you in Sidmouth. You see, I'd only just arrived at the refuge, and I took my daughter Josie for a walk on the second day, and, as we went along Manor Road, I saw your car there.'

'And on the strength of that you decided to hang out there in the rain, dressed like a man, to follow me, hit me and snatch my handbag?' Eve's voice rose to almost a screech of indignation. 'Not only is that far-fetched, but it's an awful thing to do to someone who had just refused to be interviewed. Do you really expect me to believe you?'

Button ladled three spoons of sugar into the coffee Eve handed her.

'You've done worse. I know you started the fire that your ex-husband died in,' she retorted, her dark eyes flashing with scorn. 'Some of your old neighbours told me they thought the same because they'd seen you with black eyes and other injuries. But as a wife who has been beaten myself I kind of admired you for it; he sounded a right bastard. But, lucky you, you not only got rid of him permanently, but you ended up with the house and the insurance.'

Eve's eyes widened with shock and her pulse rate increased. 'Of course I didn't start the fire,' she said. 'That's poppycock. So which of the neighbours said they thought that, and told you I'd gone to Devon?'

'I can't remember her name now.'

'If you'd been beaten as I was, why on earth would you want to inflict that kind of pain on someone who had done nothing to you?'

'Jealousy, I suppose,' Button said, her tone sullen. 'I was angry with you because you wouldn't talk to me that day in Grove Park. Then, once I was here, I found things had improved for you. While I was skint and homeless, I discovered you doing up this place – no expense spared. I watched you here a couple of times. Once you were laughing about something with the curly-haired builder and you looked so happy. I hated you for it.'

She stopped her rant and was shaking so much she had to put down her mug of coffee. 'I can't justify myself for attacking you,' she went on, 'but had you told me your story and had I got a foot in the door with journalism, I could've landed a good job and become a success. Instead, things got far worse for me and Josie. We lost everything and had to come here to the refuge. So, when I discovered where you were living, I got angry and hatched the plan to lie in wait for you, and the day it was raining seemed perfect.'

Eve was stunned that this woman had convinced herself that writing a story for a newspaper would immediately transport her to a better life. What planet was she living on? Just because you could string a few words together didn't mean a newspaper would take you on as a journalist. Yet even more astounding was that she'd take her revenge in such a ridiculous way.

'Well, you certainly did hurt and frighten me. And you stole my bag.'

'I know and I'm ashamed of that.'

Eve looked hard at the woman and tried to be objective. She was just a worn-down woman who'd had the stuffing kicked out of her by a brute. She clearly wasn't that bright either. And Eve remembered only too well how it felt to be trapped with a violent husband and no money to escape. But Button had been brave enough to come here and apologize, so Eve had no desire to punish her further, just to make sure she didn't bandy stories about her around.

'And now?' Eve asked, looking right into the other woman's eyes. 'I applaud the apology, Dawn, and I admire your courage. But why do I have the feeling you have some other motive for coming to me? There is something more, isn't there?'

'Yes, I want you to let me interview you now. I could do a brilliant rags-to-riches story.'

The hope on her face was laughable. Surely she didn't really believe Eve was that much of a pushover?

'No, Dawn, no,' she said firmly. 'I don't want any kind of story in the press – not written by you or anyone else.'

'A glossy local magazine offered me six hundred pounds for your story. I could get even more from one of the nationals if I called it something like "Getting away with Murder", and said how I think you did it. But I don't want to do that. All I want is to earn enough for a deposit for a little flat for me and Josie. My time with Marianne ran out and our home now is a room in a grotty bed and breakfast. Josie suffers from asthma, and it doesn't help that the room is so damp.'

Eve knew immediately that they had finally arrived at the bottom line. With or without her permission, Button was going to write a story about her. It would probably never be bought by a magazine or newspaper, much less published, but editors would read it, and they were likely to send out one of their own experienced journalists to dig into the story. Eve had to stop her. Just the suspicion of murder could ruin her business and her children's lives, to say nothing of the police opening the case again.

'I do feel for you, Dawn. I remember that feeling of complete hopelessness –' she paused, wondering just how to word it – 'but I don't like that you're trying to blackmail me. You do know it's a criminal offence?' She let her words sink in.

'It's not blackmail; I don't want money from you.'

'It is, Dawn. You're holding something over me to make money. I've done nothing wrong; those old neighbours of mine were just spiteful gossips.'

'Please help me, Eve,' the woman pleaded, and she looked so desperate and hopeless that Eve did feel for her.

'OK, Dawn, I will help you. Not because you're threatening me, but because I know you're in a bad place, and I've been there too. I'll give you some money for your deposit.'

'You will?' The woman's eyes widened. 'You aren't winding me up, are you?'

'No, I'm not. But first you must make me a promise.'

'About what?' Button asked.

'You forget writing about me. And never come back for more. If you do, I'll bring the law down on you so fast you won't know what's hit you. Are you willing to swear on Josie's life that you'll never come near me again or talk about this to anyone?'

'Yes, I will.'

'Swear then.'

'I swear on Josie's life I won't come near you again or talk about this to anyone.'

'Wait here.' Eve went into her workroom and opened the desk drawer, taking out a thousand pounds she'd been given that morning as a deposit on some curtains. She then put two brown and orange velvet cushions into a carrier bag.

She went back to Button and handed her the thousand pounds. 'Now, remember your promise, Dawn. I hope you find a nice little flat and get a job; there's always work in Sidmouth in catering or in shops.' She then handed her the carrier bag. 'This is a little housewarming present. But don't ever come near me again.'

Eve watched Dawn Button walk away with the bulging carrier bag, and although it felt like a victory she knew it wasn't. Giving the woman that much money was almost an admission of guilt. As she started to get the tea ready for Tabby and Olly, she found herself crying; she didn't think she'd ever felt so alone before. Or so scared.

In the days that followed, Eve thought of Sylvia's advice for when things were difficult. 'Count your blessings' was one of them. And she surprised herself by how many blessings she had: two healthy, happy children, a great business and a lovely home. Tabby was loving working for George; she spoke about him as if he could walk on water. Instigated by George, Tabby had joined an amateur dramatic group in Sidmouth with one of her friends. She said for now she would only be backstage, sorting costumes, props and making scenery, but she was enjoying meeting people and hoped eventually she might get a small part. Olly had started to learn to play classical guitar at school back in November, and he was so enthusiastic that Eve had bought him a guitar of his own for Christmas. But in January when she saw how serious he was about playing it, she found a private teacher who lived just five minutes away by the River Sid. Both he and Tabby had a lot of homework to do, but Olly would do his in a hurry and then practise his guitar.

Eve was happy that the move to Devon had proved to be a good one for them, although she only saw George at weekends, sometimes only on Saturday nights as he was busy with charity work. But she had a new job too, as she'd finally got the contract to decorate, furnish and stage a flat in the apartment block George had told her about when they first met. The budget was a good one, and it was exciting to do a whole flat, and to source the tableware, ornaments and lighting, along with all the soft furnishings.

With all this going on, Eve put aside her worries about Dawn Button and whether the thousand pounds she'd given her would come back to bite her. She also gave up on worrying about George. He stayed with her twice in January, and he was talking about them taking a holiday in Italy in spring. His lack of passion didn't seem to matter to her any more. They were friends after all; perhaps that was more important.

February was cold and bleak, but finally March arrived with a hint of spring. Marianne came round one day, looking fresh, slimmer and happy. Eve asked her to come in for a coffee.

'I've had a long holiday. George Mulberry, the estate agent you recommended, found me a buyer for the house, so I'm looking for a small flat now,' Marianne said.

The last time they had met was back in October when Marianne was getting decorators in to smarten her house up before she approached anyone about putting it on the market. Eve immediately wanted to know more. George had never said he'd met Marianne, but then she realized he would have no reason to; he didn't know Eve knew her, much less that she'd lived in her refuge.

'Well, this is lovely,' Marianne said, stopping short to look around the kitchen. 'I couldn't see it properly the night of your launch party; there were too many people about.'

'I'll give you the full tour later if you like. But sit down and we'll have coffee first.'

Marianne told Eve about her holiday and how good she felt at finally giving up on the refuge. 'I'm told everyone who runs one gets burnout after a few years – other people's misery and misfortune can be very debilitating. But now someone is due to complete on the house and give me more money than I expected, I've got a new lease of life.'

'I'm glad you used George Mulberry,' Eve said.

'Well, you did say how helpful he was to you. I actually thought you fancied him, and who could blame you?'

Eve blushed. 'I did, but it never came to anything. Though, funnily enough, I am seeing him now. But be careful what you say to him, as he doesn't know I was at the refuge.'

'I wouldn't ever tell anyone how I met you, or any woman who came to the refuge,' Marianne said indignantly. 'But how long have you been seeing him for? I thought you were going out with Tom the builder.'

'I was, but that fizzled out, remember, and I've been seeing George for a few months,' Eve said.

'Well, that would be a record for George. I'm told he's famous for seeing women a couple of times then dropping them. He's very handsome, though.'

'Who told you that?' Eve asked.

'One of my decorators. His sister went out with George and he seemed mad about her, then suddenly he didn't call or phone. Apparently that's what he always does. He left his wife when their son was just a baby with no real explanation.'

'People do like to gossip and embellish things,' Eve said. She was a little shaken by this, remembering her own early experience with him. But she wasn't going to react. 'I'll let you know if he suddenly does that to me. By the way, why didn't you ever tell me that Dawn Button admitted to you that she'd attacked me? She came here to apologize.'

'She was a very odd one.' Marianne shook her head as if bewildered by the woman. 'She'd only been with me a few days when she claimed she'd attacked a woman. She seemed to want absolution.'

'Really?' Eve said incredulously.

'She just started ranting about attacking a woman and stealing her handbag, then suddenly she said "Eve Hathaway", your married name. I thought, *Christ Almighty, what's going on here?*'

Marianne paused for breath. She looked at Eve with an anxious expression. 'I didn't tell her you'd stayed in the refuge, but she took me by surprise, Eve. There she was claiming you'd started the fire that killed your ex-husband. How could I not shout her down and tell her I'd known you for years and you couldn't have done such a thing? But afterwards I was horrified I'd told her I knew you.'

'It's OK,' Eve said. 'I know you wouldn't have deliberately given out any information about me, or any of your women. And I think I've been a first-class prat because I've given her a thousand pounds.'

Marianne clutched at her throat as if she was being throttled. 'Oh no, Eve. Why?'

'Because I felt sorry for her, guilty because I had so much more than her – take your pick.'

'Eve, you are a kind and loving woman, but didn't you learn anything from your brutish ex-husband? To survive in this world you have to stay strong, and that means when maggots crawl out of the wood-work and make demands on us, we have to learn to squash them.'

'It's always easy to see the mistakes you've made after the event,' Eve said ruefully.

'Is that an admission that you started the fire, or just giving Button money?'

'Of course I didn't start the fire, but I may have been foolish giving the woman money.'

Eve was tempted to tell Marianne the truth about the fire, because she could see by the way her friend was looking at her that she didn't entirely believe her. But she couldn't.

'Secrets can be a terrible burden, dear,' Marianne said, confirming it. 'I've had so many laid on me over the years. Babies who didn't belong to the man they'd married. Women who only married a man to give them children. Women who married only for money. Women who married to please their parents. Strangely enough, all these different secrets ended in violence and often hatred. I'm so glad to be stepping away from it all now.'

Eve got to her feet. 'Come and let me show you round the house,' she said. 'And by the way, I'm working on plans for the show flats George will be selling. You should get him to give you the details; they're lovely.'

After what Marianne had said about George, in the weeks that followed Eve found herself observing him more closely. He was certainly thoughtful, kind, very affectionate, always interested in her latest work project, and asking Olly how school was and how the guitar lessons were going. He didn't need to ask after Tabby as he saw her on Saturdays unless he was called away to the Exeter branch. Yet, along with his lack of enthusiasm to sleep with her, she sensed he was hiding something. She asked him direct questions about the number of houses he sold and the rent he paid on the properties his two branches were in, hoping he'd admit if he was struggling financially, but from what he said he was doing well, and so she decided his business was none of hers.

Then one evening when they had supper together in her house, the children going off to their rooms and leaving them alone, she tackled him some more. She quizzed him gently about his life with his ex-wife and why they had separated. He admitted that when Katrina had become pregnant with Noah, he had felt he had to marry her, but he wasn't happy about it because he was certain she'd got pregnant on purpose. He then told Eve a bit more about his background. His father was a high-ranking army officer, as his grandfather had been too, and home was a rather grand estate near Barnstaple.

'I was expected to follow the family tradition,' he said with a sigh, 'but I had no interest in soldiering, or even farming our land, while my younger brother loved the farm and worked long hours on it. But Katrina imagined we would inherit the house and land once my father died. When I told her he had left it to Harry and that I was relieved about it, as it would be nothing but a millstone around my neck, Katrina was savage. She said I should buckle down, get involved with the farming, the horses and every aspect of country life, so that my father would change the will in my favour. I refused.'

'That was very brave of you,' Eve said. 'But, just out of interest, what was so bad about that life?'

George pulled a face. 'Buried in the country, up to my shins in mud and muck most of the time? It's a struggle to keep an estate in profit these days, Eve. Besides, Katrina was even less suited to country life than I am. She doesn't ride – in fact, she's afraid of horses – so I can't imagine her feeding chickens or growing vegetables, let alone being happy in a big draughty house with absolutely nowhere to wear glamorous clothes. Just running a bath is an act of faith the boiler won't go out. Mostly it does.'

Eve smiled. It didn't sound that appealing to her either. 'So what happened?'

George sighed dejectedly. 'She walked out on me. Taking Noah with her. We were living in Exeter at the time. I was working in the shoe shop I mentioned when I first met you, and by night I was the sommelier at Exeter's only hotel smart enough to call the wine waiter by that name. But we were struggling to make ends meet and she didn't help by buying expensive dresses. Anyway, to cut a long miserable tale short, she met Harrison Bixby, a lawyer. Apparently he was in Exeter for an important, rather long trial. I assume she was having an affair with him, as when he had to go back to his law firm in Eastbourne, she and Noah went with him.'

'How awful for you,' Eve said.

'It was a shock at the time, but quite honestly we weren't happy, Eve. Katrina had found a man who could give her what she wanted. I saw an opportunity to do what I wanted to do without the financial strain of a wife and child. I got a job in an estate agent's in Exeter, kept the sommelier job on too, and built myself up a nest egg to start my own business.'

'What about Noah?'

He grimaced. 'That's not my finest hour. I try to see him as often as I can, but the distance makes it difficult. Katrina doesn't do anything to make it easier. She'd like me to bow out on fatherhood and let

Harrison become his dad. She's pregnant now, baby due in a few weeks, and no doubt she'll claim it's time for me to clear off for good.'

'How does that make you feel?'

'Honestly? Relieved. I can't be Noah's dad. I haven't spent enough time on the job, and he's been influenced by Katrina to despise me – he barely speaks to me. No point in banging my head against a brick wall.'

Eve got up from the table and went to him, wrapping her arms around him and kissing him. She thought it was a sad story; he was probably terrified of any woman who might turn out to be another Katrina. He was probably ashamed too that he wasn't brave enough to follow his father and grandfather into the army. Though she saw nothing to be embarrassed about. Katrina sounded terrible, and Eve hoped Harrison Bixby might turn out to be less of a pushover than she had planned for.

18

Eve felt happy that spring had finally arrived. It was lovely to see the daffodil bulbs she'd planted last September bursting into flower and the touch of green on trees which said that leaves would be unfurling any day.

With the swimming pool just down the road, she started to go at seven in the morning daily to keep in shape. She was a little concerned about Tabby, who seemed distant, often disappearing after school with no explanation other than she was seeing a friend. But Eve put this down to normal teenage behaviour and assumed it would end before long. Despite her fears there had been no further visits from Dawn Button. But she had sent a little card, thanking Eve for her kindness.

Although she had niggling anxiety about Tabby, the business was continuing to do well. People kept coming in to spend a couple of hours browsing her sample books. Orders for wallpaper followed, and usually requests for her to come to their home to give them a quote to make curtains.

Although Sophie was flamboyant in her clothes

and her nature, she was at her best with clients who wanted a more traditional style, as her background was the country house look. Eve might look more conventional, but she adored wild, crazy designs, and it was said she had the courage to use them and make something fabulous, so together they were a perfect fit. They had a lot of laughs during the day, especially about the people who came in, looked around, saw the price of some of the fabrics and shuffled out saying, 'There's a price!', muttering they were off to the market for something cheaper.

'I just hope that one day we don't get someone coming in here with a carrier bag full of cheap and nasty fabric and ask us to make it up,' Sophie giggled.

'A couple came in the other day when you'd popped out and asked me how to put up a curtain track,' Eve said. 'That's like going into a dentist and asking him how you could fill your own teeth. I was very polite, however, and said I didn't know as I only make the curtains, but suggested they borrowed a DIY book from the library.'

Her relationship with George she likened to floating down a calm river. He was as charming, kind and thoughtful as ever. On Saturday nights during the winter, they often ate out locally or Eve would cook and they'd stay in watching television or a DVD. Sundays they mostly took bracing walks along the clifftop and had lunch in a pub. Olly often came on these walks, but Tabby often used the excuse she had schoolwork or that it was too cold. George stayed over some Saturday nights but always in the guest room. Eve would have preferred a little turbulence rather than endlessly calm water. But she accepted that was the way George was and reminded herself that, after living for so many years in a maelstrom, perhaps she should be careful about what she wished for.

Some early mornings after her swim Eve would do a spot of gardening and put in some new plants. She gave the old wooden garden table and chairs a new coat of cream paint and made a note to ask Brian the odd-job man to put up some brackets both in the garden and on the veranda for hanging baskets. She was finding peace and tranquillity she'd never known in the past.

'Do you think Tabby's got a boyfriend?' Eve asked Sophie one morning as they'd paused work for a coffee break. 'She seems very jumpy and excitable, but also more moody than usual. And she's lost her usual appetite. Plus, she's often very late home from school or runs in to get changed and goes out again. It's always "Promised I'd meet a friend" or an after-school club, but she never tells me which friend or what club.'

Sophie sipped her coffee thoughtfully. 'It's quite likely she's seeing a boy. She's fifteen and very attractive; all I'd be surprised about is that she hasn't had one before. Have you asked her?'

'I don't like to. She'd just clam up,' Eve said. 'But if she has, I ought to warn her about pregnancy, infections, etc. I know you aren't going to stop a girl having sex if she gets carried away, but at least suggesting a condom would protect her.'

'Difficult one that,' Sophie said. 'I mean, if you suggest a condom, you're giving her the green light. She's underage too, but maybe just tell her a few cautionary tales about girls you know who had shotgun weddings or caught STDs.'

Eve thought that a very good idea, and in the next few days looked for films that might come under that category. She found one, but every time she asked Tabby if she wanted to watch a film, she had homework to do.

The weather was gradually getting warmer by April, and it was good to see tourists coming back to Sidmouth again. Olly delighted in swimming in the sea with a friend, despite how cold the water was; he said it made him feel powerful, which amused Eve. She was also pleased and proud at how well he was doing with the guitar. His teacher praised him highly and said she wished all her pupils were so dedicated. Just before school broke up for the Easter holiday, he played solo in a school service. Parents weren't invited, but even Tabby admitted her brother played brilliantly.

George had asked Tabby to work three days a week during the school holiday, from ten till four, saying she was an asset to the agency. So, for the first time Eve could remember, her life seemed to be on an even keel with both children doing well and life being good for all three of them.

On the Wednesday afternoon before the Easter weekend, Eve got a call from the Victoria Hotel. It seemed George had enquired about tickets for the Easter dinner and dance, but they had all been taken by guests who had booked in for the weekend. Due to a cancellation two tickets were now available if George wanted them. The receptionist said she'd been unable to get hold of him and she needed his answer today.

Eve thought it best to walk round to his office to ask him, as he was obviously very busy. Mentioning first to Sophie where she was going and that she'd be back within half an hour, Eve set off.

George wasn't in the office. Muriel his secretary was talking to a couple and showing them details of a house. Tabby wasn't there, and had Muriel not been busy Eve would have asked if she'd arrived for work today, thinking her daughter had bunked off and gone out with a friend.

'George?' Eve asked, and Muriel pointed upstairs

to his flat. Eve ran lightly up the stairs at the back of the office, something she'd done dozens of times before, through the partly glazed door at the top and into the flat.

George's living room-cum-office was a big room at the front overlooking the high street. She could see at a glance he wasn't in there and opened the bedroom door.

She froze at the sight in front of her.

Tabby was naked on her hands and knees, and George, also naked, was entering her from behind, grunting with relish. Nothing Eve had ever encountered was as horrible as the sight of her little girl, blonde hair covering her face, and the little bleat coming from her.

Spotting a golf club by the door, Eve picked it up and brought it down with all the force she could muster across George's back. 'You bastard!' she yelled at the top of her voice. 'She's fifteen, you sick fucker.'

George tried to both ward off further blows and cover himself.

Tabby's shrill cry of 'Mummy, stop!' cut her to the quick. In a flash of enlightenment Eve suddenly realized why he had never wanted to sleep with her. Tabby had always been his target.

'Muriel, call the police!' Eve yelled down the stairs. 'Tell them your boss has just been caught raping a fifteen-year-old girl.'

There was a yelp of distress from Muriel, but then Eve heard the ping of the telephone, so she knew she had picked it up.

Tabby scrambled off the bed and tried desperately to get her clothes back on. She was white-faced and shaking, but whether this was from what had been taking place or terror at her mother catching her, Eve didn't know. George had curled into a foetal position, seemingly too stunned to say or do anything.

Eve caught hold of her daughter's arm with one hand, picked up the remains of her clothes with the other and dragged her out of the bedroom and pushed her into the living room. 'You will stay there till the police come,' she ordered, and locked her in.

Ignoring Tabby's pleas to let her out, Eve returned to George who was still on the bed. She picked up the golf club again and poked him with it. 'Get up, you piece of shit,' she snarled. 'I see it all now and what a fool I was to be taken in. You're a paedophile, not a normal human being. You preyed on my trust while you coerced my daughter into your nasty twisted world.'

'I f-f-f-fell in love with her. It isn't like you th-th-th-think,' he said, stuttering as he tried to get his boxer shorts on.

'Save that for the police,' she shouted. 'I hope they lock you up and throw away the key.'

To be sure he couldn't make a run for it, Eve took

the key from the glazed door at the top of stairs, went through it and locked it behind her.

Downstairs, Muriel, usually such a stern, controlled woman stood white-faced and shaking in the corner of the office.

'Did you know Tabby was up there with him?' Eve asked.

'No,' Muriel bleated. 'I thought George was alone doing his accounts. Tabby must've arrived and gone up there before I got here.'

She was saved any further questioning from Eve by two police officers arriving.

'They're up there –' Eve pointed upstairs – 'I've locked them in. George Mulberry is in the bedroom at the back and my fifteen-year-old daughter Tabitha Taylor is in the living room.' She held out the keys and then slumped down on to a chair, afraid she was going to be sick with the shock.

'I'm so sorry,' Muriel said, putting a soothing hand on Eve's shoulder. 'What a terrible thing for you to see. Can I get you some tea?'

'That's kind, Muriel,' Eve said haltingly. 'But no. Just tell me, did you know this was going on?'

Muriel wrung her hands and shook her head, glancing up to the ceiling at the sound of heavy boots marching about up there. 'No, I had absolutely no idea. I wouldn't have stayed working for him had I known.'

An older man in plain clothes arrived, accompanied by a younger constable.

The older man introduced himself. 'I'm Detective Inspector Baytrum, and this is PC Webber. And you two are?'

'Eve Taylor. I'm the mother of Tabitha Taylor; she's the girl with George Mulberry up there.'

'I'm Muriel Parkinson. I work at this office part-time. It was me who telephoned you.'

The constable stayed with Eve and Muriel, while DI Baytrum went up the stairs.

George began protesting his innocence loudly. He said something about believing Tabby was seventeen, but within minutes one of the two officers who'd arrived first led him down the stairs, handcuffed. He gave Eve a pleading look, but she turned away in disgust and he was led out to the car and driven away.

Yet another police car arrived, this time with a mature female police officer, and Tabby was brought downstairs. She was crying hysterically, calling for Eve, but the PC hushed her gently and said she was putting a jacket over her head so she wouldn't be recognized by anyone outside. With that she quickly led her out and into the waiting car which sped away.

'I had no idea Tabitha was up there,' Muriel said to the DI, so upset she could hardly get the words out. 'George rang me at my home at one o'clock and asked me to come and man the office because he had some accounts to do. I don't usually come in on a Wednesday. As soon as I arrived, he gave me some instructions about people I had to ring and then he went up to his flat.' She paused, overcome by emotion and shock.

'When Eve arrived, I was speaking to some clients,' she went on haltingly. 'Eve waved and ran on up the stairs, just the way she's often done before. Then when all the commotion and swearing broke out, I suggested the clients left and Eve shouted for me to call the police, so I did.'

The constable was writing all this down in his notebook, including her full name and address. The DI suggested that she could go home. 'This is a crime scene now. I'll lock up here and take the keys. But we'll need a formal statement from you tomorrow.'

Once Muriel had gone, he sat down with Eve and got her to tell her side of what had happened. She admitted hitting George with the golf club and locking them both in.

'He was my boyfriend,' she said, and that made her cry again. 'I don't know if this has been going on for weeks or if it was just today. I trusted him with both my children. I can't believe he would do such a thing to my little girl.'

'We're going to drive you home now, Ms Taylor,' Baytrum said, gently patting her on the shoulder. 'We'll take your statement there if that's all right with you?'

'I can't leave my daughter alone in the police station,' she said and began to cry even harder, not only with the shock of what she'd seen, but remembering the brusque way she'd been with Tabby.

'I understand how upsetting this is for you, but your daughter will probably find it easier to tell the truth about what happened without you nearby. She'll be looked after and seen by a doctor and, as she is underage, she will only be questioned with a responsible adult present.'

Sophie came to the door as soon as she saw the police car on the drive. 'What on earth?!' she exclaimed when she saw Eve's swollen eyes. 'Have you had an accident?'

When Eve didn't or couldn't speak, Sophie sensed this was something more than an accident. 'Come in. Whatever's happened I'll stay here and see to Olly when he comes in,' she said, taking command. 'You go on up to the sitting room. I'll bring a pot of tea. If you need anything else, just shout.'

Telling the police sergeant what George had been to her and then to find him doing that to her daughter was the worst thing Eve had ever been through. She felt she would rather be back in a hospital having been beaten half to death, than to have that sordid scene imprinted on her mind.

'Was it my fault?' she asked Baytrum. 'Should I

245

have seen some signs that it was my daughter he wanted?'

The DI had a very lined face like he spent too long in the sun, and his eyes reminded Eve of a spaniel, but there was kindness and understanding in them. 'You mustn't blame yourself. Men like Mulberry are very cunning; they plan everything they do meticulously. I'm sure he bought you expensive presents, flowers and perfume, told you he loved you. Why wouldn't you believe such a plausible man?'

Eve looked down at the gold bracelet on her wrist, but then she remembered he'd given Tabby a bracelet for Christmas too. It was a cheaper one, yet bracelets for both mother and daughter was sick. She wrenched the bracelet off her wrist and threw it on the floor.

'It's betrayal of the worst kind!' she cried out. 'To make out he wanted to share a life with me and all the time he is creeping closer and closer to my child. Do you think she went to bed willingly with him? How long has it been going on? What do I do now?'

'Ms Taylor, I can't answer those questions. I wish I could. Neither can I tell you how to get through this. But once we have all the facts,we will pass them on to you. But you mustn't blame yourself. When you met that man, you couldn't possibly have known what was in his mind. He has been edging closer to your daughter for a long time, and as a normal person you'd have been glad to see them bonding, that's only natural.'

'You're being very kind,' she said, sniffing back tears. 'But I feel so foolish that I never suspected. As a mother you think you will notice even the slightest different thing. I did think Tabby was a bit odd lately, moody, then overexcited, no appetite, going out and not saying where. But that's just typical teenage girl behaviour, isn't it?'

'I'm not qualified to comment on that, I'm afraid. But we may want you to speak to someone who is soon. But for now may we look around Tabby's room?' he asked. 'We need to look for evidence of grooming: any letters, cards or photos. Then we'll get out of your way. Will your friend downstairs stay with you tonight? I think it would be for the best.'

'Will Tabby come home tonight?' she asked.

'Again, I don't know. It depends on what the police doctor reports, whether he thinks she needs to see a counsellor. He or she might think it preferable to take her somewhere safe for the night.'

'I'm not going to hurt or punish her,' Eve said, horrified to think he might suspect that.

'I realize that, Ms Taylor, but feelings will be running high on both sides. Tabby is very young and she needs to process what has been happening. Just as you do.'

*

He had some papers in his hands as he said goodbye to her an hour later.

'We'll be in touch and will keep you abreast of what's going on,' he said. 'Try to get some sleep tonight, Ms Taylor, it will help.'

'Nothing is going to help,' Eve said to Sophie once the men had gone and she'd told her friend the whole story.

'A large brandy might,' Sophie said. She looked at the clock. 'Now, Olly will be home soon, so we must decide what to say and do. Obviously it's not a great idea to blurt out the truth straight away, but you can't lie to him either as the police will be ringing. Tabby isn't here, and he'll soon suss something is badly wrong.' She paused to think. 'What if you go and get into bed and I tell him you feel poorly? I could make him some food, and then perhaps he could come up to you afterwards, when you've had a chance to assemble your thoughts and what you need to tell him. How does that sound?'

'Better than anything I could come up with, but, Sophie, you aren't going to want to stay tonight to babysit us.'

'How could I not want to help you through a ghastly situation like this? We don't know if the police will want to come again or bring Tabby home. Besides, I really don't think you should be alone at such a time.'

'I keep thinking on how rough I was with Tabby,' Eve said. 'I'm ashamed of that. What if he forced her?'

'From what I know about such things, which I might add is very little, paedophiles groom their victims. You told me that Tabby was always praising George, so I suspect she was there willingly. Perhaps not expecting to have sex with him – maybe she even tried to get out of it – but she wasn't dragged into that bedroom kicking and screaming. I think putting her into the other room and locking the door was a wise thing to do. She could have made a run for it and ultimately that would've made it worse.'

'You're an angel, Sophie, so calm and sensible,' Eve sighed. 'And, yes, I will have a brandy.'

Eve took the brandy up to her room, put on pyjamas and got into bed. She could talk to the police on the phone from here and meanwhile she could think how to explain the situation to Olly without being too graphic.

Olly's sensitive nature made him realize as soon as he got home that something bad had happened.

He had a front door key, so Sophie didn't need to be waiting for him, and he was perfectly capable of making himself some tea.

'What exactly's wrong with Mum?' he asked, his brow furrowed with suspicion. He was sitting up on a stool on the other side of the kitchen island and watching her mashing potatoes.

'She's had a bad shock,' Sophie said. 'She needs time to process it before she tells you. But she'll tell you later.'

'And where's Tabby? Is it something to do with her?'

'Why do you ask that?'

'I don't know exactly, but she's been hiding something for ages. I've just got a feeling.'

'Tonight we have sausage and mash, my boy.' Sophie hoped that was a suitably jovial voice. 'By the way, how was today's guitar lesson?'

'Really good,' he said, as Sophie handed him a plate of food and a knife and fork. 'She said maybe I could go on to a music college when I leave school. I'd love that.'

Sophie suddenly felt saddened for him. However gently Eve told him what was going on, at fourteen it was going to take away his innocence and spoil the good memories he held of George and perhaps his hope that he would become his stepfather.

Olly went up to see his mother about an hour later. As soon as he looked round the door Eve could tell he was very worried, and she wondered how on earth she would be able to tell him the truth.

'It's about Tabby, isn't it?' he asked. 'Where is she?'

'At the police station.'

'Has she been shoplifting? She told me some girls at school do it.'

Eve knew she must tell him a palatable truth.

'No, she hasn't been shoplifting. I caught her with George.'

'Your George?' Olly frowned and sat down on the bed.

'He was my George, but he won't be any longer. When I found them together this afternoon I had to call the police because she is underage.'

'You mean they were doing that?' he said in horror. 'But he's old. Why would she do that with him?'

'That's the question I need answering,' Eve said carefully. 'I think he's been grooming her. Do you know what that means?'

'Creeping round her, sending messages?'

'Yes, with the intention of getting her on track for something more.'

'Sex.' He blushed scarlet, and Eve remembered how he couldn't even bear to watch people kissing on TV.

'That's it, Olly. Muriel, who works for George, rang the police and George was taken away to be questioned and probably charged. Tabby is at the police station too, she has to be questioned and examined by a doctor, and she will probably be taken to somewhere else tonight until the police have investigated. They were here earlier and took some papers from Tabby's room but they didn't tell me what they were.'

Olly didn't say anything. He just swung his legs up on to the bed and wriggled closer to Eve to put his arms around her. 'That must have been awful for you,' he whispered. 'We all thought he was such a good man. I can't really believe it of him.'

'Nor me, but sadly I saw something I can't unsee,' she whispered back. 'I was a bit harsh with Tabby, but it was the shock.'

'What do we do now?' he said. 'I mean, we can't pretend it didn't happen.'

'She'll be found a counsellor, I expect. Maybe they'll counsel me too. I don't know where it will all lead, darling.'

'I wish Tom was still around,' Olly said. 'He'd know what we should all do.'

Eve had nothing to say to that; she couldn't tell her son it was her fault he wasn't here now, and that if he had been, George could never have preyed on Tabby.

19

DI Baytrum rang Eve the following morning. He knew he hadn't got anything to tell her that would lift her spirits, but he had to do it.

'Tabitha spent the night at a children's home, and she said she'd rather stay there than come home,' he said apologetically. 'She also said she intends to stand by George Mulberry because she loves him.'

'Hell and damnation!' Eve exclaimed. 'So she was a willing partner?'

'On the face of it, it would seem so. But in her room and on her phone –'

'Her phone?' Eve interrupted. 'I wouldn't let her have one; they're far too expensive.'

'It looks as if George bought it for her; all the easier to send her messages,' Baytrum said. 'Anyway, we read all the messages and they are pretty damning. He was sending her little hearts and things from soon after you moved to Sidmouth. Gradually they got a bit saucy and there is one where he says he's going to give her a Saturday job so he can see more of her. That comes with winks, etc. I can't and won't reveal some of the more sleazy recent messages, but it all reads like textbook grooming.'

Eve felt quite faint. Unwanted, sickening images ran through her head. 'Can I insist on seeing her?'

'You could, but at this stage it would be detrimental. I think you must leave her to stew. Without George, Olly and school friends around her she's going to get lonely very quickly. At that point she might want to apologize to you and ask to come home.'

'So what about George? What will he get?'

'We've found some unsubstantiated accusations that he had underage sex with two other girls. But it seems the parents of the girls didn't take it any further; whether this was because George bribed them, or they didn't believe their daughter or were afraid of any publicity they'd be caught up in, we don't know. But we are following many more lines of inquiry, and we have arrested him and are holding him on the charge of sex with a minor. If you wouldn't mind packing a case with some of Tabby's clothes, I'll send a female police officer round to collect it later. The counsellor we've appointed will want to speak to you too.'

After Eve put the telephone down, she burst into tears. Sophie had gone home to change, and Olly had gone out. She had never felt more alone. All at once her successful business, her lovely home, meant nothing. Was this payback time for what she had done to Don? It felt like it.

She cried as she folded Tabby's clothes and packed them in the case. Whatever Tabby had done, she was still her little girl and she loved her.

Olly was not with a friend as Eve had thought; he was up near the house they'd rented in Manor Road. He'd been up here with a friend a couple of weeks ago and had spotted the van belonging to Steve the electrician who had worked on their house. Unfortunately Olly didn't know the man's surname to look him up on the internet at the library, but his van was dark blue with a big yellow flash of lightning as his company logo. He hoped he might find him still working here.

He couldn't remember which house it was, so he began knocking on doors to ask if they'd had an electrician there with a van like that. In the whole road there were only five houses where someone came to the door. Three of those just said no and shut the door. Of the other two neither remembered seeing a van like that. But just as he was turning away from the last house, the man suggested he asked at an electrical wholesaler.

'I can't tell you where there is one, but I bet he'll have been in there at some time to buy cables, power points and such like.'

Dejectedly Olly walked back into town. He didn't know any electrical wholesalers, but he knew a shop called Handy Man, which was close to Marianne's refuge. He'd been in there once to buy a battery. The owner might know Steve by his van. It was a long walk, and he was getting tired and hungry.

The man in Handy Man tried to be helpful; he looked through a little box of business cards to see if there was one with the name Steve. But though he found tilers, builders and plumbers, there were no electricians called Steve. 'Sorry, son,' the man said. 'Get the local paper and look at the advertisements. You might find him there.'

As Olly began to walk back towards town, he heard someone calling his name. He looked round to see it was Marianne.

'What are you doing up in this neck of the woods?' she asked, giving him a very welcome hug, but to his shame it made him cry. 'Oh, Olly, love, what's wrong? Shall we go and get a cup of tea and you can tell me?'

When she realized he was hungry she bought him a full English breakfast and had a fried egg sandwich herself.

Olly began with telling her how he was trying to find the electrician.

'But what for? Surely your mum would have his number if he worked for her before.'

'I didn't want her to know,' he said. 'You see Steve was Tom's friend. I hoped he might give me a number for him.'

Marianne's kindly face said that she found this mysterious and wanted to know more.

'Mum needs Tom,' Olly said. 'She wouldn't admit it because she knows she hurt him. But I know Tom; he'd come like a shot if he thought she was in trouble.'

'So what sort of trouble is she in?' Marianne said quietly. 'You can tell me; I promise I won't breathe a word to anyone else.'

Olly blurted it out. He knew he'd told it badly, but she seemed to get the gist of it.

'That George has a reputation for being a ladies' man, and I've heard a few stories. I did tell your mum a few of them, but we both thought they were made up. Let's eat up and then I'll come home with you and see if I can help in any way. You've been a very kind boy to try and find Tom. That's a lovely idea, and we'll put our heads together and try to work out how we can contact him. Don't tell your mum, though; she'll just say you mustn't do it.'

Eve had walked miles that morning too, but once she got home and saw Sophie had given the case of Tabby's clothes to the police, she went up to her room and began crying again.

A short while later Sophie looked relieved to see Olly at the door. He introduced Marianne by saying they'd stayed at her B&B once and that she and his mum had remained friends.

'She's upstairs, and quite honestly I don't know what to say to her now. But perhaps you will, Marianne. Go on up, and Olly, you can give me a hand in the showroom. I've had a delivery of trimmings and we need to arrange them in colours.'

Marianne knocked on the bedroom door and said, 'It's me, Marianne. Can I come in?'

There was a muffled yes, and in she went.

Eve was lying on the bed and she'd obviously been crying for a long time.

'I met Olly and he told me,' Marianne said, and sat on the bed beside her friend and began rubbing her back. 'I wish I'd told you more strongly what the word around town was about George. But it's awful when you're dating a man and other women tell you nasty things. It always smacks of jealousy.'

'What had you heard?'

'Well, aside from the showering with flowers and chocolates thing I told you about, I heard that two women he was dating claimed he seemed keener on their daughters than them. Always including them on a date, flattering them. But another woman who came to the refuge, and like you stayed to live in Sidmouth, met George. After seeing her for a few months he dumped her, then her daughter admitted she was pregnant. The girl was sixteen and wouldn't say who the father was. The mum suspected it was George – he'd always been a bit too touchy-feely with her – but she couldn't prove it, and as her daughter wasn't underage, legally he'd done nothing wrong. Anyway, the baby, a little girl, was found to have some inherited disease; I don't know what it was. Then the girl told her mother about George, thinking that if she went to him, he would help as it must've come from his family. Needless to say, he didn't help, and said that the baby was nothing to do with him as he'd had a vasectomy. Awful business.'

'Did that woman tell you anything personal about her and George?'

'Well, she said he showed little interest in sleeping with her. She said it was odd, but at the time she believed he was holding back as she was damaged.'

Eve nodded. She didn't want to admit George's lack of appetite for sex with her, but to be told something so relevant to her own experience confirmed it was a true story. 'Yet you used George to sell your place, knowing this?' Eve said.

'He hadn't done anything bad to me, and I saw how well he looked after you when you were buying Mill Lane. To be honest, I heard so much gossip about so many people in the time I ran the refuge that it washed over me. By the time I found out you were seeing him, how could I say anything, Eve? I also thought that if it was true about him, you were smart enough to sniff it out.'

'I wasn't,' Eve said. 'But I suppose if you had

hinted at anything I wouldn't have believed it anyway. I'm still thinking it has to be a mistake, even though I saw it with my own eyes.'

'What are you going to do about Tabby?' Marianne asked.

'I'm waiting for the counsellor to ring me. I'm in her hands really. If I insist on Tabby coming home, that might make things worse. But let's change the subject. Tell me, Marianne, what are you doing? Have you found a new home?'

'Yes, I moved in a couple of weeks ago. I was going to ring you and give you the new telephone number and invite you round. It's lovely, brand new. Ivory walls, all mod cons, nothing to do. It's on the third floor, but that gives me a view to the sea from the balcony. All it needs is for someone to make some curtains for me. But this time I'll pay.'

'I'd be glad to, at mates' rates,' Eve said, suddenly so glad to have Marianne here, the one person she didn't have to pretend to.

'I have to go now, Eve,' Marianne said sadly. 'I've got a dental appointment. But you've got my number. Ring any time if you need to talk. Or we could have a drink and find something to laugh about. My advice is not to push too hard with Tabby – give her time to think about what's happened and examine her feelings for that man and her family. I always think when you apply pressure to make people bend to your will, later they snap back and resent you. When you do get to see her, or write to her, make it clear that you still love her . . .'

Eve sighed. 'You are very wise, Marianne, and you've made me feel a lot better. Thank you.'

'Any wisdom I may have acquired was by listening to so many sad stories over the years,' Marianne chuckled. 'One thing I do know is that the vast majority of people will listen to advice, but then go ahead and do whatever they want to do. Yet the fact they've talked over their problem with someone is the part which ultimately leads to healing.'

While Marianne was with his mother, Olly confided in Sophie about how he wanted to find Tom.

She ruffled his dark hair and smiled. 'I agree with you, Olly. Tom was good for her. But she's too proud to go cap in hand to him. But let's have a sneaky look at her files; we might be able to find Steve the electrician. Wasn't there a carpenter called James and Ian the plumber? One of them must be in contact with Tom.'

The filing cabinet in the workroom had a file labelled BUILDING WORK. Sophie got it out and flicked through it. There were plans for the building drawn up by Tom, which had his old address and phone number on, and hundreds of invoices for materials, and then finally she came to quotations from the tradesmen and their invoices when work was completed.

'Here's James,' she said triumphantly, and jotted down his details. 'And Ian's too. We'd better put this lot away now in case your mum comes down and catches us snooping.'

'But what about Steve?' Olly said.

'We didn't see anything for him, but you could ask either James or Ian about him when you get through to them.'

Just then they heard Marianne's voice on the landing.

'Quick,' Sophie said. 'They're coming down.'

The file went back in the drawer and Sophie pretended to be showing Olly how to use the sewing machine as the two women came down the stairs.

'That's right. Don't try to go fast – just hold the material steady,' Sophie said, as Olly put his foot on the pedal and fed a strip of material under the needle.

'Learning to make curtains, Olly?' Marianne asked as she came into the workroom to say goodbye.

'I'm a bit scared as it goes too fast,' he said.

Eve was standing in the doorway, but he noted her red swollen eyes and he hoped that if his plan worked, he would never see her crying again.

'Have I got an apprentice now?' she said. 'I thought you were going to be a better guitar player than Eric Clapton and set the world on fire?'

Olly laughed. 'I don't think I'll ever be a champion seamstress. But it's good to try new things.'

The following day was Good Friday and the desk sergeant at the police station rang Eve to inform her that the clinical psychologist Helen McCluskey had had an hour with Tabby the previous evening and would like to talk to Eve now too. 'Unfortunately she has already booked off the Easter holiday weekend, but she will see you on Tuesday morning at ten thirty.'

'Does that mean Tabby has to stay in the children's home?' Eve asked. Her heart had sunk down into her stomach and it was all she could do not to cry. 'Or can I go and get her and bring her home?'

'I'm very sorry, Miss Taylor, you can't do that. A counsellor will be talking to her today, and the police haven't finished interviewing her yet either. But I can tell you your daughter is OK. Very quiet, but that's to be expected.'

Knowing that to argue with the police would only alienate them, she didn't attempt it. A small part of her also knew that if Tabby was to come home now, they'd probably be fighting within the hour. It was for the best.

But Easter had always been a special time for them as a family. On the Saturday they would go out for the day. As Don rarely joined in, usually this was a train journey to somewhere different. Sometimes just to Chislehurst to catch tiddlers and sticklebacks in the ponds or a walk in the country and lunch in a pub, but once it had been a boat ride down the Thames and another time London Zoo. For Easter Sunday Eve usually made a chocolate cake, iced to look like a nest, which she'd fill with Mini Eggs and tiny fluffy chicks. They had an Easter egg hunt in the garden, and a special roast dinner with trifle to follow. Then on Easter Monday there was the fair on Blackheath.

Eve knew she must find something exciting to do for Olly's sake; he looked so sad, lonely and worried. Tabby had always been the dominant one, but Eve knew she must let him see he was every bit as important as his sister. She discussed this with Sophie who, although by rights was having the weekend off too, had called in during the morning to see if there were any developments.

'Why don't you go to Bristol or Bath?' she suggested. 'You can't do anything for Tabby, but he needs your attention too. You don't know either place, so get on one of those open-top buses and take an overnight bag and get a hotel if you don't feel like coming back the same day.'

'Won't it look like I'm running out on Tabby?'

'No, because you've already been told nothing will happen until Tuesday. Besides, she won't know.'

'OK, I'll do that. I'll tell Olly when he gets back. I

don't know where he's gone. I heard him leave just before you arrived.'

Sophie said she thought he might be having a dip in the sea, but she was pretty certain he was phoning James and Ian from a phone box somewhere, trying to find Tom.

20

As the open-top bus went around Bath, Olly was only half listening to the guide telling them about the city on his earphones. In his pocket he had Tom's telephone number, and as soon as he could he was going to try it again.

James had given it to him. He said Tom had rung him a week ago to ask if he wanted to join him on the same job as him in Bath, as they were short of a carpenter. James had said he'd like to, but was tied up with work in Sidmouth for the next two weeks.

James had asked Olly what was wrong and was it a building emergency that he needed Tom for? Olly didn't really know how to reply to that; all he could say was that he really needed to speak to him.

'Well, I know he was planning to go to Tenerife,' James said. 'He might be there now or he could be going this weekend; he didn't say. But I'll give you his number and you can keep trying. If he contacts me, I'll tell him you wanted to speak to him.'

Olly had tried the number four times now, and it just kept ringing and ringing. But when his mum had said they were going to Bath today, his heart leaped, thinking they might just run into him. But as Olly looked down from the bus to the streets below and saw how many tourists were milling around, he realized it was very unlikely they would bump into him.

He knew his mum was struggling with anxiety about Tabby, and at the same time trying to give him a good time. He tucked his hand into hers and saw her smile. He guessed she was thinking he hadn't held her hand for years and was liking it.

He took off his earphones and so did she. 'It's a beautiful city. I read somewhere it's the second-favourite tourist destination, London being number one.'

'We could stay tonight if you like,' she said. 'Then we could take a more scenic route home tomorrow and find some other interesting and pretty towns. I packed an overnight bag just in case.'

'That would be good, but we'd better listen to the commentary or the guide might get cross with us.'

Their car was in the park and ride on the outskirts of Bath. Eve rang a small hotel very close to it and luckily they had a double room free. At five in the afternoon they caught the park and ride bus back to the car park to pick up the overnight bag and leave a few bits of shopping in the car, then walked back to the Avalon hotel, leaving the car parked till tomorrow.

As they'd walked miles during the day, they didn't want to go back to the city centre in the evening to get some dinner, so they decided to eat at a Chinese restaurant near the hotel.

Olly had managed to get away from his mother for a little while during the afternoon to try Tom's number again. But he hadn't answered, and Olly resigned himself to the fact that he'd left for Tenerife already. He had wanted to ask James if Tom had a new girlfriend but didn't as it seemed too personal.

'It's been a lovely day today,' Olly said when they'd got back from the Chinese restaurant and into the single beds to watch a bit of TV. 'Thank you, Mum, for being kind to me and brave enough to go somewhere when you're so worried.'

'Oh, Olly, you are a sweet boy,' she said with a little catch in her voice. 'Let's hope this horrible business is resolved soon and we can get back to normal.'

At ten thirty sharp on Tuesday morning Helen McCluskey arrived at Mill Lane to see Eve. Sophie was in the workroom and Olly had gone out to meet a friend.

Eve took the rather formidable-looking woman up to the sitting room. She was at least five feet ten tall and broad. Her face was somewhat flat, with pale skin and small eyes. She was warm, however, saying immediately how distressing this must be for Eve.

'May I call you "Eve"?' she asked as they sat down opposite each other with the coffee table between them.

Eve had made a pot of coffee only minutes before Helen arrived and laid the tray with a plate of biscuits too. 'Yes, of course,' she said, and pushed the plunger on the coffee pot down. Eve was wearing a black dress and tights, but thinking she looked like she was going to a funeral she'd added some multicoloured beads. 'May I call you "Helen"?'

That sorted, Eve poured the coffee, passed over the sugar and biscuits, before asking how Tabby was.

'Scared, defiant, anxious about you and her brother and brave all at once,' Helen said. 'I have ascertained that Mulberry groomed her over a long period. He only got her to agree to have sex about three weeks ago. She didn't want to do it. Her actual words were "I knew it was wrong. I was too young, and he was Mum's friend. But he had made me crazy about him and I had to do it." She broke down in tears after she said this, and I came to the conclusion this was the analysis she'd arrived at after thinking about it all carefully.'

'Is that a good result then?' Eve asked.

'Very. She has acknowledged she was too young, that he'd cast some kind of spell over her, and she was horrified that she'd hurt you. But right now she's still saying she wants to be with him. And that she doesn't want to come home to you.'

Eve's eyes filled with tears.

'That's normal,' Helen said gently, picking up the

coffee Eve had poured. 'She is, of course, afraid of facing you. And at her age girls have romantic ideas that mostly don't make much sense to us adults. I mean by that she doesn't understand that men like Mulberry love the chase if you like. Once they've got their chosen victim in their clutches they will not be quite so attractive as they once thought. Mulberry would never have imagined Tabby as his wife, someone to grow old with, have children with. He wants youth, a perfect body, not domestic bliss. Yet Tabby will have been imagining all that.'

'How do we teach her that isn't going to happen?' Eve said.

'Time will do that. Even if he gets bail today in court, which I very much doubt, he won't dare try to contact her as he'll be in breach of bail conditions. He can't anyway as the police have Tabby's phone.'

Helen went on then to ask many more questions, about Tabby's father and how she had reacted to his death. Was she angry about being moved away from London and had she made any close friends here?

It was only then that Eve realized Tabby hadn't spoken of any friend in particular; she had always talked of 'friends' loosely as if she hung around with a bunch of them, but now Eve recalled that it was very rare for anyone to telephone her.

'So did all this come out of loneliness or feeling she didn't fit in at school?' Eve asked Helen.

'Possibly, but she didn't reveal that to me. Of course, we all know that girls of her age can be very mean to one another, especially when the new girl is as attractive as Tabby.'

The questions seemed to go on and on, some seemingly unrelated to Tabby, like what Eve's aspirations were, and how she felt about Mulberry's betrayal.

'I'm not upset that he didn't care about me. I was at first, but this has made me realize just how wrong our relationship was, and that I should have spoken about it to him. But I am furious that he used me to get to my daughter, and that it will affect Olly too.'

'Tell me, Eve, when your ex-husband died, did you grieve?'

'I did, in as much as it was a horrible way to die, but it wasn't real grieving for him. He'd hurt me too many times; my heart was hardened to him.'

'And the children?'

'Olly was glad it was finally over. Tabby occasionally accused me of not caring, but her real fear seemed to be about me getting a new man in my life.'

Eve explained about Tom and how she'd tried to do what she thought was the right thing but had lost him. 'That's when George Mulberry stepped in,' she said with a grimace. 'He was such a gentleman, didn't push me. He got on well with the children. The only thing that was odd about him was that he didn't really want a physical relationship. Of course I now see why that was.'

They continued to chat for a while longer, then Helen said she had to go. 'I'll be seeing Tabby again tomorrow, and we'll take it a day at a time.'

'Will you tell her I'm not angry with her?'

'Yes, of course, but as long as she holds out hope for being with George, that is going to make you angry, isn't it?'

Eve nodded glumly.

Helen got up, packed her file away in a briefcase and shook Eve's hand. 'Chin up, it will be resolved eventually. You're a good mother, Eve, and Tabby knows this. Time is a great healer. A cliché, I know, but it's true.'

After Helen had gone, Eve went down to the workroom, and as she'd had a couple of quite large cheques arrive from clients in the post that morning, she thought she'd go to the bank and pay them in.

She took the yellow bank bag out of the filing-cabinet drawer and removed the paying-in book from it. Finding the bag surprisingly light suddenly reminded her of the three thousand pounds in cash she'd been paid for a job some ten days ago. She frowned; she didn't remember taking it to the bank, but perhaps Sophie had. She pulled out the paying-in book to see if there was a bank stamp on the stub, because she did remember filling in the slip.

When she saw the slip was still attached to the book she felt sick. The cash was gone.

'Sophie,' she called out, 'the cash I left in the bank bag has gone.'

Sophie came in. 'What do you mean it's gone? Are you talking about the three thousand pounds from Mrs Willoughby? You said you were going to pay it in that same day.'

'I know I said that. I even filled in the paying-in slip, but we had a delivery of fabric if you remember that day, so I put the bank bag back into the filing cabinet intending to go later. But by the time we'd sorted the fabric the bank had closed. And then I forgot about it.'

'Who has been in here aside from us?' Sophie asked. She was frowning, pacing up and down. 'Please don't say you suspect me?'

'As if I would.' Eve was horrified Sophie might think that. 'Only the kids have been in here and they wouldn't take it. Besides, they don't even know where we keep cash and cheques. Clients never come in here unless we're showing them something, even the delivery man only dumped the fabric in the kitchen. I can't think of anyone else coming in here. Can you?'

'There's George – he was in here on the fifteenth; he was looking at the mood boards you were working on.'

Eve gasped. 'Oh shit! Don't tell me he's been stealing from me on top of everything else?'

'Ring the police,' Sophie suggested. 'If he's paid money into his own account, they'll find it immediately.'

Eve got on to the police and reported the theft. She was told someone would get back to her later in the day. She left Sophie spreading a large roman blind out on the cutting table to fix the rings and cords on the back and went upstairs. This felt like the last straw. She didn't think she could take any more.

21

Two days after the cash went missing, Eve was waiting for a phone call to confirm if Tabby would see her today. She kept looking at the clock, hoping hours had passed since she last looked, but each time it was just thirty minutes or so. Normally as she made curtains the time flew by, often she would remark to Sophie that there weren't enough hours in the day to get all the outstanding work done. It was now Friday midday, nine days since her life fell apart, and all she wanted to do was to hold Tabby in her arms and tell her she loved her.

George had been remanded in custody and Eve had been told by the police that there was a vigorous ongoing investigation into his past. They were also looking into the theft of her cash.

Helen had telephoned last night and reported that Tabby was much calmer since she had been told George had been refused bail and was in custody. 'I saw that as a suggestion she'd finally realized he was a predator, and she was his victim. However, that might not be the case. She's a clever girl. She knows very well that if she says she intends to wait for him, you're not going to like that.'

'No, I wouldn't,' Eve admitted, 'but maybe I can help her recover if she's willing to at least try and forget about him.'

'Then it's stalemate,' Helen said. 'She'll be totally aware she can't lie to you and pretend she's given up on him so she can come home with you – not if she intends to run to him the minute he's released. That would bring the whole nightmare back for you, wouldn't it?'

Eve could only agree that it would.

There were many telephone calls that morning, but all were enquiries about curtain making or for appointments and from stockists. But finally at two Helen rang back.

'Is it OK to visit her?' Eve asked breathlessly.

'I think you may need to sit down,' Helen said.

'I am already. Is it something bad?'

'Tabby has just had a pregnancy test and it was positive.'

Eve felt her heart plummet. 'Heavens above!' she exclaimed. 'What else can happen? Surely the police doctor did tests when she was first examined?'

'It seems not. There may have been a reason for not taking one then, like they felt it was too soon, but

I haven't been informed of that. I'm sorry, Eve, this is another shock you didn't need.'

Eve found her heart was racing. She felt faint and had to bend over for a moment and put her head between her knees. She heard Helen calling to her but couldn't respond.

Sophie came over to her, put her cool hand on Eve's neck and took the telephone receiver from her. 'Hello, this is Sophie Fox. I work for Eve. She appears to be unwell – can I help?'

'I'm afraid I gave her some unwelcome news. I'll call her back later.'

Sophie kneeled down beside Eve. 'What is it? Whoever that was, she said she'd ring back later. Was it about Tabby?'

'Yes,' Eve croaked out. 'I think I'm going to be sick.'

Sophie watched as her friend staggered across to the washroom. Seconds later she heard her vomiting.

Eve emerged some ten minutes later, her face chalk white.

'If there is a god, he's certainly punishing me,' she said. 'Tabby is pregnant by that bastard. How on earth do I deal with that?'

Sophie just put her arms round Eve and rocked her comfortingly. 'I've got no words of wisdom,' she whispered. 'I'm as shocked as you.'

'I always thought when I heard I was going to be a grandmother it would be the best, most wonderful thing ever.' Eve's voice cracked with emotion. 'But not this! What do I do, Sophie?'

Sophie's eyes filled with tears for her friend. She wanted to say 'A baby is a special gift, no matter what the circumstances'. She'd wanted a baby so badly, but it wasn't to be, and her marriage broke up because of that. But this was a different scenario. Eve was big-hearted but Sophie couldn't see her ever accepting George's child.

'Let me get you a brandy or a cup of tea,' Sophie suggested. 'Then maybe call Helen back and talk to her.'

'I don't know what to say, not to Helen or Tabby,' Eve said. She was hanging her head and looked so desolate it was frightening.

'The first thing you need to know is how Tabby feels about being pregnant. She might be horrified, aware she's too young, that it will prevent her from having a career. But if she's thinking this is great, my very own baby, then that's going to be far harder to deal with. But, Eve, you have no choice – you must speak to her.'

'I know you're right,' Eve said dolefully, 'but I'm afraid I might lose it and shout at her. That would make everything worse.'

'Maybe it would get your feelings out into the open, though,' Sophie said thoughtfully. 'I think we all pussyfoot around people too much these days, especially kids. We've all been indoctrinated that we mustn't speak our minds. Our parents did, and flexed their right to box our childish ears. We all turned out quite normal and took responsibility for our actions too. Don't we have to give kids boundaries?'

'I thought I had,' Eve said.

'Go upstairs and ring Helen to talk it over,' Sophie said, and pointed to the staircase. 'I'll bring you up a cup of tea.'

Eve disappeared up the stairs, albeit a little unsteadily, and Sophie went to make some tea in the kitchen. To her shock Olly was sitting there and it was clear by his stunned expression he'd heard everything.

'We thought you were up in your room or gone out,' she said.

'So Tabby's going to have a baby?'

'It looks that way, sweetheart. Not what your mum planned for her!'

'Not what Tabby planned for herself either,' he said in his sister's defence. 'She's the one who will have to bring the baby up, not Mum.'

'So, clever clogs, what do you suggest?'

'Mum should find out how Tabby feels. If she can't, maybe I should talk to her.'

Sophie made the tea. She couldn't help thinking Olly had a point.

*

Taking the tea into the sitting room, Sophie found Eve crying. She repeated what Olly had just said, then added, 'He might be right. Why don't you suggest Olly talks to Tabby? He's young and unworldly but he loves you both, and he's kind and thoughtful. He could be the best mediator.'

'I'm willing to try that,' Eve said. 'I feel as if I'm going mad. I need someone to take over.'

'Well, let Olly speak to her. I know he's only fourteen, but Tabby will probably tell him the truth about how she feels. He's maybe too young to understand exactly, but he's not going to push her into an abortion clinic or start saying he'd love to be an uncle. Listening is his gift.'

Eve felt like the burden on her shoulders was being lifted a little. 'You know, Sophie, you are a wise old bird.'

Sophie chuckled. 'Less of the old. Now drink this tea and get on that phone.'

When Sophie came back to the kitchen, Olly looked at her expectantly. 'I think your mum can see the sense in your suggestion,' she said. 'She's speaking to Helen, the woman who's working with Tabby now. So we'll see. By the way, any luck with ringing Tom?'

Olly shook his head. 'But I'll try again in a minute. He can't have gone away forever.'

*

Tom Bolton unlocked the door of the tiny studio flat in Bath, flung his suitcase down and winced at the smell. He'd forgotten to empty the kitchen bin before going away and that last takeaway curry had clearly gone bad. He'd been in Cape Town, a spur-of-the-moment change of heart when a building job he had accepted was suddenly put on hold indefinitely, so he thought Cape Town would be better than Tenerife.

He opened the window, then, gagging at the stench of the bin, took out the plastic bag, tied it up and put it in a second bag to take down to the dustbins.

As he returned to his flat, the telephone was ringing. He frowned – only a couple of people knew the number here, and those that did knew he'd gone away – but, assuming the job that had been postponed was now back on track, he picked up the receiver. 'Tom Bolton speaking,' he said.

He heard what could only be described as a whoop of joy. 'Who is this?' he asked.

'It's Olly, Eve's son. I thought I'd never get hold of you.'

Tom was so surprised he almost fell on to the sofa. His flight had been delayed two hours and he couldn't seem to sleep once he was on the plane. It had been eight in the morning when he had landed at Heathrow, and it had taken another hour after clearing customs to get the bus to the car park. The rush-hour traffic was terrible all the way to beyond

Reading. What he really wanted to do now was to crawl into bed.

'Hi, Olly, what's the problem?' he asked. Eve had torn his heart out, but he'd been very fond of her kids and he couldn't bring himself to be nasty to either of them.

'It's Mum, and Tabby too. They're in a terrible state and you're the only person I know who might be able to help.'

'Your mum doesn't want me in her life any more,' Tom said. 'She made that quite plain. I'm sorry, Olly, but whatever's going on in her life now is nothing to do with me. I can't help.'

'She never wanted to lose you,' Olly said. 'She was thinking of how Tabby and I would feel if you stayed over. But we wouldn't have minded; we loved you. We wanted you there. We told her that too.'

'Did you now?' Tom said, touched to hear that. 'So, go on, tell me what's wrong at home.'

'It's that man George Mulberry. He was doing stuff to Tabby, and now she's pregnant. I heard them saying he's a paedophile.'

A pang of guilt shot through Tom. It was George who had recommended him to Eve, something he had been very grateful for, but an old friend had told him that George had a reputation for going after very young girls.

He hadn't thought any more about it until after he'd

split up with Eve and heard George was taking her out. He thought he ought to warn Eve but didn't – she would have only thought it was jealous spite.

'Are you sure about this, Olly?'

'Yes. George gave Tabby a Saturday job, and Mum went up to his office before Easter and he was in bed with Tabby. She called the police and he's been remanded in custody.'

'And what about Tabby?'

'She's staying in a children's home. The police are still investigating and Mum's all over the place. I've been ringing you for a week now. You're the only person who can help.'

Tom thought for a moment. It was very flattering that a fourteen-year-old believed he had the powers to sort this out, and his heart went out to both Eve and Tabby. But should he get involved? He didn't think he could stand any more heartbreak.

'I don't think I can help,' he said eventually. 'I'd like to punch George's lights out, but as he's in custody I can't do that. As for your mum, what can I say to her?'

'You could say you love her and you'll stand by her,' Olly said in a small voice. 'Please, Tom. I know you can make everything better. We've all missed you so much.'

Tom was touched by Olly's sincerity. He wouldn't have expected a fourteen-year-old to understand an adult relationship, yet Olly seemed to recognize that

Tom loved Eve, and to turn down his request would perhaps ruin his belief in the strength of love.

'OK, Olly, I'll come. I've only just got back from South Africa, though. I need a shower, a little sleep, but I'll come this evening. You look after your mum until I get there.'

Sophie drove Olly to Chard to see Tabby. It was only forty miles away, but Sophie felt Eve was too upset to drive to a place she didn't know and then to sit outside and wait.

Sophie kept glancing sideways at Olly as she drove. She could see he was nervous; he was picking at his nails, fidgeting in his seat and not saying a word. It was understandable. All he had in his armoury was his love for his sister, but Eve had been told that a social worker would be on hand to supervise and intervene if things got difficult.

'You'll be OK,' Sophie said, patting his arm with her left hand. 'Tabby will be bowled over by how handsome you look in your new jeans and that smart jacket.'

'I wish we could take her home with us,' he said. 'She must be feeling so scared and lonely.'

'She won't feel that way when you get there; you just try to get her to talk about how she feels and what she wants to happen, but if she doesn't want to talk about any of that, just listen to whatever she wants to say. The whole point of this visit is to make her realize you and your mum love her and want the best for her.'

'Why haven't you got children, Sophie?' he asked, and the gentle question and his soft brown eyes on her brought a lump to her throat.

'For some women it just doesn't happen,' she said. 'I would have liked some very much, but we can't always have what we want. I've got nieces and nephews I love. I've got you and Tabby too. And a big fluffy cat called Marmaduke. That's enough for me.'

'If Tabby wants to have this baby, I'll be an uncle,' he said thoughtfully. 'One of my friends at school is an uncle.'

'Does he like his niece or nephew?'

'Not much. He said his big sister always plonks the baby on him and says it's good practice for when he gets one of his own.'

Sophie smiled at that. 'I suppose that's true. Maybe your friend will like the baby more when it can walk and talk.'

Olly lapsed into silence then and Sophie didn't try to talk to him any more. She guessed he was wondering what on earth he was going to say to Tabby.

The home was a detached Victorian mansion-style house behind a ten-foot stone wall on the outskirts of Chard. Sophie drew up at the wrought-iron gates, opened her window and pressed the bell. 'Sophie Fox to see Tabitha Taylor,' she said into the speaker, and the gates slowly opened. The drive was quite short, with lawns and trees either side.

Sophie parked at the side of the house. 'I'll come with you to the front door,' she said. 'I'll wait inside if they let me, but if not, I'll come back to the car.'

'I'm scared, Sophie,' he said in a small voice. 'It's an awfully big house.'

'It's a nice house,' she said, and she put her hand on his shoulder. 'And you are going to make your sister feel so much better when she sees you.'

Olly felt very small and insignificant when a woman in a white overall with grey hair in a bun, a stern face and small eyes told him he was to follow her and that Sophie was to wait in the hall.

On the first floor, they turned right into a long corridor with dark green polished tiles on the floor. There were framed prints of flowers on the pale green walls and the occasional mirror. As it was a children's home Olly had expected it to be noisy, but he couldn't hear anything except someone playing a piano downstairs. They didn't see anyone else either, which he found a bit creepy. A big house like this should have dozens of people in it.

Finally at the end of the corridor the woman

unlocked a door. Olly bristled at that. Why was Tabby locked up?

His first impression was that it was a very pleasant room with windows to the front and the side overlooking the garden, large sofas, art on the walls and attractive pale blue wallpaper. Tabby was sitting on a chair by the side window and she rose to her feet as he came in, but didn't rush to him. She just looked scared.

'Hello, Tabs,' he said. 'Can I hug you?'

Before she moved towards him he became aware of an older woman sitting by the fireplace. 'Don't take any notice of me,' she called out. 'I'm only here in case you need anything.'

Suddenly Tabby had her arms around him and she was whispering in his ear. 'Be careful what you say.'

He hugged her back, noting she smelled of lavender, and that her hair was newly washed. She was wearing a denim skirt and a pale blue T-shirt. When he pulled back from her he saw she had been crying. 'Don't cry, Tabs,' he said and led her to sit down on the sofa furthest away from the watching woman.

Meanwhile the woman who had brought him up spoke. 'Ring if you need me, Miss Havers,' she said. 'Shall I get someone to bring up some refreshments?'

'That would be good,' she responded. 'Coke OK for you two?'

'Lovely, thank you,' Olly said, and smiled at her.

'I'll have tea,' she said to the woman. 'Perhaps some cake for all of us.'

'So, Tabby, is it all right here?' Olly said in a low voice. 'All this must've been horrible for you. Where is everyone? There's not a sound beyond that door. And why are you locked in?'

'In the afternoons they all go out to play games and stuff. You'll know when they come back; it gets really noisy. They lock the doors because I tried to run away at first,' she whispered. 'But it's OK now. It was a daft thing to do. Like, where did I think I was going? Is Mum very angry with me?'

'Not angry, just sad and worried. Especially today when she was told you are . . .' He paused, saying the word was too hard. 'How do you feel about that?'

'Shocked.'

She looked so stricken Olly put his arm around her and drew her to his shoulder.

'You don't have to have the baby,' he said. 'You're too young for that.'

She tried to smile at him. 'Says you! Like you're a grown man and not my little brother!'

'This has messed up your life, but don't let it mess you up any more,' he said, taking her hand and squeezing it. 'I'll stand by you whatever happens.'

'And Mum? Will she?'

'She'll look after you, care for you, but you have to understand that she doesn't feel able to ever see

George again. She found out two days ago he stole three thousand pounds from her on top of everything else. The police are looking into that too.'

'Oh, Olly,' she said, big tears running down her cheeks, 'I can't believe he did that. I've been really stupid, haven't I? He wasn't honest about anything, was he?'

Olly wiped her tears away with a tissue. 'No, he wasn't honest, but how were you to know that? I thought he was a good man too. But we all do stupid things sometimes or get it wrong about people. Have you made a plan? Like, what do you want to do?'

She sighed deeply and cast her eyes down at her lap. 'I'd like to be able to go back several months and start again. If only I could wipe it all out and go home with you right now to watch TV with Mum and play board games the way we used to. Go and paddle in the sea. Just normal things. But nothing will ever be normal again, will it? People will point at me, talk behind my back. Mum won't trust me.'

'We can make it normal again,' he insisted, squeezing her hand tightly. 'I'll shout at you for staying in the bathroom too long. I'll insist you're cheating at board games, and Mum will make you lay the table and accuse you of not cleaning the bath round after you.'

Tabby smiled weakly. 'I'm different inside now,' she said. 'He made me different.'

The door opened and the woman came in with a

tray. She put two cans of Coke down, two glasses and two slices of Victoria sandwich on the coffee table in front of them. Then she went over to Miss Havers and gave her a cup of tea and a slice of cake. Olly noticed that she turned back to look at him and Tabby, then whispered something to Miss Havers. He got the feeling she was saying Miss Havers should be sitting closer to them so she could hear what was being said.

'Are you still convinced he's "the one"?' Olly asked.

Tabby laughed, surprising him. 'Did you get that out of a girls' magazine? "The one". It sounds so old-fashioned.'

'So what would you call him?'

'A snake,' she said, grimacing. 'I did believe he was everything in the world. But being here, remembering Mum's shock, the things the police doctor asked me, thinking about how it must be for you and knowing I'd be too ashamed to ever talk to our grandparents about it, made love go away. If he'd really loved me, he would've protected me, wouldn't he?'

'He should never have thought about you in that way,' Olly said, and he began to cry. 'It's creepy, sinister and dirty. I'm sorry,' he sobbed. 'I was told not to say anything like that to you.'

Tabby put her arms around him and kissed his cheeks. 'Maybe I needed to hear it from you, Olly. I mean, I care more about your opinion than anyone else's. So stop crying and eat your cake or I'll eat it for you.'

Olly attempted a laugh then; she'd always tried to eat his sweets, cakes or anything he really liked. And it made her sound like his sister again.

They talked for a bit longer and then Miss Havers told them that the visiting time was up. Olly hugged his sister once more, and with his eyes full of tears he went out through the door Miss Havers had unlocked.

'Tell Mummy I love her,' Tabby called out after him.

22

'So what did she say, Olly?' Eve said, pouncing on him as he came through the door. Sophie had driven off home asking him to tell Eve she'd be back in the morning.

Olly sighed deeply, as if sad he hadn't something positive to pass on. 'I think Tabby knows now that George is bad. But I couldn't go on about what she's going to do about the baby.'

'Why not?'

Olly rolled his eyes. 'I don't know stuff like that. I just said she needs to think it over.'

He took some orange juice from the fridge and slumped down on a chair by the table to drink it. 'I think she's ready to come home.' He went on to tell Eve a bit about the children's home and what they'd talked about.

'But how did she seem?' Eve asked. 'Weepy, scared, what?'

'Quieter, afraid people are going to talk about her when she gets back. But she's missing you.'

Eve relaxed a bit. 'Thank you, Olly – you are such a good boy.'

'Maybe not a good idea to keep saying that when she gets home,' he said with a cheeky grin.

Eve laughed. 'OK, point taken. Now what shall we have for tea?'

They were watching *Coronation Street* upstairs when the doorbell rang.

'Who can that be?' Eve said grumpily. 'Surely customers can read the opening times on the door.'

Olly made no comment, and she went down to see who it was.

'Tom!' he heard her exclaim. 'What brings you here?'

Olly crept out on to the landing so he could hear better.

'Olly traced me and asked me to come. He told me what had happened, and he seemed to think you needed my support.'

Olly could see Tom but not his mother's face. He wished he could.

'Oh, Tom, how like you to be so kind,' she said, and Olly guessed she was crying. 'Please come in.'

He closed the front door behind him and they moved out of Olly's sight towards the dining table. There were several minutes of silence, and he guessed they were hugging and hopefully kissing.

'With hindsight I should have got heavier with you and insisted we got married,' Tom said eventually, and his voice had a little catch to it as if he was overcome with emotion. 'That pervert would never have got a foot in the door then. But don't let's go over that old ground. Just tell me what's happening.'

Olly went back into the sitting room; he so wanted to go down and watch the reunion, but he knew that wasn't a good idea.

Tom was overwhelmed with emotion. Just one kiss had taken him right back to the first one ever and how he knew with utter certainty that Eve was meant for him. He was still a bit bruised though, afraid to give his all just yet. But he sensed Eve felt the same as him and right now he had to get the whole story about Tabby and find out how he could help.

He listened carefully. While indebted to George for recommending him to Eve for her property renovation, he had never liked the man. He was the sort that saw manual workers as inferiors and talked down to them. He recalled that about four years ago George had asked him to look at a rundown property further along the coast. It was in a superb position with a sea view, but Tom had spotted so many serious problems with it that demolishing and rebuilding was the only possibility. George had treated that like a joke, and asked Tom to write a report just mentioning the roof and windows needed repairing, and leaving out subsidence, dry rot and all the other issues. Tom had refused and George had got another less scrupulous builder from Brighton to write a report. Cash buyers were found, who had paid a very high price for what they considered to be a good investment.

But a few months later an outside wall on that property collapsed, bringing down the roof. Tom had just started Eve's renovation when he heard about it. He also heard that George blamed the builder who had made the report.

But there was something else about the man, though nothing Tom could put a finger on – too smooth perhaps.

'So you don't yet know how Tabby feels about the pregnancy?' Tom asked.

'I don't suppose she thinks anything much about it other than terror,' Eve said, wiping tears from her eyes. 'Girls of that age never think it can happen to them. The maternal feelings don't usually kick in immediately either, so hopefully she'll agree to a termination and then get on with her life.'

'And if she doesn't?' Tom asked.

Eve looked troubled. 'Under most circumstances a baby is pure joy, but not only would I not like to see my young daughter putting her life on hold, I also don't know that I could love George's child. And, let's face it, Tom, I'd be expected to be the major carer. Tabby couldn't manage alone.'

'No, she couldn't,' Tom said thoughtfully. 'And I'd hate to see you having to shelve your plans.' His mind turned to the daydreams he'd had of them getting married and having children. He had grown to love both Olly and Tabby and he believed they were at an age now when they'd like having younger brothers or sisters. But George's child was likely to be the cuckoo in the nest, however hard they tried to not let him or her be that.

'And, Olly, how is he coping with this?' Tom asked. He knew by the effort the boy had gone to find him that he was deeply troubled. He'd heard the tremor in his voice; it was a plea that came from the heart. It was flattering to think Olly believed Tom could sort anything, but right now Tom didn't think he could solve this problem.

Eve got up and went to the fridge and took out a bottle of wine. 'I think we both need a drink,' she said. 'I can't quite believe you're actually here again or that your heart is big enough to care about my problems.'

'I left my heart in this house,' he said simply.

Tears started up in Eve's eyes. He had a knack of saying the perfect thing. Just looking at him, taking in the unruly curly hair that was in need of a trim, the sincerity in his blue eyes and his physical strength which showed in his broad shoulders, muscular chest and arms – there was absolutely nothing artificial about him. He was pure truth. She knew he had put his all into this property, not just out of professional pride, but because it was to house the woman he loved. She wondered how she could ever have thought she could live happily without him. Not for just the lovemaking, but for the laughter, the teasing and that incredible kindness he had.

'So what are your plans, Tom? Are you still working in Bath?' She was hoping against hope he would say he was coming back to Sidmouth.

'A job was postponed, and I don't know when or if it will be on again. My flat here has been empty all this time and so I'll stay for a few days now to sort things and decide whether to sell it or let it out. As for work, there's plenty in Bath, but I'd really rather be here. The next few days should make the picture clearer.'

'I hope you'll stay,' Eve said, taking a glass of wine over to him. 'I've no right to say that, I know, but I've missed you so much and I could kick myself for being so unfeeling to you.'

'You had the best of motives, trying to protect your children's innocence. I have to say I was thrilled when Olly rang me – not happy, of course, about Tabby, but to know he thought I could put everything right. I can't, of course, but I'll be around to support you, help, comfort, whatever else you need.'

'Tragic irony that I let you go to protect my children, and then I let a sexual predator in the door.'

Tom half smiled. He guessed it took a lot for her to admit that. 'Hindsight is a wonderful thing,' he said. 'I've bitterly regretted saying you'd got too big for your boots.'

'But I had.' She shrugged. 'I can see that now. I began to believe I was the best interior designer in the West Country.'

'I suspect you probably are,' he said. 'Just as I'm the best builder. But maybe we'll just keep that between ourselves.'

She laughed then, and perhaps that was exactly the signal Olly had been waiting for, as he came haring down the stairs and flung himself into Tom's arms.

'Tom, Tom, I've missed you so much,' he said breathlessly.

Tom looked a little teary too, as he hugged Olly and ruffled his hair and said he'd missed him and Tabby. 'I'm really glad you tracked me down; it more than made up for my nightmare trip home from South Africa.'

They all chatted for a little while about general things – Olly learning the guitar, gardens, good restaurants – and that brought to mind that Tom must be hungry.

'Can I get you something to eat?' she asked. 'You've had a long flight and then the drive down here. I don't suppose you've eaten anything.'

'I can get some fish and chips,' he said.

'Oh no, you won't. I've got a lovely steak pie, and mashed potato and veg won't take long to do.'

As Eve cooked, she watched her son and Tom

talking. Tom told him about a safari he'd been on, and how he'd been in a shark cage off the Cape. 'It was a bit worrying,' he said. 'A huge one came right up to the cage and his teeth terrified me. I had visions of him snapping off the chain and getting the cage door open. But I had to pretend I wasn't worried as there was a boy of about seventeen in the cage with me and I couldn't let him see I was a wimp.'

'I think I'd be too scared to do that,' Olly said. 'Especially now you've told me you were.'

'I saw whales breaching too; that was incredible,' Tom went on. 'They're even bigger than you imagine. Maybe we can all go there one day once Tabby is over this.'

'Do you think she should keep the baby?' Olly asked. 'I mean, it isn't the baby's fault, is it?'

'No, it isn't the baby's fault, but in my opinion babies need two loving parents to bring him or her up together. I know you and your mum, and me too, we'd all muck in and help, but that isn't the same. Besides, in a few years' time, Tabby might meet the right boy and fall in love, and that boy might not be too keen on taking on someone else's baby.'

Much later, food eaten, a bottle of wine drunk, a lot of chat and catching up, Olly finally went off to bed, and Tom said he was going home. Eve went to him to kiss his cheek and thank him.

He caught hold of her arms and leaned in to kiss her.

All the passion she remembered was still there. They clung to each other, kissing ever more feverishly, their bodies straining to get closer.

It was Tom who broke away first. 'I'd give anything to carry you up those stairs and make love to you, but it wouldn't be right tonight, Eve. I still love you. I always will, but we need to get everything else sorted, don't we?'

She wanted to tell him that the day he walked out she had felt her heart would break. But she just smiled and agreed he was right.

DI Baytrum telephoned the next morning to tell Eve that Mulberry's bank had confirmed he had paid in three thousand pounds in cash just two days before she had caught him with Tabby.

'He is, of course, claiming it was a little nest egg he'd been holding on to – some of it wins at the casino in Exeter, some from an oil painting he'd sold. He said he had to put it into his business account as there were bills to be paid.'

'Can you check on that?' Eve asked.

'Some of it maybe, but it's always a hard thing to prove. But the same amount so close to when you found it missing is pretty conclusive. However, Eve, I need to warn you, his father has got him a hotshot lawyer, and there's every chance he might get bail.'

Eve had been feeling happy that morning, optimistic about Tabby and Tom, but hearing that was like her balloon had just been pricked and all the good thoughts disappeared.

Sophie comforted her. 'You might have known his family would pull strings,' she said. 'Their sort always do. But he won't dare set foot in Sidmouth. He might have a flat above the shop but he's likely to have stuff thrown at him if he goes there. His business will collapse. I can't see Muriel Parkinson running the show for him; she's probably in the "let's run him out of town" brigade.'

'I feel sorry for her,' Eve said. 'She doted on him, and she loved her job. What a shock it must have been for her.'

'Yes, poor woman. There are always people caught up in things like this that don't deserve it. But you have enough of your own problems to deal with. Like, are you going to insist Tabby comes home?'

'Yes, I am,' Eve said resolutely. 'I want her where I can see her, and I'm going to try and be terribly adult about whether she keeps the baby or not.'

'That's the spirit, Eve.' Sophie put her arms around her friend and hugged her. 'I've spent so many years wanting a baby that it comes as second nature to me to say no to abortion, but mothers usually know the right thing to do and say, and ultimately we all know you'll end up doing most of the mothering if Tabby keeps it.'

'It's a cruel world, isn't it?' Eve sunk down in a chair. 'There's you, ideal-mum material, but it never happened, and my teenage daughter gets pregnant straight away. People used to think adoption was the solution, giving the baby from the mum that might not make the grade to someone who has everything. On paper it's a brilliant idea. But the truth is we've got thousands of people adopted at birth who don't feel they belong.'

'That's a very jaundiced view, Eve,' Sophie said, and put the kettle on for some coffee. 'I suspect you're trying to talk yourself into accepting this baby.'

Eve looked at her friend with an expression of utter dejection. 'It will be my grandchild. I'll see Tabby and Olly in its face, the shape of its hands and feet. I might even see Don, though I hope not. I thought when he died all links with him died too.'

'Why do I always feel you've got a burden of guilt about him?' Sophie asked. 'Excuse my nosiness, but I can't help it.'

Eve felt a tremor of fear run down her spine. Was her guilt about Don so strong that people could see it? What if George had picked up on it and handed his idea to the lawyer to try to discredit her?

'Don't look so scared,' Sophie said lightly. 'Don't all women feel guilty about something? Not loving their kids enough or being mean to their parents?'

Eve sniggered. 'That's right. I suppose I think if

I'd been stronger, he might not have been such a swine.'

'Well, there you go, in one sentence you've stated that you're glad you've got Tabby and Olly, regardless of Don's genes in them. So does it matter that Tabby's baby has some genes from George? They might be the good-dancer genes, they might be the liking-films genes or even the smooth-talking, good-to-have-at-a-party genes.'

Eve roared with laughter; she couldn't help it. Sophie was so good at changing people's opinions with half fact, half imagination, and making complete sense. In this case Eve felt she'd done really well to prepare her for a grandchild that she could love.

'Right –' she put Sophie's coffee in front of her – 'we've got curtains to make, and I've got to get on the phone to Helen McCluskey and tell her I want Tabby home and that I'm coming to get her this afternoon.'

At two in the afternoon Eve was in Chard to collect Tabby.

'Are you sure you want me home with you?' Tabby said doubtfully as Eve stuffed her daughter's belongings into her suitcase.

'Would I be here if I didn't?' Eve said. 'I could have gone to Exeter airport and gone to the first place that was sunny and warm.'

Tabby giggled. 'Oh, Mum, you can be so funny. As if you'd get on a plane and leave Olly and me!'

'Don't tempt me, girl!' Eve retorted with laughter in her voice. 'I've decided that whatever you want is what we'll do. No pressure from me.'

Eve found it odd that when she said that it felt like a weight was lifted from her. She looked at Tabby and saw not her little girl but an almost woman who was the same height as her. The blonde hair, blue eyes, pretty face and slender yet busty figure had something more now. The teenager who had danced around her bedroom pretending to be Britney Spears, holding a hairbrush as a microphone, singing 'Oops! . . . I Did It Again', had morphed into someone who had partially and perhaps reluctantly entered the grown-up world. But the door had slammed behind her; she couldn't go back now, and it was Eve's job to take her hand and lead her right into adulthood.

23

After consultation with Tabby's teachers, who knew enough of her story to be concerned at her coming back to school just now, it was decided she would stay home for a few weeks to let the dust settle.

'She's a very bright girl,' Mr Cox the headmaster said. 'I know she'll work at home at the lessons we set her, and all this upset will disappear before long. After all she was never named as Mulberry's victim.'

The headmaster had no idea that included in 'this upset' was pregnancy and Eve wasn't about to tell him. She was even avoiding the subject with Tabby too. In fact, the only person that spoke of it was Olly.

'What do you want to do?' Eve had heard him ask his sister. 'If you do want an abortion, the sooner you get it done the better.'

Her reply chilled Eve to the bone. 'I'm waiting to see what George wants me to do.'

It was all Eve could do not to charge into Tabby's bedroom and tell her that George would be locked up for at least five years and he didn't care about the son he had already. But she took deep breaths instead.

Lessons were sent from school and Eve or Sophie

helped her with them. Tabby had to read *Jane Eyre* for English literature, and as Eve discussed it with her, she wondered how Jane would have fared if she'd been seduced by Mr Rochester. Eve even felt a little like Bertha Rochester in the attic, wanting to stop her daughter's feelings for George Mulberry and looking for vengeance for the trouble he'd caused.

Tom brightened things by coming by daily. He hugged Tabby and told her she could have the world at her feet if she chose. He told Olly he was special, clever, kind and loved by all.

Three weeks later George got bail at Exeter Court and was told he wasn't to go within a mile of Eve Taylor's home or to try to contact Tabitha Taylor. His estate agency business was just within that mile radius, and Eve couldn't see him not attempting to go there, but she hoped he would so he'd be rearrested.

It was a waiting game for Eve. Waiting for Tabby to announce whether she wanted an abortion or to keep the baby, waiting to see if George broke bail restrictions, and waiting for Tom to make a move. He still hadn't said whether he'd cancelled the job which had been postponed, given up his flat in Bath or decided whether to sell his flat in Sidmouth. Eve knew it was better not to press him, but it was hard not to ask questions.

Late one afternoon, after working on some particularly difficult curtains all day for a hotel in Lyme Regis, Eve needed a change of scene and went out on to the front veranda to plant up the tubs with some geraniums. Tabby and Olly had gone to the swimming pool and Sophie was busy in the workroom planning an intricate patchwork design of several different embroidered fabrics joined by braid for a huge headboard. The clients had taken photographs of one they'd seen in a hotel in New York and wanted one just like it.

Eve was pulling the old plants out of the tubs and putting them and some of the soil into another tub, when someone suddenly grabbed her by the shoulder and put something cold and sharp to her throat, clearly a knife.

'Gotcha,' he said. 'Don't try to scream or I'll slash your throat.'

She hadn't heard him come up behind her, and it was frightening, but she knew it was George, even doing a pathetic James Cagney imitation.

'You know I've got CCTV?' she lied. 'So if I were you, I'd turn round and walk away.'

'You think you're so bloody clever,' he said. 'Not satisfied with ruining my name for having sex with your little scrubber, you tell the police I'm a thief too. Now get up off your knees. I'm taking you somewhere more private.'

Eve got really scared then, but she was angry too and tried hard to think how she could knock the knife out of his hand. But he was holding her left arm very tightly and if she tried to lash out with her right one, his knife would go in her throat.

She stood up, and the knife was still at her throat. She willed someone, anyone, to come up the lane and see him, but there was no one around. 'Look, George, you're in enough trouble without doing this,' she said, and could hear her voice wavering.

'Move it,' he responded, and he pushed her into the car park. He was breathing heavily like he'd run a mile.

'What do you hope to gain by this?' she said, as he nudged her out on to the lane. 'You'll get a longer stretch in prison, so for God's sake go now while you still can. The children are only in the swimming pool, and if they see you, they'll raise the alarm.'

'Tabby won't – she'll think I've come for her.'

'You're deluded,' Eve spat out. 'She knows what you are now.'

Standing close behind her he kept nudging her towards the lane and she guessed he was planning to take her to a patch of waste ground between a couple of buildings. Was he angry enough to kill her? The knife was hurting her neck – perhaps not cutting her skin yet, but just a bit more pressure and it would. He must think he had nothing to lose now; his name was ruined, his business in tatters.

She frantically scanned ahead of her and saw a half-brick lying in the middle of the lane. He was controlling her direction, but she could gradually take each step sideways as long as he hadn't seen the brick. It seemed possible that she could step over it then kick it back at his feet or shins. With luck he'd stumble and she could knock the knife out of his hand.

Every step was slow, and her heart was pounding. She braced herself as she got nearer, but she was wearing sandals so knew it was going to hurt to kick the brick. But a sore foot was better than a cut throat.

There were people in the car park now, but to shout was too dangerous.

As they reached the brick, she paused for a second to concentrate.

'Move,' he snarled, bringing the knife closer still to her neck so that it cut her.

She stepped over the brick, then, using her heel, kicked it back at him.

'Shit!' he exclaimed, and he wobbled, letting go of her left arm to steady himself, but the knife was still at her throat.

Taking a chance, she bent her elbow and thrust it into his chest as hard as she could.

He staggered back.

'Help!' she yelled at the top of her voice. 'He's trying to kill me.'

He recovered himself and came back towards her, but she grabbed up the brick and hurled it at him.

It hit him on the temple and with that he dropped his knife in shock. She kicked it away and snatched up the brick again, still yelling for help.

'Come on, I'd like to bash your head in,' she screamed at him. She could hear feet running towards them but suddenly she felt faint.

Her legs were turning to rubber, her head was reeling and just as she felt herself sinking, all at once she felt someone was holding her. 'It's OK, I've got you,' she heard a man say and she was lowered to the ground.

She came to on hearing a loud whack. She opened her eyes and saw Tom was there and that he'd just knocked George to the ground very close to her. Tom then hauled George up on to his feet and punched him again. This time he was out cold.

It was odd that a few minutes ago there hadn't been a soul about, but now the area was positively crowded, as people pushed forward to see what was going on.

Tom kneeled down beside her and smoothed her hair back from her face. 'Just stay there for now until the police and ambulance come,' he said. 'Someone yelled out to me that they'd called them and they're on their way.'

'I can get up,' she said.

'No –' he gently pushed her shoulders down – 'your

neck is bleeding, not badly, but you'll be in shock. I want the police to see what he was trying to do.'

She found it strange that until he'd said her neck was bleeding, she'd felt nothing, but suddenly it hurt enough for her to take Tom seriously.

Sophie appeared above her then, her face wreathed in concern.

'Oh, bloody hell, Eve. I can't leave you alone for a second,' she said.

'She's going to be OK, thank goodness,' Tom said. 'But where are the children?'

'The swimming pool,' she said. 'Shall I go and get them, or will you?'

'No, you go, but try not to alarm them too much. But we need them indoors together.'

George was coming round and he tried to get up.

'Oh no you don't, you bastard!' Tom exclaimed and he positioned the man's two arms back on the ground behind his head. 'I'd like to beat you to a pulp and then stamp on you, so don't tempt me by moving.'

The police and ambulance arrived then. After just a cursory look at George, he was to be taken to the police station as his injuries didn't warrant hospital. Eve was examined by a paramedic and it was decided they would take her home and patch her up. A policeman said they would follow to take her statement. But before they could move either George or Eve, the children arrived with Sophie.

Tabby looked from her mother with blood on her neck and T-shirt and then to George, and gave a howl of savage rage. 'You animal!' she shrieked, moving to attack him herself. 'To think I tried to defend you. Well, not any more. I hope they stick you inside now and throw away the key.'

Olly caught hold of his sister's arm and pulled her away. 'I'll take her home and look after her, Mum,' he said. He then looked at Tom who was nursing sore knuckles. 'Thank you, Tom. Please come back to the house too.'

Once indoors the paramedic checked Eve's throat and found it was only a superficial wound. He cleaned it and put a loose dressing over it. He suggested tea and a lie-down until she got over the shock of what had happened.

'You did so well to disarm that man,' he said. 'When fight-or-flight switches on at times like these, it's wonderful, but it can leave people very shaken.'

Tom helped her upstairs to her bedroom, covered her with a throw and went back downstairs.

The paramedic recommended Tom put some ice on his knuckles, and as he packed up to leave he said that if Eve was to feel worse later, with sickness or blurred vision, to call a doctor or ring 999.

Tabby came into Eve's bedroom and sat on the bed next to her mother. 'You were so brave,' she said admiringly. 'But if it helps to make you feel it was worth it, I suddenly saw what a louse George really is.'

'That's the best news ever.' Eve reached up and caressed Tabby's cheek. 'I'm not going to press you now about the baby, but please think on it.'

'I'm going to give evidence against him,' Tabby said. 'I told the police I couldn't at the time, but I realize now that I must. For other girls' sakes. But, Mum, will you tell me the truth about Dad's death?'

'What do you mean, Tabby?' Eve said in alarm. 'You know the truth.'

'I know what you told Olly and me,' she said, taking Eve's hand and holding it gently between her own. 'But I saw you that night. I'd gone into Olly's bedroom to get a magazine I'd left there earlier. I heard a little sound, like the back door opening and so I looked out of the window. The first thing I saw was the light of Dad's lamp in the shed window, and I thought he'd come back again to frighten us all. But then you came into view walking across the lawn with something in your hand. It looked like a stick. You stood on tiptoe and pushed the lamp over with your stick. Then you went back in the house.'

'That's ridiculous,' Eve said. 'How can you believe that of me?'

'Because it all came back together in my head while I was away. Maybe leaving Grove Park and starting a new and better life here sort of blanked it out. But the shock of being taken to that children's home brought back how Dad had pushed you too far too often.' She paused for a moment, tears running down her cheeks.

'I know how badly he hurt you that night before we got taken away to the refuge. And I haven't forgotten that time he screamed at you from the street, calling you horrible names. It was really frightening. He'd hurt you so often before, Mum. I didn't realize it then, not until after what happened to me. But you were broken. Dad broke you!'

Tears were cascading down Tabby's cheeks. Eve reached up to wipe them away.

'You said to me that I needed to face the truth,' she went on, her voice wobbly with emotion. 'And I have. It came to me then that you need to do the same. I believe guilt plays on your mind, eating away at you.' She bent to kiss her mother's cheek tenderly.

'I love you, Mum, and together we can sort this. You've got to admit to it or be tortured forever. I know you didn't intend to kill him, just to scare him, and heaven knows he deserved it. But own up. I'll support you and give evidence.

'George said once he knew you'd done it. I realize now he said it to make me hate you. But he said he'd spoken to a friend in the south-east London police and they did too but couldn't prove it. I never told him what I remembered, but I bet that after today he'll be talking about it to anyone that will listen. If they open the investigation and haul you in, that's going to be far worse than you owning up now.'

Eve felt panicked and didn't know what to say. Yet she knew she couldn't continue to deny it. Tabby was telling the truth. But to go to the police and admit what she'd done, that was a big ask. How long would she get in prison for it?

The bedroom door opened and Tom put his head round it.

'Hey, who wants to eat? Olly wants to go out for a burger, but I thought we ought to all stay here. I could whip up some pasta.'

Their serious faces worried him, so he came right in. 'OK, what's wrong?'

Eve put her hands over her face. He knew then that whatever it was went a long way back. And she wasn't able to tell him.

But Tabby was. She laid it out to him how cruel Don had been to her mother and also to Olly, but stressed that Don's death had not been planned. She could've been a lawyer; she stated the facts clearly and concisely but with such empathy.

'You two won't have a future together unless she owns up to it,' Tabby finished, looking up at him. 'Lies and secrets just destroy happiness.'

The new maturity in Tabby astounded Tom. This

wasn't a petulant teenager only concerned with herself but a young woman who had considered her mother's problems and wanted to solve them, just as Eve was trying to solve hers.

'And what made you so wise suddenly?' he asked her, reaching out to wipe a tear from her cheek.

'Because I faced up to what I'd been doing. I think I let George seduce me to hurt Mum. I'm ashamed of that now. But there was more to it than that. I sensed she'd been brooding on something, and there was this vague memory which bugged me. Then suddenly it came to me while I was in Chard.

'You see for a long time I thought I'd dreamed seeing her walk to the shed. But all at once I knew I really had seen that. I didn't want it to be true. I was tempted to just push it aside. You can't imagine how terrible it feels to say something which could be so serious for her. But if you two want, you can ignore what I've said. I'll never tell a soul. It's up to you.'

Tom was shattered by what Tabby had said and the way Eve was covering her face, though with shame or fright he didn't know, which was alarming. She had told him that Don had hit her, but always almost casually as if it wasn't anything too serious. But now, after hearing what Tabby had told him, it was entirely understandable why Eve had snapped and set fire to Don's shed. Yet he knew in his heart she hadn't intended to do anything more than scare him.

Tom also believed it was important that Eve, Tabby and Olly could count on there being good men who didn't hurt women. He didn't care whether Eve was right or wrong in what she'd done; she deserved peace of mind and justice. He felt that no judge on earth would punish her severely for scaring her ex-husband when he'd scared and hurt her for so many years. She was a good mother; she had done everything she could to protect her children. Surely with the right defence no jury would want to put her away in prison?

'Right, Eve, I know now what happened, and I want to help.' He watched as Eve slowly took her hands away from her face. 'I agree with Tabby that owning up about what happened is the only way forward. I bet it's been on your mind constantly?'

'Yes, every few days it rises up like some horrible smell. I thought it would pass with time, but it hasn't.'

'I recommend that tomorrow we ask DI Baytrum to call and I'll be with you as you tell him the whole story. George is a rat, Eve. I bet even as we speak he's spilling out anything he can to get you into trouble. Let's put a stop to it all.'

'I want to, Tom,' she said in a weak voice. 'But hasn't Tabby got enough to worry about just now, and why should Olly have people pointing their finger at him and gossiping?' She paused for a moment. 'And what if I do get sent to prison? Who will look after them and the business?'

'I don't think you will get prison with the right defence,' Tom said evenly. 'Even if you're detained for a few weeks, I can look after the children, and I'm sure Sophie will stay on to run the business.'

'You make it all sound so simple,' she said. 'But it isn't, Tom. I killed a man. Granted, I didn't mean to, and he was a very nasty person, but I deserve to be punished.'

'I think you've had too much punishment in your life,' he said, sitting down on the bed and drawing her into his arms. 'Years of terror with that brute, and then George targeting Tabby. I'd like to see all that end – no more guilt, time to be happy ever after.'

'That only happens in fairy tales,' Eve retorted.

24

DI Baytrum sat at the kitchen table, a young constable standing by the door, both listening intently to what Eve had to say. Tom was also at the table, but Tabby and Olly were next door in the studio with Sophie.

There was coffee and a plate of biscuits on the table, and sunshine was streaming through the back window, almost mocking the seriousness of what was taking place. But Eve's white face, the vivid red line above the open neck of her white shirt, and the quaver of fear in her voice as she spoke, told the true story.

'So you saw him go into the shed from your bedroom window?' Baytrum asked for clarification. 'You had seen him defecate on the lawn just seconds before, and that made you angry on top of your fear, because you knew he was taunting you?'

'That's right,' she said in a small voice. 'He had always made me feel powerless and useless. I was afraid that this was how it was going to be forever unless I stood up to him.'

'Did you decide then that you were going to scare him?'

'No, I got into bed. But I couldn't sleep knowing he was there and I got up some ten or fifteen minutes later. I looked out again, and I could see he'd fallen asleep with the Tilley lamp still lit, as his head was lolling back by the little window. So I put on my dressing gown and went downstairs and got the wooden spoon.'

She had already drawn a rough sketch for him of where the shed was in relation to the house, and that Don always locked himself in and had the only key. She went on to tell him the final part of the story of how she stood on tiptoe, reached through the window and pushed the lamp over.

'I thought he would wake up with the crash. There were no flames then; in fact, there was no light to see him any more. I was back in bed and dropping off when I heard the whooshing noise of the fire. When I looked out and saw the fire I assumed he'd got out, but I rang 999 immediately.'

'Well, Eve – I hope you don't mind me addressing you informally – the Metropolitan Police will have your original statement on file in London, and I'll liaise with them about this. But I will have to consult a more senior officer than myself about this. I think the outcome will be that he will want to make an appointment to see you with your solicitor at Heavitree police station in Exeter.'

'I've only got the solicitor I used to buy this place,'

she said. 'This isn't likely to be their kind of case, is it?'

'No, it won't be, Eve. You need someone well versed in criminal law, but I can give you the number of an appropriate solicitor.'

DI Baytrum then had to take her formal statement about the previous day's events. The constable took notes about George Mulberry coming to the house and holding a knife to her throat.

After he had finished with Eve, he took one from Tom too.

'I will get these typed up and you can sign them later today,' the sergeant said, and smiled warmly at Eve. 'Just to get back to the fire. Tell me, Eve, off the record, what made you decide to confess to your involvement so long after the event? Was it triggered by George Mulberry attacking you yesterday?'

'It did in as much as I'd begun to think everything bad happening to me or my family was punishment for what I'd done. You see it has preyed on my mind ever since that night,' she said, tears filling her eyes. 'Guilt's a terrible thing. I'd forget what I'd done for days, then it would come back. Yesterday, after the incident with Mulberry, my daughter shocked me by telling me she'd looked out of her brother's bedroom window that night and seen me push the lamp over. But she was half asleep and didn't think it was real.

'It was only when she was away from us in Chard

that it came back to her clearly. Let me make it clear, Sergeant, she wasn't trying to betray or hurt me – far from it, she was speaking out of love. She said I'd often impressed on her the importance of telling the truth and she thought it was time for me to own up because she knew the guilt was eating away at me.'

Baytrum sighed. 'Smart child. This is one of those times when I wish I wasn't a policeman. If I was a priest I could listen to your confession and give you absolution. In my heart, Eve, I think you've suffered enough. But I do have to uphold the law and not let my personal feelings affect that. As I've said, a more senior officer will need to be consulted, but it strikes me that although it is basically manslaughter, I see it more as an act of reckless endangerment. Given that you suffered grievously at this man's hands and have come forward to admit what you did completely voluntarily, with a good psychiatric report and character witnesses, I can't see the courts giving you a custodial sentence. But leave it with me, Eve, I'll talk to my superiors and get back to you.'

He took out a notebook and jotted down the name of a solicitors' firm in Exeter. 'Ask for Robert Mason,' he said. 'He's an excellent solicitor and I think you'll like him too.'

'I bet you wish you'd ignored Olly's plea for help and stayed away?' Eve said sadly to Tom as they came out of Heavitree police station in Exeter. It was Wednesday, the day after they'd seen DI Baytrum at her home. 'And now I've been charged with manslaughter.'

Tom put his arm round her and drew her close for a hug. 'I'm still glad I came. As for the charge, the police always start at the top and drop the charge to a lower one as more facts come to light. Robert Mason is a good man, as is Detective Inspector Wyles. He gave you bail, so clearly the police don't see you as a danger to anyone or likely to flee. I got the impression they were entirely sympathetic and would love to be able to brush it under the carpet. So let's go and get me a decent cup of coffee, and something stronger for you, and just be happy it's all out in the open now.'

Sitting in a bar a little later, Eve poured the brandy Tom had bought her into her coffee. 'Hmmm,' she murmured after she'd sipped her drink. 'That's good. But what will happen about the business? Do you think people will stop ordering from me?'

'I doubt it. People love drama. They might get a twisted sort of delight knowing the woman who made their new kitchen blind was a killer.'

'Oh, Tom,' she said in mock horror, knowing he was only trying to make her laugh, 'I can't believe you'd call me that.'

'Killer Queen!' he said. 'Like the song. Now, let's be serious, this is likely to take a while to be sorted.

But for the kids' sake and your business you've got to stay calm and trust it will all work out. I've got to go back to Bath tomorrow to sort out leaving my flat and cancelling that job. No problem there – they know they've messed me around too much – but I'll be gone over a week. Then I'm starting a big extension job in Sidbury. At least that's not far away. I'll be able to visit you in the evenings and weekends.'

'I'll be fine,' she said. 'You've done enough for me.'

'Is that a thinly veiled "get lost" message again?'

She giggled. 'No, it's not. In fact, I'm hoping that before long we can get back to where we were before silly stuff got in the way.'

'Time enough for that when we know what Tabby is going to do. I know Olly has been asking her, and now, after George showing his true colours, she must surely want to go ahead with a termination.'

'She's had too much else on her mind,' Eve said. 'But with George back in custody and me owning up, I think she'll decide now. I'm not going to force her hand.'

Tom didn't stay after he'd dropped her back home. He said he was going to drive to Bath and start sorting things. But when he kissed her goodbye they both felt the old passion rising. 'I'll see you on Saturday,' he said reluctantly. 'Behave yourself.'

It was a week later when Eve woke to hear Tabby calling her. As Tabby had never been one to have nightmares or call out in the night, Eve was out of bed in a trice and into Tabby's room.

'What is it, darling?' she asked.

Tabby didn't speak but pushed back the bedclothes to reveal blood-soaked pyjamas.

'Oh my God!' Eve exclaimed. 'Are you in pain?'

'Yes, Mummy,' she said in a thin voice. Eve knew then that Tabby must be feeling very poorly as she only called her 'Mummy' at such times. 'I'm miscarrying, aren't I?'

'It looks like it, baby,' she said. 'I'll just get my phone and call for an ambulance, then I'll be right back to sort you out.'

'Will it get worse?' Tabby asked.

'Maybe, but they'll give you medicine for that. Just try and stay calm while I phone.'

Eve telephoned and was told the ambulance would be there within ten minutes. She grabbed a bag and put some toiletries, clean pyjamas and slippers in it. Then she rushed back to Tabby, who was writhing in pain.

'Is this God's punishment for what I did?' she asked breathlessly.

'No, my darling, neither God nor I would punish you. I think your body knew it wasn't ready to hold a baby yet. It happens to hundreds of women every week.'

She found a pad for Eve and changed her pyjamas

for her, trying very hard not to be frightened by the amount of blood.

The ambulance arrived and Eve rushed downstairs to let them in. As the two male paramedics carried Tabby down on a stretcher, Eve hastily wrote a note for Olly saying where they'd gone and that she would ring in the morning with news. Then, grabbing the bag with Tabby's overnight things, she left the house and got in the ambulance.

They were just approaching the hospital when Tabby said she was going to be sick. Eve held the dish, but as Tabby vomited she clutched at her stomach.

'I think something came out,' she whispered.

'We'll soon have you in the hospital,' the paramedic said as he took her blood pressure.

It transpired it was the foetus that had come away and she was taken off to see a doctor. Eve sat in the waiting room biting her nails with anxiety, and it was well over two hours before a sister came to tell her Tabby was recovering.

'May I see her?' she asked.

'I think it's better that you come back in the morning; she's very woozy with painkillers and she's in a ward with other people you might disturb. Don't worry, we'll look after her. Ring just before eight when we change shifts and we can tell you how she is.'

Eve called a taxi to take her home and it was only

when she noticed the sun was coming up that she realized it was now five o'clock.

Despite being drained and exhausted she was unable to sleep. It was one of those times she'd experienced so often before, when she felt totally alone. 'What else could happen in one day?' she murmured to herself as she went downstairs again to make some hot milk. She wandered into the studio, a place filled with colour that normally lifted her spirits, but she caught sight of her face in the mirror and thought she looked at least fifty. Not thirty-three.

Before long she would need to face the court case, and however much her solicitor and the police claimed it was unlikely she'd go to prison, they couldn't guarantee that. She had, after all, killed a man, her own children's father. Perhaps prison was what she deserved.

Then there was George's trial. She would be called as a witness for the prosecution. Once again she would be forced to look at how he had betrayed her trust and coerced her fifteen-year-old daughter into a sexual relationship.

Eve felt she ought to be happy that Tabby was now spared the painful decision of whether to terminate or keep her baby. But as Eve stood there with early-morning sun coming through the workroom window, she began to cry for her grandchild. She hadn't asked if it was a boy or girl; it was probably far too early to tell. Huge tears rolled down her cheeks, and she slumped on to a chair, her shoulders heaving with emotion. She had achieved so much since they had left Grove Park and all the disturbing memories behind. Yet money and a good business had not brought the happiness for her and her children as she had expected. It had brought heartache.

25

Tabby was sad and frail for over two weeks when she returned home.

For a girl who had always been prickly, opinionated and rather self-centred, it was as if the girl Eve and Olly knew so well had been replaced by a watered-down version. She didn't argue about which TV programme to watch, she volunteered to make tea or coffee, she made her bed when she got up, and when Olly asked her to play a game with him, she agreed readily. On several occasions Eve found her sweeping the kitchen floor, something she'd never done before.

'You don't have to do a penance,' Eve said one day, on finding her cleaning fingermarks off the front door.

'What's a penance?' Tabby asked, her blue eyes seemingly almost too big for her face now because she'd lost weight.

'It's like a self-inflicted punishment for wrongdoing or sin,' Eve said. 'Catholics go for it mostly. But you haven't done anything wrong, my darling. I'm sure you feel sad at the moment – that's natural after losing a baby – but don't mistake that sadness for badness.'

'But I hurt you, Mum,' she said, her lips trembling. 'I can't forgive myself for that.'

Eve put her arms round Tabby and hugged her. 'You didn't hurt me, darling; the hurt was done to you. George is where he deserves to be now. And we have to pick up our lives, love one another and forgive.'

'But it's my fault you have to stand trial for Dad.'

Eve put her finger on Tabby's lips. 'No, it isn't, you were just like Jiminy Cricket in *Pinocchio*, pricking my conscience. And I'm glad you did.'

'But I'll never forgive myself if you get sent to prison.'

'If the judge decides that's what is needed, then so be it. But everyone tells me it's more likely to be a supervision order or a suspended sentence. So let me see you smile again, blast out your music, make a mess, that way I'll know I've got my Tabby back in residence.'

She smiled weakly. 'I'll make you regret you said that.'

It was the next evening that Tabby decided to tell Eve how it all came about with George. Olly was at his guitar lesson and Tabby had wandered into the studio as she so often did. She stood for a moment watching Eve pasting fabric and wallpaper samples on a board.

'Would you like to do one too?' Eve said. 'There's tons of samples here and I've got all the ones I need.'

Tabby sat down, took a board and started to fish through the samples.

'I think I should tell you how it all started with George,' Tabby said suddenly. 'I know you don't like to ask, but when his case goes to court, you'll hear it then.'

'OK then,' Eve said. She felt it might be good for Tabby to spill out everything.

'It kind of began when we first got to Sidmouth. Nothing bad or anything – George behaved like an uncle to me. He bumped into me one day after school and took me for an ice cream. I told you around then that the girls at school all wanted to be my friend, but that wasn't true, some of them were really mean and called me the Cockney Girl. Well, I was sad that afternoon and I told George about it. He was lovely, saying he'd be my friend, and that those girls would soon lose interest if I ignored them. But they didn't, Mum. They got worse, George came past the school a few days later when it was raining and offered me a lift home. Olly was at an after-school club so I was alone.

'It went on like that for a little while. He'd pick me up from school on a Thursday when Olly wasn't with me and take me to a cafe or something. He always said how much he liked you as a friend, Mum. I think by then he wasn't dropping by any more. Then one day he gave me the phone as a present.'

'As early on as that?' Eve said in surprise. She realized this must have been soon after they moved into the new house.

'He put his number in it and said I could phone him or send a text message any time I liked if I felt sad or lonely. I thought it was fabulous having a phone, with him paying for it; none of the other girls at school had one. But I hid it from you as I knew you'd make me give it back to him.'

'And then?'

'Well, you always seemed to be busy. Olly was engrossed in his guitar lessons, and it was fun sending text messages to George as he wrote really funny ones back. Then they started getting to be loving ones, like how his heart leaped when he saw me and stuff. I think it was just before our first Christmas at the house when he sent one telling me he loved me and would wait for me until I was sixteen.'

Tabby went on to tell how the text messages became a bit 'rude', and she'd told him off. But after a month or so she texted him again because she missed him. 'I told him I loved him about that time. I really thought I was in love, Mum, as I couldn't think of anything else but him. I lived for the times I met him for a burger or a drink. You were seeing Tom then, and I saw George as my boyfriend, never yours. But then Tom went away and George came back to you. He kissed me properly for the first time when he spent Christmas with us. He even told me he was only seeing you to be with me. I hated it if he held your hand or anything when we were together as a family.'

Eve could hardly bear to hear this. It made her feel she ought to have noticed something and perhaps that Tom had been right when he had said she had been too obsessed with her business to notice anything or anyone.

'Are you all right, Mum?' Tabby's question brought Eve out of her private and bitter thoughts.

'Yes, I'm fine,' Eve lied. She needed to know all this or spend the rest of her life wondering.

'It was when I went to work at the estate agent's it all got scary,' Tabby admitted. 'After Muriel went home on a Saturday, he'd get me to go upstairs with him. It was just kissing at first, but then it got a bit more –' she stopped, blushing furiously – 'well, you know.'

Eve did know. It would've been awful to think of a boy of Tabby's age doing such things to her daughter, but a million times worse knowing it was George who had actually made love to both of them.

'He did force me the first time, Mum. It was

horrible,' Tabby admitted, hanging her head. 'I knew it was all wrong. It hurt and I hated the way he was, like an animal. But he talked me round afterwards and said it was only because he loved me so much. He said it would never hurt again. I said it would never happen again. I meant it too. I wanted to tell you about it. But he managed to bring me round by being sweet. The time you caught us was the fourth time. That was the worst time of all. Not just because you walked in, but because he was hurting me.'

'Oh, Tabby.' Eve could hardly bear it. 'But why did you keep on saying you loved him and wanted to be with him?'

Tabby put her hands over her eyes. 'Because I felt so dirty. I thought I could make that feeling go away if I made out it was real love. Can you understand that?'

Eve could. Hadn't she told herself a million times that she loved Don? Even as she lay on the floor wounded, bleeding and humiliated. Women at the refuge had told her the same thing. And they were old enough to know better. But Tabby was just a child – how could she know?

Eve got up, went to Tabby and pulled her up into her arms, holding her tightly. 'Do you feel better for telling me?' Eve asked, trying hard not to cry.

'Yes, Mummy, I think I do. But I wish I could've found a kinder way to make myself feel better. That must have hurt so much.'

Eve rocked her in her arms. 'My darling, being a mother doesn't come with any warnings or advice. I don't think there's a child in the world that hasn't done something that hurts their mum. But love heals all wrongs. The fact your child is still alive and healthy is enough to forgive and forget. One day when you have a child you'll discover exactly what I mean.'

As summer arrived and it became warmer, slowly Tabby became her old self again. It was three weeks after she'd come out of hospital that Eve finally agreed she could go back to school for the last few weeks of term.

A new girl, Clara, had arrived in her class while Tabby had been away and perhaps she was finding it hard to fit in because she made a beeline to be friends with Tabby. Within days Tabby was saying 'Clara says this' or 'Clara does this', and though Olly rolled his eyes at it, Eve was delighted because Tabby really needed a new close friend to help her recovery.

It was so good to hear Tabby chatting on the phone, looking at clothes and make-up in magazines, and practising dance moves in her bedroom. Eve knew this was what fifteen-year-olds were supposed to do, and what she had been doing till George had begun to move in on her.

She was so glad to have her prickly, opinionated and sometimes extremely irritating, much-missed, darling daughter, back.

Muriel Parkinson unlocked the door of Mulberry's Estate Agency at nine a.m. on Monday 24 July.

She had not intended to continue working for George after the police took him away for having a sexual relationship with an underage girl. She was horrified that was what he'd been doing and felt she wanted nothing more to do with him or his estate agency. But then George had telephoned her while he was on remand in Exeter and begged her to keep the office going. He pointed out that many of the sales of houses were at the stage of exchanging contracts, and others close to completion. It was unfair to the sellers to just close up. However much she abhorred George's behaviour, she cared about the clients, some of whom she'd got to know well. They had to be protected.

Muriel was unmarried. At fifty-one she supposed most people would call her a typical spinster. She attended church, sung in the choir and painted in watercolours for a hobby. She didn't like one bit that word had got around about his arrest. Every day people came in, engaged her in conversation and then tried to pump her for information. So for the first time in her life she put aside her principles and agreed to work full-time six days a week until such time as George was able to wind up the business.

As she came into the office she saw some property details on the office floor. She tutted. George had managed to get bail once again the previous week, as long as he stayed at his parents' home in North Devon. He certainly wasn't supposed to come here.

'Maybe he didn't,' she said aloud. 'He could have sent a friend round to collect some things from his flat.'

She picked up the property details and put them on her desk and that was when she saw the handwritten letter from him. It was dated 23 July.

To Muriel,

I feel unable to continue living with all the hurt and sadness I've caused. I have decided I will end it tonight. Please, Muriel, don't go up to my flat; just call the police and let them see to it.

You have been a tower of strength, Muriel, in these past weeks, thank you. Please tell my family I'm sorry I let them down. You will find my will in the drawer of my desk upstairs, not that I have anything much to leave. Tell Noah I'm sorry I wasn't a better father, and please tell Eve Taylor I'm sorry I frightened her so badly. I think I lost my mind momentarily.

The world will be a better place without me.

George Mulberry

A chill ran down Muriel's spine. She really didn't need to go upstairs to see if what he said in the letter was true. But she couldn't help herself.

As she opened the door of his living room, there he was hanging from a beam, a small stepladder kicked to one side. She screamed and covered her face then turned and ran down the stairs.

The police came very quickly, and she heard the doctor who was with them say George had been dead for at least twelve hours. They took his body away and the upstairs rooms were checked by forensics, the suicide note sealed in a plastic wallet.

A young constable drove Muriel home and it was only when she was in her apartment with a sea view, where she'd lived alone for over twenty years, that she broke down. What affected her most was knowing how alone he must have felt. She'd had times in her life when she'd felt that way. She recalled being ill in bed with flu once and realized that if she was to die, no one would find her for weeks, because no one ever came to see her. Maybe the vicar would begin to wonder why she wasn't there every Sunday, the staff at the local library might wonder why she no longer came in on Thursday evenings, their late night. But would they bother to call round? She doubted it.

Even as she sat on her sofa stroking Cleo her Persian

cat and crying, she thought it awful that she wasn't crying for George but for herself.

The news of George's death didn't reach Eve until Tuesday, when Marianne telephoned her.

'George Mulberry has hanged himself,' she blurted out without any kind of easing into it. 'My heart nearly stopped when my solicitor rang me. My first thought was about my deposit. I mean, had George stolen it? Thankfully it seems he hadn't, and my solicitor said he has all he needs to finalize the sale, but he had to inform me as the estate agent's office would be closed.

'Where was this?' Eve asked, just a little offended that Marianne appeared to only be thinking of herself.

'Above his office, in his flat. Muriel went in on Monday morning and found a suicide note on her desk. They think he did it on Sunday evening.'

'But I thought he was in custody,' Eve said.

'I was told by a friend that his parents stood surety a few days ago on the understanding he had to stay with them. I expect you'll want to celebrate, won't you?' she went on, her voice full of excitement. 'You and Tabby won't need to stand up in court.'

Eve made excuses to ring off as Marianne's glee was too hard to stomach. As Eve saw it no one would kill themselves unless they were absolutely desperate. Although it seemed his family were supporting him by putting up bail, maybe their disgust at what he'd done was too hard to bear. He must have been in serious financial trouble too, or why would he have stolen that money from her?

Eve was relieved she and Tabby wouldn't have to go to court and face the publicity that would come with it. Yet a small part of her felt sorry for George despite everything. But she still had to worry about her own trial. Robert Mason had told her when they had first met that the trial would probably not be heard until late autumn. To Eve that sounded like an eternity as she was having frequent moments of panic that she'd be going to prison.

Both Olly and Tabby had insisted that Tom move in. From the very first day it had made all of them feel happier, safer and optimistic, especially when George attacked Eve. Tom was very stoic and optimistic about the trial; he said that if the worst happened and Eve was sent to prison, then he'd be there to look after the children. But however lovely it was to go to bed nightly with Tom, and to see Olly and Tabby so happy at having him there, it was hard to concentrate on her business with this black cloud hanging over her.

When Robert Mason called her and said her trial had been brought forward and would be heard on 1 August, she felt like cheering. She liked Mason very much. He was a stocky, no-nonsense man in his fifties, with almost completely white hair, yet looking fit and healthy. He was so easy to talk to. Non-judgemental and very understanding of what she'd been through. Not just about Don, but more recently with Mulberry and Tabby. He even understood how she felt about George's suicide, when no one else seemed to.

'Despite what he did to Tabby, for a long time he was your friend and companion,' Robert said in his calm, deliberate way. 'I think it's an admirable trait in you, Eve, that you have kept your compassion. Don't be ashamed of that.'

He went on to speak about the trial. 'It's unusual for such a case to be held so quickly. But the public prosecution service have examined all the evidence and, knowing what recently happened to your daughter, they feel it is in your family's interest to deal with this as quickly as possible.'

'Does that mean they want to quickly throw me in prison and chuck away the key?' she joked half-heartedly. Her mouth had gone dry and her stomach churned; 1 August was only one week away.

'On the contrary, I feel they're sympathetic, and they have many trials booked for September which are likely to be long and complicated. Yours should be quite straightforward. Time to tell you now that my staff have contacted Hannah Gordon the solicitor who arranged for you to go to the women's refuge in Sidmouth, and she has agreed to be a witness. Also, Marianne who ran the refuge then and I believe is still in contact with you. Along with Joanne Monday who told me you were at her son's birthday party the evening the fire started. She told me that many people in Briar Road were aware your late ex-husband was a violent man and can testify that you often had black eyes and other injuries.'

He paused to ask if she was happy for those people to speak in her defence, and she agreed she was.

'We also have hospital records of the many times you went to Lewisham Hospital with broken limbs, ribs and other serious injuries. That will be presented to the judge too.'

'My goodness, you've been busy,' she said, a little embarrassed that so much of her old life was being revealed. 'But isn't it a bit much to expect Hannah and Joanne to come down to Exeter to give evidence?'

'You underestimate how much people care about you, Eve,' he said. 'Both agreed without hesitation. Surely that should give you confidence?'

The truth was it made Eve cry. She realized then that she hadn't completely changed from the timid woman who once took everything Don threw at her and felt she hadn't a friend in the world. And she hoped that now she knew people did care, it would inspire her to stand up for herself in court.

Tom was delighted to hear the trial was to be in

August when he came home that evening. 'I'll make sure I book that week out to be with you,' he said.

'What if I don't come home with you on the last day?' she said fearfully, already imagining herself being driven off in a prison van and being stripped of her own clothes and given prison ones.

'We are not even going to consider that,' he said. 'And I hope you will agree to marry me as soon as possible after the trial, then the four of us can gad off somewhere hot and exotic for a well-deserved holiday.'

'Is that an actual proposal?' she asked, ruffling his curly hair and loving the way his lips curled up at the corners as if permanently smiling.

'It is, or do you want me to get down on one knee?' His blue eyes were shining and she thought he had the loveliest face she'd ever seen.

'No, that's not necessary. I'd agree if you wrote it on a shopping list,' she said, and threw her arms around him.

'Would it be tempting fate to book the registry office before the trial?' he murmured into her neck.

'I think it might.'

26

During the night before the trial Eve was so scared she had to get up twice to vomit. After the second time she left her bedroom where Tom was sleeping peacefully to walk around her home. Everyone and everything she loved were here in this house, and the thought of not coming back to it this evening was hideous.

She stopped first to look in Tabby's room. As always, she'd left the pretty rose-vine fairy lights attached to her headboard switched on. She looked like a rose herself, with a pink blush to her skin and her blonde hair cascading over the pillow.

Next, she went into Olly's room. He was lying on his back, arms and legs splayed out like a starfish. His dark hair needed cutting, something he was resisting as he thought boys with long hair were cool, and besides if he was going to become a famous guitarist, long hair was almost essential. Eve bent over and smoothed his hair out of his eyes, kissed her fingers and then touched his cheeks. Lately he had talked of nothing more than his intended career as a musician but seeing him here he still looked like her little boy.

Downstairs she wandered into the studio, switching on the spotlights to see the display she and Sophie had created recently of curtains with an animal theme. She particularly liked the one with elephants and acacia trees, the background a very pale yellow. They had recently got an order from one of the big hotels on the Esplanade for huge curtains to be made in this fabric for the drawing room, plus two sofas to be reupholstered in the same green as the trees on the curtains. She thought it was going to look fantastic.

She ran her hand over the cutting table, remembering when she had to make do at Sylvia's on a board. She had rung just yesterday after receiving Eve's written confession to her about Don and then about Tabby and George. True to form Sylvia was wonderfully supportive, saying she had often suspected Eve was hiding something and she was touched she was prepared to confide in her. She hoped Tabby was on the mend now and that it would strengthen her character for the future. She said she had no words of sympathy for George. She was, however, delighted Tom was back and said she would be going to church to pray that Eve would be treated kindly in court as she'd suffered enough. Finally she said that she loved Eve and both her children and remembered their time with her as one of the happiest ones. That meant more to Eve than anything.

She had also written to Don's parents and told

them, a far more difficult confession to make, but so far there was no response. It was understandable that they'd be angry with her, but she felt she had to tell them the whole truth.

In the workroom she sat at her sewing machine for a little while. There were two in the workroom now: hers, and the other one for Sophie. They had a pressing machine too. Back in Grove Park she couldn't even dream of a setup like this. Braids and other trimmings were on shelves in colour order, along with a display of different kinds of poles and tracks. Rolls of fabric were stacked against the walls; mostly this was for orders they were about to start on. She hoped Sophie would be able to cope with all the work if she was sent to prison. She was being confident that she could, but had said she knew a seamstress who would come in if necessary.

Glancing out of the window she saw the sun was just coming up, and on impulse she slipped a raincoat over her pyjamas and a pair of plimsoles on her feet, and taking the house keys she went out and made for the Esplanade.

It was too early even for dog walkers; there were just a few seagulls hoping to find someone's abandoned chips from the night before. The sea was like a millpond, pale lemon from the first rays of the sun. She broke into a run, going as fast as she could, on past the Victoria Hotel and kept going till she thought her lungs would burst. A stitch in her side stopped her. She had to bend over double to make it go away, then she sat on a wall till she stopped panting.

She walked back slowly, taking in the magnificence of the sun on the orange cliffs ahead, the stillness of the sea and the lovely Regency architecture of the hotels. She suddenly knew this was where she belonged. A few weeks ago, she was convinced she would have to leave after the trial and the awfulness of George. But Tabby was managing well, no one had asked her any questions at school, and with George gone now the story would soon fade.

As for her own wrongdoing, well, if she was sent to prison, then she wasn't sure what would happen. But if they gave her a suspended sentence and any-one asked her questions, she intended to laugh it off.

Whatever will be, will be, she thought philosophically. *But we won't leave Sidmouth.*

She felt a little bubble of laughter welling up inside her and giggled like a schoolgirl. Knowing this was not appropriate behaviour for a woman facing a manslaughter trial today made her giggle even more. As she marched home, she planned to slip into bed beside Tom and tempt him into a quickie, and then cook him bacon and eggs. So even if she were in a prison cell tonight, she'd have something good to look back on.

27

'Remember, deep breaths,' Tom said as they walked into Exeter Court. He had left the small bag of underwear, pyjamas, slippers and toiletries in the car, which she would need if she was sent down. It was unlikely the case would end today, but he could get it if it was needed. Sophie had told Eve to only take old stuff as anything good might be stolen. How Sophie knew this Eve hadn't asked. But she'd taken her advice anyway because it felt she might be stepping into a lion's den.

Olly and Tabby had clung to her like leeches when she was leaving. Sophie had to virtually prise them off her. 'Go to the beach,' Eve said to them, wiping the tears from their eyes, and fighting back tears of her own. 'Don't sit around waiting for news. Have a good day for me.'

Robert Mason was waiting for them, smiling them a welcome as if they were going into a dinner party, not a court.

'You look very nice, Eve,' he said, noting the newly washed and trimmed hair shining like a new penny in the sun. He approved of her light grey trouser suit with a white blouse beneath the jacket. It was a sober outfit, but it also said who she was, a woman who knew the seriousness of the charges against her but was doing her best to put things right. 'I'll take you down to the holding room, and Tom can go into the court when the case is called. It's first on the list, which is good. So say goodbye now and I'll go with Eve.'

Tom kissed her and then rubbed his nose against hers. 'Stay strong, look the bastard prosecutors in the eye and dare them to send you down,' he whispered. 'But my love will be with you, guarding you.'

Eve had to turn from him quickly so he didn't see her eyes well up.

Robert Mason had advised Eve to plead not guilty to manslaughter when they had done the plea and trial preparation some time ago. Robert had mentioned something else called reckless endangerment, which meant there had been no intent to kill or maim, but that the defendant ought to have known it might happen. Robert explained that meant like someone killing a person while driving drunk. He also said there would be no jury and that her guilt or innocence would be decided by the judge or magistrate. She felt Robert was playing everything down to keep her confident; he was almost implying today was just a formality. That was kind of him, but she didn't believe it.

She met the barrister Duncan Sanders-DeVere, who would handle the case, for the first time while in the holding room. He was tall, thin and had a long, craggy face which needed more flesh on it. His voice was as she had expected, classic BBC and Oxford, and it resonated round the small room as he asked her a few questions. They were mostly how soon after marriage Don started hitting her, how frequent were the attacks, and why didn't she call the police again that last time he got in the shed. He then moved on to ask why so long after the event was she compelled to admit what she'd done.

She said simply that the guilt was eating away at her.

He touched on the witnesses to be called, the ages of her children and that she had a successful business now, and that was that. Eve was surprised he didn't want to know more, but before Robert left her, he said she was not to worry, DeVere would have read all the information thoroughly that Robert had given him. He just needed to get the measure of his client.

'I hope I measured up then,' Eve said nervously.

'You did. I could almost feel his relief; sometimes we get clients who fall apart in court, and witnesses too. We know you won't, and I have high hopes for each of the witnesses too.'

'But what about when I'm cross-examined?' she asked, fear running through her veins like acid.

'You just stick to the facts. You look the prosecutor in the eye and always remember he or she has no grudge against you, even if it feels like it. It's just their job.'

The trial began with barrister Michael O'Dowd for the prosecution opening the case and laying out the facts. Eve didn't like the look of him. He had very small eyes and a complexion like corned beef. He was short and portly and he looked like he'd enjoy tearing someone to shreds.

He stated that Eve Taylor had pleaded not guilty to manslaughter but had admitted reckless endangerment in knocking the Tilley lamp over through the window of her ex-husband's shed to scare him. But that Donald Hathaway had died in the ensuing fire.

As he was speaking Eve looked around her. The courtroom was quite small, with pale walls and daylight coming in from long vertical windows high up. Aside from court officials there were only a few people who had presumably come to watch, and a young man who she suspected was a reporter by the way he was studying her so intently. Tom was there too, keeping his eyes on her steadily, as if by doing that he could give her courage.

Eve had been told that Joanne, Hannah and Marianne, her witnesses, were all here, but they had to wait outside the courtroom to be called.

Apparently there was only one witness called for the prosecution and that was Detective Inspector Radcliffe who had attended both during and after the fire.

O'Dowd started things off by questioning DI Radcliffe. 'When you were called to the shed fire in Briar Close in November 1998, can you describe the demeanour of Mrs Hathaway, or Eve Taylor as she is now called?'

'She was scared, anxious about the fire spreading further. It had set a tree on the garden boundary alight.'

'Did she tell you how the fire had started?'

'Yes, she said that Mr Hathaway was in the habit of getting in there when he was drunk and falling asleep. She said she had watched from the bedroom window as he lit the Tilley lamp he kept in there. She got into bed then and hoped he'd be gone by morning as he had on previous occasions.'

'Did she telephone the police to tell them he was intruding on the property?'

'No, as I said, she hoped he'd be gone by morning. She told me she was wakened by a whooshing sound, looked out and saw the fire, then rang the emergency services.'

'Did she tell you or the emergency services that she thought Mr Hathaway might still be in the shed when it was on fire?'

'No, she only said that a tree on the garden boundary was catching fire.'

'That was rather odd, wasn't it? Surely by telling you that she thought her ex-husband was in the shed, you'd come quicker.'

'Yes, I agree it was odd, but she was half asleep. She did tell the firemen the moment they arrived that he'd been in there and she hoped he'd already run out when it started. They asked her for the key. But that was irrelevant by then, as the whole shed was ablaze. They kicked the door in.'

'And what did they find?'

'Mr Hathaway was still in there, dead, still sitting in the chair.'

'How did Miss Taylor take this news?'

'She was horrified. She said she couldn't believe he wasn't woken by the fire and hadn't rushed out.'

'Did you believe her?'

'Not entirely. I believed that, however drunk a man was, if he knocked over a lamp, he would snatch it up immediately or rush to get out,' Radcliffe said. 'But we had no evidence of foul play. He was still in the chair, the shed door was locked from the inside. There was only one key.'

'But you did know that Miss Taylor had reported

her ex-husband for not only beating her to the extent that she had to flee with her children to a women's refuge, but that he'd done this trick of getting into the shed quite often, knowing it would frighten her. The police had even been called just a couple of weeks previously when he was screaming abuse at her from the street.'

'Yes, I did know about that.'

'So the lady in question had a great deal to hate her ex-husband for. Would you agree?'

'There was no doubt he'd behaved very badly towards her.'

'As I understand it, the Hathaways had a large life insurance policy. Did you not find that suspicious?'

'Yes, very, especially as Miss Taylor had claimed during the investigation that she felt the life insurance they'd taken out as newlyweds had lapsed.'

O'Dowd had no further questions for DI Radcliffe. DeVere got up to cross-examine him for the defence.

'It seems to me that the police were derelict in their duty for a great many years.' He waved a sheet of paper in his hand. 'This is a report from Lewisham Hospital of a great many injuries to Miss Taylor: broken wrists, cut and burnt legs, black eyes and broken ribs. She had called you when he was screaming abuse at her from outside the house, and she reported at that time that he was in the habit of coming round when he was drunk and sleeping in the shed. She is a gentle-natured woman and he was doing this to terrorize her because I believe he had no opportunity to beat her any more.'

'I think that is very likely,' Radcliffe agreed. 'But the police's hands are often tied in domestic situations like this. The time he was yelling abuse in the street it was thought that under the influence of drink he was just letting off steam at losing his home, wife and children. He showed no sign of attempting to hurt his ex-wife.'

'Back to the night of the fire. Would you say a man capable of driving to and parking his car up perfectly in a nearby road, then walking to Briar Close and defecating on his ex-wife's lawn, was so completely inebriated he didn't know what he was doing?'

'Possibly not,' Radcliffe admitted.

'Quite so,' DeVere said. 'I would say he came to my client's home with the sole purpose of distressing her. He had been told weeks before by the divorce courts that he was either to remove the shed if he wanted it, or to give her the key.

'But the reason we are here today to look at Mr Hathaway's death is because Miss Taylor has confessed that on the night in question his behaviour was the straw that broke the camel's back. She fought back for the first time ever by waiting until he fell asleep in the shed, then poking a wooden spoon through the small window to knock the lamp over. It was not her intention to kill him, only to scare him enough that he wouldn't come there again. Would you say that was the truth of the matter?'

'Yes, I would say that was the truth.'

'However, before Miss Taylor admitted pushing the lamp over and you discovered they had a large life insurance policy, did that suggest foul play to you?'

'I was suspicious, yes.'

'But who took this insurance out?'

'Mr Hathaway, soon after their marriage in 1986. But he had increased the premium in 1998.'

'Was Miss Taylor's signature on either of these two documents?'

'No. They were taken out by Mr Hathaway to insure both him and his wife. When I asked her about insurance she knew one had been taken out in 1986 but she thought it had lapsed. She said she didn't know if it was still active because her ex-husband had never let her look at bank statements or any correspondence.'

'Did you believe that?'

'Not really.'

'But is it likely a woman who had been beaten mercilessly many times would risk looking for papers she'd been told were her husband's province?'

'Perhaps not.'

'When you searched the house at Briar Road

immediately after the fire, did you find these documents, bank statements or this insurance policy?'

'No. It transpired he had taken all these things to where he was living at the time of his death.'

'So that is proof Miss Taylor had no idea there was an insurance policy! So I think we can be clear she was not expecting an insurance payout!'

DeVere said he had no further questions for DI Radcliffe, who left the witness box. As the prosecution had no further witnesses, O'Dowd called the first of the defence witnesses, Joanne Monday, the mother of Sam, Olly's friend in Briar Road.

Eve was touched that she'd agreed to come. She looked very nervous and shot Eve an 'I'll do my best' look.

When O'Dowd asked if she had ever seen Mr Hathaway attack his wife, she said she hadn't witnessed anything but had heard shouting and screaming coming from their house. She went on to say she'd seen Eve many times with her arm in a sling, a bandaged wrist or leg and black eyes. But Eve had never told anyone he was hurting her.

O'Dowd went on to ask her about the night of the fire. Joanne said that Eve and the children had come to a firework party at her house. She said Eve had been happy and relaxed and left about ten to go home.

'Did you go out in the street when the fire engines came later?' O'Dowd asked.

'No, we didn't, and it wasn't until the next day that we learned Don had died in the shed.'

'Did Miss Taylor tell you what happened?'

'Yes, she said he'd got into the shed again when he was drunk and he must've knocked the Tilley lamp over.'

'Did you believe that's what happened?'

'Of course. Eve's not a liar. She's a kind, caring person. And we all knew he was always going in that shed to annoy her.'

O'Dowd said he had no further questions.

It was DeVere's turn then. His questions were far more gentle, getting Joanne to tell the court about one time when Eve had a broken arm and black eyes and she'd driven her friend to Lewisham Hospital. She said how a nurse said she knew Eve had been beaten and urged her to get help.

'But we all know when the police come to beaten women they might arrest the man, but the man just comes back and does it again. Eve had nowhere to run to and no money of her own. I was so glad when she finally went away to a refuge.'

'Do you believe she meant him to die in the shed fire?'

'No,' Joanne said. 'Not for a moment.'

Hannah Gordon was called next by O'Dowd, and she was ice-cool and composed as Eve expected of a solicitor.

He asked Ms Gordon why it had taken Eve so long to get help if her husband was beating her on a regular basis.

'It takes great courage to take your children and leave your home, especially with no money or transport,' she said. 'Years of abuse can convince a woman she deserves it, and their self-esteem becomes so low they don't even try to defend themselves. The day she came to me was because her children had begged her to get help. Even then she was doing it for them, not for herself.'

'But she rallied round after her time in the refuge! She sued for divorce and to regain her family home. That was hardly the action of a downtrodden woman.'

Hannah shot him a look that said she believed he was a misogynist. 'That was because I was advising her and giving her encouragement. She had recovered her strength and it was right to permanently sever all connections with such a brute.'

'Did she regain her strength so well that when her ex-husband began to frighten her by coming back and getting in his shed she wanted revenge? Didn't she wait till he fell asleep and using a wooden spoon she stood outside the small window and pushed his lamp over to burn him to death?'

'Never.' Hannah spoke out loudly. 'She is not a malicious woman.'

'Maybe you don't know the whole truth yet, but we

are here today because Miss Taylor did exactly that and went to the police and admitted that she knocked over the lamp that caused the fire. What do you think of that?'

Hannah didn't miss a beat. 'I think it is typical of her honesty that she'd admit her guilt. But I don't believe she's capable of cold-bloodedly starting a fire with the intention of killing him. She hasn't got that in her. In a moment of anger and desperation she may have felt she had to do something that would make him leave her alone. In her position I think all of us would do the same. But I am certain she thought he would be able to get out in time, suitably chastened.'

O'Dowd had finished his questions and DeVere began his.

'Ms Gordon, I understand you acted very quickly to get Eve and her children away from Mr Hathaway the very same day she came to you. Is that right?'

'Yes, as soon as she saw her children off to school, she went to the police, reported her husband and had her injuries photographed. A male nurse at the police station actually took her to the hospital, that's how concerned he was. Then she came to me. She was in pain, frightened and in despair, so I organized a colleague to pick her children up from school and take them all to the refuge.'

'And later? I believe when her spell in the refuge was up, you arranged for them to have a home with a friend of yours. An unusual turn of events, I would say. Why did you do that?'

'Because I liked and admired Eve very much, and I felt she needed a bit more support than women in her position normally get. As it was, there were a couple of incidents when Mr Hathaway had found out where she was. In one he threw a brick through the window. He also laid in wait for her at the school. Fortunately that day she outwitted him. I was handling her divorce and the more I got to know about Eve, the more I came to admire her. She had the dream of becoming an interior designer, which she now is, but she started humbly by making curtains for local people.'

Her questioning over, Hannah joined Joanne on a bench.

Marianne came next and last, and as Eve had half expected she'd dressed to be noticed, in a shocking-pink dress with a purple trim. She had a bow of the same material in her hair too, and dozens of rattling bracelets. She walked into the courtroom as if she was on a red carpet and swore on the Bible as if she was auditioning for a part in a film.

O'Dowd appeared to take one look at her and dislike her. 'I'm sure all the women who come to your refuge try to outdo one another with tales of the atrocities done to them?'

'No, they don't, sir,' she snapped. 'In fact, most

of them keep it to themselves what they've been through.'

'And Miss Taylor, was she the kind to keep it to herself?'

'She was very quiet, but we could see her injuries for ourselves. She had a job to walk with broken ribs and a nasty wound on her leg.'

'Did she tell you about the fire that killed her ex-husband?'

'Only that he was in the shed that burned down.'

'Funny that she should tell you that if nothing else. Would you say that meant she'd played a part in his death?'

'No, I wouldn't,' she said with great indignation. 'Eve is kind and generous. She's a listener rather than a talker. She is not a killer.'

O'Dowd let DeVere take over with his questions then.

He encouraged Marianne to speak of Eve's peace-making ability, how she won the other women round with her cooking and taking an interest in them and their children. 'That husband of hers had drained her confidence, squashed the very life out of her, but gradually she began to grow again in the refuge. She brought out the best in everyone really. She didn't back bite, tell tales. I missed her when she had to go.'

'You said to the prosecution that you didn't believe she had a hand in her husband's death. Why is that?'

'Well, I used to tease her sometimes that she had. I said he had deserved the death he got. She said that not even he deserved a death like that.'

'You're both in the same town now; do you keep in touch?'

'Oh yes,' Marianne said eagerly. 'I love to see her and her delightful children. We will always be friends. And I'm so proud of her for getting her business together.'

The court was adjourned then for lunch and perhaps Hannah sensed that Eve wanted to be alone with Tom, because she suggested to Joanne and Marianne that she'd drive them to a cafe she knew.

There was a snack stall close to the court, and Eve and Tom bought coffees and sandwiches and sat on a nearby bench in the sun.

'How do you think it's going?' Eve asked Tom nervously. 'Tell me the truth.'

'Well, I can't see any reason why the judge would want to send you to prison,' he said. 'There's been nothing said by anyone that suggests you're a cold, calculating woman intent on killing him and getting the insurance money.'

'I suppose I want complete absolution,' she said. 'I think the police still think I did it to kill Don.'

'They're trained to be suspicious, just as that prosecution guy O'Dowd will probably be mean to you in his questioning when we get back in. It's his job. But the fact remains that Don was a brute, and you were rattled enough to give him a scare. I didn't see anyone in that courtroom for him. Not his girlfriend or his parents. He was a nasty piece of work and he got what was coming to him.'

Eve leaned against his arm and took his hand in hers. 'How lucky I am to have you in my corner,' she said. 'Even if they do send me to prison, I'll be able to stand it knowing you're waiting for me.'

'Let's walk for a bit,' he said. 'My bum went to sleep on that bench, and I'm sure you're stiff too. I think it will all be over today. I can't see what they could possibly bring up to make it go into another day.'

28

Eve braced herself as they went back in. She knew O'Dowd was going to try to discredit her.

'Well, Miss Taylor, shall we start with you explaining why you took so long to admit the truth of how the fire began that killed your ex-husband?'

'I was scared how it would affect my children. I felt people would hate me and I was frightened of going to prison,' she said, looking at him intently. 'But I couldn't live with the guilt of it. I was looking over my shoulder all the time, thinking any day I could be exposed. I often had nightmares about what I'd done, but I only pushed that lamp over to scare him. He was, after all, a horrible violent man and on the spur of the moment I thought I'd make him as scared as he'd made me.'

'So you don't regret your actions?'

'I regret that my guilt may have affected my children and relationships with other people. But I did what I did out of desperation, when all other avenues, like the police, couldn't stop him.'

'I see. But despite having said you were scared of him, you divorced him when you came back from the refuge, insisted you reclaimed the house and you expected far more than your half of the value when it was sold. And to keep the children. What made you suddenly that brave?'

'He wasn't living in the house for a start; he had a new girlfriend. Of course I started divorce proceedings, only a complete fool wouldn't. As for the children, how could I let him have access to them when he had already beaten our son many times for virtually nothing? As for the house, it had been bought with money my parents had bequeathed to me. It was fair for me to have the lion's share, but I had agreed with his solicitors for him to have some of the profit made on it.'

'Yes, of course,' O'Dowd said with a sneer. 'And you have flourished since his death, haven't you? Your own interior design business, a lovely home by the sea. The insurance payout, which you say you knew nothing about, has been good for you.'

'Has it occurred to you that Don might have been intending to bump me off and that's why he increased the premium?' she snapped at him. 'And, yes, I have a successful business that I have worked extremely hard to build. Now I have a legacy to leave my children or to help them if they need it. Which is far more than their father would have done.'

Eve felt satisfied she had put him down, as he ended the prosecution questions.

DeVere also seemed to have run out of steam. He asked a couple of questions about the children's schooling and what Eve's plans for the future were.

'I intend to marry Tom Bolton, who has been my love and my rock ever since I arrived in Devon and is here with me today. For my son Oliver I hope I can get him into a music college as he wishes to pursue music as a career. Tabitha hasn't told me about her hopes for her future, but she is clever enough to go to university. But most of all I wish us to be a normal happy family and I would like to apologize to the court for not admitting what I had done before. But, as you can imagine, I was afraid for my children.'

The judge, who hadn't interrupted the proceedings once, beamed at her. 'You may sit down now, Miss Taylor, and I will adjourn for a short while to discuss this with counsel.'

As O'Dowd and DeVere followed the judge out, Robert Mason came over to Eve. 'He didn't even want a summing-up,' he said incredulously. 'I've never experienced that before. But I am assuming this is because he's finding it all cut and dried, and just has to decide whether to hang you or kiss you.'

For just a nanosecond Eve thought he was serious, and then laughed. 'I'll happily kiss him if he lets me off.'

Robert was very complimentary. 'You were very

good, Eve,' he said. 'Straight to the point. I loved the bit about Don bumping you off; I think the judge did too. But saying that about getting married and the kids was brilliant. If it doesn't get us off, I might be tempted to eat the judge's wig.'

The judge and barristers were gone no longer than ten minutes, but in that time, which seemed endless, Eve wished she could get up and go over to her friends and Tom who were all chatting together. But various court people were still there so she didn't think she should move.

As the judge and barristers came back in Eve stood up. For the first time Eve noticed the judge was quite old, probably at least seventy, but he had a kind face and bright eyes. Furthermore he smiled at her.

'Miss Taylor, I didn't need to agonize overlong about this case. You were badly wronged by Mr Hathaway and had a miserable pain-filled life with him. You were very brave to admit your guilt, and because of that I feel it would be very wrong to punish you with any kind of custodial sentence. Your children need you home with them. I am going to give you a suspended sentence, however, mainly because people like to see justice done. But I wish you happiness in your forthcoming marriage and that your children achieve their dreams.'

Eve closed her eyes for a moment, thinking she

was dreaming, but clapping from her friends and Tom brought her out of it, and then she began to cry.

Robert came forward, beaming from ear to ear, and said he'd talk about what a suspended sentence meant the next day. 'Basically if you stick Tom under your steam presser when he's getting on your nerves, you'll be locked up pronto,' he joked. 'So off you go and enjoy the rest of the summer.'

Eve went over to Joanne, Hannah and Marianne, hugged them tearfully and thanked them for supporting her. 'You were all wonderful,' she said, and her tears began to flow even faster.

'Home!' Hannah said, nudging her out into the hallway. But she stopped for a minute to turn and speak to Tom. 'Thank you for bringing her happiness,' she said. 'Eve deserves it.'

It was something of an anticlimax as they drove home. Eve felt she should've been wildly excited, desperate to tell the children the good news, yet she suddenly felt very low. The first two men in her life were both dead. Don had died in the fire, and George had hanged himself. She felt she was responsible for both deaths, at least in part. Tabby had miscarried and may very well carry the scars of that for years and Olly might have as yet unseen scars.

How could she agree to marry Tom believing in happy ever after?

Epilogue

'Happy, Mrs Bolton?' Tom whispered in Eve's ear as the plane gathered speed on the runway.

Tabby and Olly had seats across the aisle, and Olly was nervously clinging to his sister's arm. It was their first flight and, as excited as they were about going to Turkey, they were a bit scared.

'I'm extremely happy, Mr Bolton,' Eve whispered back. 'And our wedding was beautiful.'

She leaned back in the seat for take-off, remembering how she had been straight after the trial, guilty, frightened, convinced she should've been locked up and horrified about newspaper reports. As it was, the case only got a couple of lines in the Exeter local paper. Her children had been so thrilled she was home with them; they clearly didn't have any hidden issues with it. And Tom, always the wise, kind one, had convinced her she was a wonderful mother and that what had happened to the two nasty men in her life was not her fault but their own.

The biggest surprise came, though, the following day when the doorbell rang and standing there were Patty and Ernest Hathaway, Don's parents, both smiling ear to ear and carrying a huge bouquet of flowers.

'We got to the court just as the case was over,' Ernest explained. 'We were caught up in heavy traffic on the M25, but we weren't too worried as we imagined the trial would go on for several days. One of the court officials told us the good news, and that you'd gone home.'

'Come on in,' Eve said breathlessly, delighted they were not angry with her and bearing a grudge. 'When I didn't hear from you, I thought the worst.'

Over a cup of tea Patty explained that they'd been away when Eve's letter had arrived. 'We were shocked, of course, but by then it was too late to do anything but come to the court and offer our support. God knows we knew what our son was. What an ordeal for you, my darling! You must know that Ernie and I had come to see you as the daughter we never had and that we'd always be on your side whatever happened.'

They refused her offer of the spare bedroom and insisted on going to a hotel for the night. 'You, Tom and the children need time together alone, but we'll come down later on in the year to see you.'

The Hathaways' reaction to Eve's confession did feel like absolution, and it was wonderful to know that they still wanted to be in her life and see their grandchildren, but in the days that followed, as Tom and

Eve rushed about getting a special licence to get married and planning what they would wear and who they would invite, Eve was able to put that trial behind her.

It was a very simple wedding but made fabulous by a beautiful sunny day. Eve wore a very pretty pink and green silk sheath dress, with a matching fascinator. Tom looked remarkably smart in a blue checked jacket and grey trousers, his fair curly hair cut and tamed a little. He'd even had a manicure, as his builder's hands were not in good shape. Olly had a new navy-blue linen jacket, and Tabby was a picture in a turquoise short dress. James, the carpenter who worked with Tom, was his best man. Sophie, Marianne and Ian the plumber and his fiancée Julie were the only other guests.

Tom's mother had died of cancer years before and his father was in a nursing home in Exeter and unable to come. They planned to visit him when they returned from their honeymoon.

After the wedding ceremony they had lunch at the Hotel Riviera on the Esplanade. They were on a big round table by the window to enjoy the sea view, and Tom had booked a room for him and Eve that night too. Sophie would be staying at the house to keep an eye on the children.

Eve couldn't help but compare the wonderful day

with her wedding to Don, when he'd invited several of his most noisy, rude and drunken friends, and Eve's parents had felt they had to scuttle away right after the wedding breakfast to escape the embarrassment. Don hadn't invited Patty and Ernest and, of course, that was the start of Eve believing they were mean to him and had no interest in her.

It was bliss to spend the night at the Riviera; there were no memories of anyone else, just new delights for her and Tom to store away forever. Through the open window they could hear the waves lapping on the shingle beach, and Tom said he wanted to build a house for them overlooking the sea, so they could grow old together with that sound every night.

But right now Eve wasn't thinking about old age, only the excitement of going to Turkey and beautiful Bodrum. Tom had booked a four-day trip along the coast on a wooden sailing boat called a gulet. She could hardly wait to dive off the side into crystal-clear turquoise water and eat barbecued sardines on a deserted beach.

'A penny for them?' Tom said, breaking into her little dream world.

'Just imagining the gulet, swimming and barbecues,' she said, suddenly aware the plane was up in the air and she hadn't even noticed. 'Sophie told me a couple of days ago Turkey is also brilliant for fabrics, and she thought I ought to bring some home with us.'

'I forbid you to think about curtains or fabrics for this entire holiday,' he said in a mock-stern fashion. 'You will think only about pleasing me, nothing else.'

She turned in her seat to cup his face in her hands. As always she thought what a lovely face it was. 'That will be my pleasure,' she laughed. 'But I expect you to think of things to please me too.'